PRAISE for ~~————~~

"Robert Randisi has long been held as a master
of the genre. . . . He's one of the best."

Michael Connelly

"The astonishingly prolific Randisi may be
one of the last true pulp writers."

Booklist

"Randisi is a masterful writer."

James W. Hall

"A skillful, uncompromising writer, Randisi knows
which buttons to press—and how to press them."

John Lutz

Robert J. Randisi, winner of the Private Eye Writers of
America's Lifetime Achievement Award in 2009, is a
publishing phenomenon. With more than 500 novels under
his belt, he shows no sign of slowing down. He is the
author of a new novel for Perfect Crime Books
—***The Bottom of Every Bottle***.

The GUILT EDGE

Other Books *by* Robert J. Randisi

Novels

The Bottom of Every Bottle
You're Nobody 'Til Somebody Kills You
Hey There (You with the Gun in Your Hand)
Luck Be a Lady, Don't Die
Everybody Kills Somebody Sometime
Alone With the Dead
Arch Angels
East of the Arch
Blood on the Arch
In the Shadow of the Arch

Anthologies (Editor)

The Shamus Winners
Hollywood and Crime
The Eyes Have It
Mean Streets
Greatest Hits
Justice for Hire
Eye for Justice

The GUILT EDGE

And Other Stories

ROBERT J. RANDISI

Perfect Crime
Baltimore

Perfect Crime Books. www.PerfectCrimeBooks.com.

Library of Congress Cataloging-in-Publication Data
Randisi/Robert J.
The Guilt Edge and Other Stories/Robert J. Randisi
ISBN: 978-0-9825157-3-0

First Edition: February 2010

Contents

Introduction

Way back in 1982 I picked up a paperback by Robert J. Randisi. It wasn't the writer's name that attracted me—I'd never heard of him—it was the fact that *Eye in the Ring* combined professional boxing with the private eye novel, which seemed to be an interesting mixture.

As I read the book I realized that this Randisi guy a) wrote as if he was on fire b) knew a lot about boxing and c) understood how the law worked.

I liked the book so much I asked my friend Max Allan Collins, who knew Bob, if it would be all right if I wrote and told him how much I admired *Eye in the Ring*. Bob was kind enough to write back and we've been friends ever since.

I should note here that Bob's also been my mentor. I grew up reading westerns but was always afraid to write one. Bob was writing The Gunsmith series as by J.R. Roberts. He patiently told me how to write my own western. I would never have gotten started in the field without Bob tutoring me. (And in case you're interested, as I write this The Gunsmith series has reached number No. 335.)

Bob's skill with westerns (besides his own name he's written them under the pseudonyms Lew Baines, Tom Cutter, Robert Lake, W.B. Longley, Joseph Meek, Joshua Randall and Cole Weston, among others) was superseded only by his skill with crime fiction. Like most of us, he began by imitating those writers he read and admired. But soon he was producing novels and stories in his own voice.

Bob is as good in the short story form as he is with the novel. You're holding in your hands the proof of that.

His sleuths include Henry Po, an investigator for the New York racing commission, Val O'Farrell, the Irish private eye, Truxton Lewis the irritable-with-good-reason sixty-something crime solver, and Bat Masterson. Yes, there really was a Bat Masterson, and after his famous days in the Old West, he really did come to New York, where he spent his last years as a journalist.

Masterson is the central figure of one of Bob's finest novels, *The Ham Reporter*. Among other the things, the book is rich in New York City history. There is a chapter in which the street gangs figure as players. I've been begging Bob for years to turn that chapter into a novel. It proves that truth is not only more often stranger than fiction but also more terrifying. Vampires had nothing on these juvenile monsters.

In addition to his writing, Bob has been busy with editing anthologies and various other projects over the years. Bob and I started *Mystery Scene* magazine and The American Crime Writer's League. On his own Bob created The Private Eye Writers of America, one of the most successful writing groups in genre history.

It's impossible to write about Bob without discussing his astonishing output. Right now the number of Randisi-written novels has passed the five hundred mark and will be even larger by the time this collection appears. In the mystery field, only one other writer has published that many books, the late British novelist John Creasy.

Yes, Bob is a phenom. Yes, Bob is proud of what he's achieved. Yes, Bob is celebrated for his astounding accomplishment.

But there is a problem with the numbers. There are those who say that anybody who writes so much can't possibly be good. The people who say this about Bob have rarely read anything of his—they just dismiss him when they see the numbers.

Well, consider the aforementioned Creasy or the Belgian Georges Simenon. If you combine his early pseudonymous work with the work we know him for, Simenon likely wrote as much as Bob or Creasy. All three men faced the same derision. They were dismissed by some critics simply for the number of books they wrote.

A look at Bob's work over the years is telling. He's grown in talent and stature. To me a hack is somebody who's satisfied doing the same thing over and over, never taking the time or interest to attempt anything new or more adventurous. Bob's career is a study in the opposite. As much as I enjoyed *Eye in the Ring*, the later books such as *No Exit to Brooklyn*, *Alone With the Dead* and his new series about the Rat Pack are richer in character and story and far more eloquent in the telling. And those are just three examples. Hard work and determination paid off. There are a few new writers who come to the task ready to do their best work. But most of us have to struggle and persevere to improve.

Now's the time to bring Bob on stage. Sit back and enjoy a master storyteller at work. I've been doing just that for almost thirty years now.

ED GORMAN

The GUILT EDGE

The Disappearance of Penny

Penny's Penny was Hopkins Stables' Triple Crown hopeful that year. The colt had been named after Benjamin Hopkins's daughter, Penny Hopkins.

"Penny won nine out of ten races as a two-year-old, Mr. Tucker," Benjamin Hopkins bragged to me. "Her only loss was to Paul Lassiter's Bold Randy—"

"Whose only loss as a two-year-old was to Penny's Penny," I finished for him. "I follow the horses, Mr. Hopkins." Hopkins and Lassiter were chief rivals in the world of thoroughbred racing. "Could we get down to why you asked me to come here?"

"As I told you on the phone, Mr. Tucker, she left the house yesterday morning and has not returned. She's never done that before. I tried to report her missing to the police, but they inform me that she's overage."

"What they mean is that she is between eighteen and sixty-five and therefore they cannot accept a missing-persons report on her unless there is some physical evidence of foul play," I explained, "or a history of mental illness."

He waved his hand impatiently. "Yes, yes, they explained that to me. They also suggested I hire a private investigator."

He had called me that morning at my office and asked me if I would come to his office at the track. He promised me a two-hundred-dollar consultation fee even if I turned down his case.

"They told me you are a specialist in missing persons."

I nodded. "I worked with the Missing Persons Unit as a detective for six years until they changed their policy to this eighteen-to-sixty-five age limit. I disagree with the new policy, which claims it is against the constitutional rights of the missing person for us to look for him if he doesn't want to be found. How are we supposed to determine whether a person wants to be found or not?" I shrugged. "I decided to go out on my own."

He tapped the desktop with a pencil. "I will pay you one thousand dollars to find her for me," he told me.

I didn't hesitate. "You've got yourself a detective, Mr. Hopkins."

"Fine. First I'd like you to—"

"We'd better get something straight right from the beginning," I interrupted, holding up my hand. "You've hired yourself a detective, not a leg man. You'll have to let me run the investigation my own way."

He digested that a moment, then nodded curtly. "Agreed."

I took some preliminary information from him, about his daughter's favorite places and people. He paid me the promised fee, plus a retainer, and walked me to the door. He was tall and stately looking, with plentiful snow-white hair, big shoulders, and a barrel chest. He must have been a hell of a figure twenty years before, but now he was sixty-five and showed every year of it.

"Please, Mr. Tucker," he said before I left, "find my daughter." I had a feeling his concern was artificial, but I told him I'd try.

Hopkins had said that Penny was a regular at almost every stable on the track, so that's where I began asking questions about who'd seen her and when. I saved Paul Lassiter's stable until last.

As I approached, I saw a man come out of one of the stalls. He was tall, at least six-foot-one, and he was remarkably handsome. Paul Newman eyes. In his early forties.

"Paul Lassiter?" I asked on a hunch.

He turned and gave me an easy grin.

"That's me. What can I do for you?"

"My name is Frank Tucker. I'm working for Benjamin Hopkins."

"In what capacity?" he asked.

I took out one of my cards and handed it to him.

"What would Benny need with a private eye?" he asked, pocketing the card.

"He's looking for his daughter. She's disappeared."

"Penny?" He seemed surprised.

"How many daughters does he have?"

"Just Penny that I know of."

"Have you seen her in the last few days?" I asked him.

"Come over to my office, Mr. Tucker. Maybe we can rustle up a drink." I followed him to the far end of the grounds where we stepped into an office very much like the one where I'd spoken to Hopkins. I turned down his offer of a drink and settled into a seat while he made one for himself. I had the feeling he was stalling for time.

He turned around, a drink in his hand, a smile on his face, and said, "I think I saw her, let me see, the day before yesterday. That would be Thursday, wouldn't it?"

"How friendly were you?"

"An old man like me?" he said. If he was acting he was doing it very well. "I'm her father's mortal—well, professional rival."

"What were you going to say?" I prodded.

He shrugged, sipped his drink. "Mortal enemy. But that's a little strong. That may be the way Benny thinks of me, but it's not the way I think of him."

"You call him Benny."

He sipped his drink again before answering. "I used to work for him. Then I branched out for myself, took some people with me. He never forgave me for that. I think he wanted me to be his protégé forever. That wasn't for me. I learned everything he could teach me, then went out on my own. I guess he considered me a traitor, probably still does."

"What was Penny doing when you saw her Thursday?"

"It was at the track lounge. She was having a drink with one of her friends, Louis Melendez."

"The jockey?"

He laughed. "Some people think of him that way"

Which didn't say much for Lassiter's opinion of Melendez's riding ability. I thanked him for his time and left, promising myself I'd be getting back to him soon.

I couldn't locate Louis Melendez anywhere on the track grounds. He seemed to have vanished right along with Penny Hopkins. Before checking out his apartment, I decided to try the lounge where Lassiter had said he'd seen them together.

"What'll it be?" the bartender asked. He might have been an ex-jockey, judging from his size.

"A ginger ale and some information," I told him, sliding a ten across the bar. "Louis Melendez. Have you seen him?"

"Little Louie? Let me think—Thursday," he answered finally.

"Was he with anyone?" I asked.

"Sure was. That little fox, Penny Hopkins."

"Benjamin Hopkins's daughter?"

"The same. Hey, if there were two of her, wouldn't that be something?"

"Why so?"

His eyebrows went up and almost touched his hairline.

"Haven't you ever seen her?" he asked.

I shook my head. Old man Hopkins hadn't had a picture of his daughter in his office.

"Come with me," the little barkeep beckoned, coming around the bar. I followed him to a wall covered with framed photographs.

He pointed to one and I zeroed in on it. It was a shot of a curvaceous young girl surrounded by a group of jockeys. She was taller than all of them and her red hair was tied with a green ribbon. Her grin was wide, her nose slightly snubbed. Her face was that of a young girl, but the body was definitely a woman's.

"If that don't make your blood boil, you're made of stone," the bartender said.

"Is Melendez in that picture?" I asked.

"He sure is—he's the guy practically drooling into her lap." He pointed to a little guy whose hang-dog look bespoke a man hopelessly in love with someone he couldn't possibly have.

"Was he in love with her?"

"Hey, you're pretty good. Just from the picture you can tell, huh?" I stared at him. "Okay, sure he was crazy for her. I mean, everybody was a little in love with her, but he was sick."

"How'd she treat him?" I asked.

"Like a trained puppy. He was her gofer, but that was his choice, you know?" He shook his head and a faraway look came into his eyes. "I'd've been her gofer, she give me half a chance."

I turned around and went back to the bar to finish my ginger ale. It was still early and the place was empty, so he came back with me and leaned on the bar while I drained my glass.

"Thanks for the information," I told him.

"Of course, I never would have had a chance with her, same as everybody else," he said and droned on. I shut him off and was about to leave when he said something that made me stop and back up.

"What?" I said.

He had good instincts, that boy. As soon as he saw my interest he clammed up, waiting for the green. I reached across the bar and grabbed his tie with the horse's face on it and twisted it just a trifle.

"Repeat, please."

"Hey, okay, okay. All I said was nobody had a chance because everybody knew she was tied to Paul Lassiter."

"Yeah," I half whispered, letting loose of his tie.

I laid a five down on the bar and left.

"It was a stupid lie, Lassiter," I said. "If it was all over the track, you had to know I'd come back with it sooner or later. Why make it later?"

He shrugged and reached for the drink he'd been working on when I burst into his office. "I saw no reason to volunteer any information—besides, isn't that an occupational hazard with you? Being lied to?"

"Only by people who have something to hide," I told him.

"I have nothing to hide, Tucker." He shook his head, "I didn't think Benny would mention it to you because he was furious at the idea. He wouldn't admit to anyone that his daughter loved me. I saw no reason to admit it either."

"You've made me think you have something to hide, Lassiter. If you do, I'll find out what, I promise."

I left him and went looking for Benjamin Hopkins. He had lied to me also, even if it was a lie of omission.

He wasn't in his office and I didn't see him on the grounds. "Where's Hopkins?" I asked his trainer, Mickey Rivers.

Rivers glared at me. He was a man of about thirty-five, retired from the races because of a bad fall some years before. Hopkins took him on as trainer because of his love for horses and it had worked out to their mutual advantage. "Mr. Hopkins," he began, "went home earlier. I imagine he's still there."

Hopkins greeted me, asking, "Have you found out something already?"

"Yes, I have. I found out about Penny and Paul Lassiter. That was something you should have told me, Mr. Hopkins."

"I don't see why that—" he began imperiously.

"I can see why you might not want to admit that Lassiter was taking something from you, especially your daughter, but if you are really concerned about finding her, your pride shouldn't interfere. That is, if your real interest is in finding her."

"What do you mean by that?" he demanded.

"Just that your main interest may not be in where she is, but in whether or not she's with Lassiter."

The look on his face told me I had him pegged right. He wasn't concerned about his daughter's welfare; his real concern was in finding out if Lassiter had taken a "property" away from him.

"I'd like to see her room," I told him, before he could gather his thoughts and decide he wanted to fire me.

"Come this way," he muttered. I followed him up a long winding flight of stairs and into a room larger than my entire apartment. The walls were covered with framed photographs of Penny with horses, Penny with jockeys, and Penny in the Winners Circle with her father.

"I have some paperwork to attend to downstairs," Hopkins told me. "If you need anything, call me."

When he left I began to prowl about the room, attempting to get a bead on how the girl's mind worked.

On her dressing table was a hardcover novel called *Price, Pride, and Passion* by someone I'd never heard of. The bookmark was between the last page and the back cover. I leafed through the book and decided to take it home with me. I continued to prowl and came up with a locked diary—under the mattress. I put it in my jacket pocket.

Nothing else in the room interested me except a framed picture of Paul Lassiter, at his probable handsomest. He was smiling and it was signed, *Love, Paul.*

He was a phony, just like her old man. He didn't love her, or he wouldn't have attempted to hide the fact that they were a "thing." Neither of them loved her. They both considered her a prize to be won from one another. I took a close-up of Penny from the wall, removed it from its frame, and slid it into the book to take with me, and found myself wondering if Penny Hopkins's disappearance had been her own idea.

When I called my service, there was a message from "Ray the bartender." He said he had some information for me. I didn't know a bartender named "Ray," so it had to be the one at the track lounge.

When I walked in, his face lit up in a smile. Considering the way I'd left him, it was a bit of a surprise, but it also meant he had something to sell and he thought he could sell it big.

"Hey," he said, "I been trying to find you. I got your number out of the book."

"Pour me the same as before," I told him. "Why did you want to see me?"

"I remembered something after you left this morning." He stopped and backed away so that his horseface tie was not within easy reach. I took out a five and slid it across the bar.

"To start," I told him. He nodded and grabbed it up.

"I saw Melendez after Thursday."

"When?"

"Yesterday. He came in here for a drink and he was filthy."

"What do you mean by filthy?"

"He looked as if he'd just ridden the feature in the mud and got thrown, you know? Only it ain't rained in weeks."

I digested that and swallowed some ginger ale. "He had a drink?"

"Yep. He came running in, all upsetlike. He even ordered in Spanish. I hadda ask him to repeat it in English. After he drank it, he looked around, scaredlike, you know? Then he ran out like somebody was chasing him."

"Why didn't you remember that this morning?" I asked.

"Hell, it happened so fast. He was in and gone in a couple of minutes." He shrugged. "Slipped my mind."

I thought about it. If what Ray had just told me was true and Melendez was that scared, chances were he wouldn't be at his place. He'd probably be hiding out somewhere.

"Who's he hang out with the most?" I asked. Another jock named Ramirez, Ray said. I asked him to get a message to Ramirez, telling him I had to talk to Melendez. I slid him one of my cards wrapped in a ten-dollar bill.

"He's to call me anytime, got it?"

He snatched up the ten. "I got it. What's it all about anyway?"

"The way I figure it, that's about thirty bucks you've made already. If I hear from Melendez, it could go up to fifty. Got it?"

He widened his eyes. "You got it!"

I went home and fixed myself a steak with onions, a baked potato, and a salad. Then I settled down with my night's reading.

I got a little deeper into the book and caught the drift of it. It was about a girl with a dominant father who didn't like her choice of a fiancé. The two, father and fiancé, hated each other. One night the girl was raped and murdered. The book ends with the two men crying on each other's shoulder.

The diary was next. I used a steak knife on the flimsy lock, got it open, and started reading. It was written in a little-girl scrawl that made the reading a task. It started when she was about seventeen, about two years before. Most of it was about her love of the racetrack, the horses, and the jockeys. There was a segment that said, "Little Louie brought me flowers again today. I know he loves me, and he is sweet, but Paul would never understand."

Another part lamented: "If only Paul and Daddy could become friends again, like they used to be." These, or words to the same effect, were repeated again and again.

Later on, dated just a few weeks before: "I can't take it much longer. I feel as if I'm being torn apart, I love them both so much."

The last pages grew even more anguished, until the final page: "I finished the book this afternoon, and I think I finally have the solution. I must go see Little Louie and ask him for his help."

That was dated Thursday. On Friday Penny had disappeared. She had been seen in the track lounge with Little Louie Melendez on Thursday. On Friday Louie was seen again in the lounge, this time dirty and agitated.

I closed the diary and set it aside.

"Are you the guy that called?" he asked. His nameplate identified him as Officer Doyle.

"That's right, officer." I took out my photostat and showed it to him. His partner, Parker, came along and took a look for himself. They'd pulled their radio car right into the meadow behind the track.

"What's this about a homicide?" Parker asked.

I shook my head. "I didn't say homicide. I said I'd found a body. It's over here."

They followed me into the brush where I had found Penny Hopkins's final resting place. I'd driven there early and had started my search of the meadow about eight-thirty. I found her at ten. I dug just deep enough to free her arm, then stopped and went back to the track to call the police.

They'd sent a patrol car first, to decide whether or not the call was a crank, but as soon as Doyle saw her arm he had called to his partner to get Homicide and the lab people.

I asked him if we could wait for Homicide before I told my story so that I'd only have to tell it once. He was agreeable and we spent the time talking horses. Neither of us looked at the grave while we spoke.

When Homicide arrived I told my story to two detectives I didn't know, Homes and Williams. I told them why I was hired, who I'd spoken to, and what led me to believe the girl was buried where she was.

"You say Melendez showed up in the bar covered with dirt?" Homes remarked. "I'll put out a wanted on him, but meanwhile if you hear anything from him, let us know."

"Would you let me know what the lab comes up with on her?" I asked him. He agreed to keep me informed.

"You got any ideas?" he asked, as we walked from the meadow.

I nodded. "Some. But I need a little more time. Ask Lieutenant Joe Garvey about me. He'll tell you it will be worth your while to give me a little rope." Garvey was my old boss at Missing Persons.

He poked a cigar into his mouth and said, "That's a pretty good recommendation. Were you on the force?"

I nodded. "Ten years."

When we reached his car he told me, "I'll talk to Garvey. If you don't hear from me, be in my office tonight." He pointed his cigar at me and added, "Ready to spill."

I got to a phone and called my service. It was a little like calling OTB to see if your horse has come in—and mine had. Melendez had called and left a message for me to meet him at the opposite end of the track, beneath the grandstand. The time he wanted was twelve-thirty, and it was a quarter-past now.

The grandstand was, as I've said, at the other end of the track so that you couldn't see the meadow from there. I hoped Melendez hadn't seen the police from somewhere else and been scared off.

But when I got there he was waiting. He was like a scared deer, ready to run at any moment.

"Meester Tucker?" he asked, primed to run if I said no.

"That's right," 1 told him. I let him see my ID and he relaxed.

"I got message saying you want to help me." He was almost five feet tall and must have weighed all of ninety pounds.

"That's right, Louis, I do."

He nodded. "That is good. I can use help."

Just then he spotted something behind me and he froze. I turned. It was Homes with his partner and two uniformed cops.

"Damn it!" I yelled. They had tailed me.

"Don't move, Melendez!" Homes shouted. "We're the police!"

Louis glared at me and yelled, "You trick me!"

"No, Louis, I didn't!" He started to run and I hollered, "Don't run, they can't hurt you!"

"You've got nowhere to go, Melendez!" Homes shouted, coming up beside me. He had his gun out and was pointing it at the fleeing jockey. "Halt!"

"Don't shoot, damn it!" I yelled, knocking his arm up. His shot went wild and I started after Louis. I had to get to him before Homes or anyone else killed him.

I knew he hadn't killed Penny Hopkins.

He had only buried her.

"Detective Homes and Detective Williams, Mr. Hopkins. They're from Homicide."

Hopkins backed away from the door into his stable office and said, "Homicide! You mean he killed her?"

"Who killed her, Mr. Hopkins?" Homes asked. Williams stepped inside after us but kept the door open.

"Why, Lassiter, of course. She probably came to her senses about marrying him and he killed her!" He sat. "She is dead, isn't she?"

"Yes, Mr. Hopkins, she's dead," Homes answered. "Mr. Tucker found her buried in the meadow behind the track."

Hopkins nodded. "So he did kill her."

"You're ridiculous," came a voice from outside. Lassiter stepped into the room and faced Hopkins, a younger version of his former mentor. "You know I didn't love her, Benny. Why would I kill her?"

"Because you couldn't take her from me," Hopkins snapped.

"That's all she was to both of you, something to take from each other," I told them.

Hopkins took no offense. "I don't have to justify myself to you, Tucker. I didn't ask for a daughter, I wanted a son. And on top of that, my wife died in childbirth. How could anyone expect me to love her?" It made so much sense to him that I pitied him.

"What about you?" I asked Lassiter. "What did she mean to you?"

Lassiter shrugged. "I liked her, but I didn't love her. She knew that—"

I shook my head. "No, she didn't know that. It says in here that she loved you both." I tossed the diary at Hopkins.

"What's this?" he asked.

"It's the diary of a young girl who was being pulled apart by the only two men in the world she really cared about."

"All right, Tucker," Homes snapped, "you brought us here to convince us Melendez didn't kill the girl—so do it." Melendez was in custody, but he hadn't been charged yet.

"Melendez only buried her," I said, suddenly bone-tired. I indicated Hopkins and Lassiter and added, "They killed her."

"What?" Hopkins barked.

"You fool," Lassiter said.

"Tucker—" Homes began, but I interrupted.

"I'm sorry. I should have said they caused her death. They didn't actually murder her, but they were the cause."

I picked up the diary and began to explain. "Penny Hopkins was a very emotional, impressionable, unstable young girl. She loved her father and she loved Lassiter, but to them she was just something to fight over, like a beautiful colt. That confused her. She wanted them to love her and she wanted them to be friends.

"I don't know exactly how long their battle for Penny went on, but this diary goes back two years and it was happening then. That's two years she was pushed and pulled between the two people she cared most about, not knowing which way to go, which one to be loyal to . . .

"Then she read a book about a girl with very much the same problem as hers. The girl in the book had her problem solved for her. She was raped and murdered and this brought her father and boyfriend closer together. It was a terrible, romantic solution, but Penny was very much alone and very much in need of a solution."

"You mean she went out and got herself raped and murdered?" Williams asked.

"I mean she shot herself."

"What?" It was a collective statement.

I turned to the last page of her diary "The last page in her diary says she finished the book and had found her solution, but she needed Melendez's help. Melendez was in love with her, he'd do anything for her. He got her the gun she asked for and afterward he buried her."

I shut the diary and concluded.

Penny, Louis had told me, had chosen the meadow for her suicide because it was behind the track and out of sight and chances were good the shot would not be heard. After it was over, after he had watched her put the gun to her head, and pull the trigger, and he had buried her, he began to realize what he'd done. Penny had not wanted to be buried—she had wanted to be found. It was part of the plan to make her father and Lassiter think she'd been murdered, which, to her disturbed way of thinking, would bring them closer together. But Melendez had panicked and buried her in the meadow, along with the gun—as a result of which, he was as guilty in the eyes of the law as if he had pulled the trigger.

And so the man who had really loved Penny Hopkins would pay for Hopkins's and Lassiter's lack of love for her, and they would go scot-free. I took the photograph of the girl from my pocket and looked at it.

The two men she had adored were playing a perpetual game of chess.

She had thought she was their queen.

I'm glad she never discovered she was just another pawn.

Author's note

Although the detective's name in this story is Frank Tucker, when the story was turned into a novel the P.I. became Henry Po. There have been quite a few Henry Po stories since then. Plans for further Po novels just never moved forward.

The Equine Theft

Three months ago no one had ever heard of a horse named Half A Buck, and the Triple Crown races for this season were generally considered to be a two-horse affair between Hopkins Stables' Mush Money and Lassiter Farms' True Crime. Now, after four easy victories, the last being an eight-length romp in his first stakes test, Half A Buck had made the Triple Crown races competitive again. Two horses did not a race make. But three? That was a race.

Half A Buck had been unraced as a two-year-old, hence he did not have the experience the other two horses had, but for pure speed you just couldn't fault him. And as for stamina, his last race had been at a mile and an eighth and he had led the field from start to finish.

I knew all of this because I keep up on the racing news. So when my boss, J. Howard Biel, chairman of the New York State Racing Club, called me into his office and asked me if I knew who Half A Buck was, I said of course.

"Henry, there's something going on out at Camden Farms," Biel told me.

Camden Farms owned Half A Buck, and the horse was trained by Wally Briscoe. Camden Farms was owned by Samuel Woodford Camden. Camden had been around racing for fifty years and, with all his success, had never come close to saddling a Kentucky Derby winner. Half A Buck was his first shot.

"Like what?" I asked.

"I don't know. I've gotten this much through the grapevine, but haven't been able to positively identify the problem."

"If you can't *positively* identify it, what do you *think* it is?"

Biel hesitated, contemplating me over the bridge he'd formed out of his hands.

"I think," he said, "they are missing a horse."

I sat up straight. "Half A Buck?"

He shook his head. "I don't know. I hope not."

"It can't be. How could they keep that quiet?"

"Again, I don't know. I want you to go out there and find out what the hell is going on."

So I went, but I was not welcomed with open arms.

Some trainers kept their horses in stables on the track grounds during the meeting, but an outfit the size of Camden Farms had their own place. This was especially useful for Half A Buck, who was notorious for being extremely high strung.

When I pulled up in front of the gates of Camden Farms in Cherry Hill, New Jersey, I was confronted by a uniformed private security guard.

I showed him my NYSRC credentials and identified myself as Henry Po, special investigator.

There were four of us designated as "special investigators," answerable only to Biel and paid by a special grant from the board of directors—a grant they were forever trying to revoke, the cheapskates!

"I'll have to call ahead, sir," the guard told me.

"I'll wait."

He called ahead. If they were trying to hide something, my appearance probably shook them up good.

When he returned from his little shack he said, "You can drive through, sir. It's about a mile ahead."

"Thanks."

He opened the gates and I drove my Pontiac through. I passed the training track on my way, and almost a mile in I came to a large, southern mansion-style house.

I recognized the barrel-chested man waiting out front from having seen him around the track and in racing newspapers. It was the trainer, Wally Briscoe.

"Mr. Po?" he asked as I got out of my car.

"Mr. Briscoe," I said, putting out my hand. His grip was like a vise, but he knew it and kept it under control. He was, after all, an ex-jockey and jocks were supposed to have incredible strength in their hands, wrists, and forearms. Shaking hands with him, I could believe it.

"What can I do for you, Mr. Po? What brings you all the way out here?"

"Would Mr. Camden be around, Mr. Briscoe?"

"As a matter of fact he stays out here whenever we're approaching a big race with Half A Buck. He likes to be near his pride and joy. He's waiting inside."

His instructions had probably been to try and handle me outside first. Failing that, he'd bring me in. I wasn't giving him much choice in the matter.

"Could we go in and see him, please?"

"This way," he said, giving me a dirty look.

I was very interested in meeting Mr. Camden. He was something of a recluse, only coming out in the open these days when Half A Buck raced. He loved the animal and was quite proud of him.

He was waiting for us inside, seated in a straight-backed chair rather than one of the sofas or softer chairs in the living room.

"Mr. Camden," Briscoe said, "this is Henry Po."

"Do you have some identification?" the old man asked me.

I nodded and produced my ID again, and a photostat of my private investigator's license.

While Camden inspected them, I did the same to him.

He was about six-two, as near as I could figure while he was seated, with closely cropped gray hair and a deeply lined face. He looked every year of his age—seventy-four—and more. Apparently, judging from the way he sat in that straight-backed chair, he suffered some sort of back ailment.

He handed me back my ID and asked me the same question Briscoe had asked outside. "What brings you here, Mr. Po?"

"I'll be very frank, Mr. Camden. My boss, Howard Biel, has heard some rumors that have disturbed him. He asked me to come out and check it out for him."

I saw a look pass between Briscoe and Camden before the old man asked, "What kind of rumors?"

"Something about a missing horse."

They exchanged looks again, trying to decide how to play it, and I gave them each time to think.

"Tell him," Camden finally told his trainer.

Briscoe grimaced, as if in pain, and said, "It's true. We are missing a horse, a very valuable horse. Too valuable to let it be known publicly."

Camden decided to speak for himself at that point.

"Fifty years, Mr. Po," he began sadly. "Fifty years I've been buying horses, searching for the right one. For twenty of those years Wally has been my trainer and together we've tried and tried to build a champion, a Kentucky Derby winner, a *Triple Crown* winner!" Leaning forward—a movement that obviously quite painful for him—he said, "Never before have we gotten our hands on an animal like Half A

Buck." His eyes, sunken and moist, came alive when he spoke the horse's name.

"Quiet Little Morning was no slouch," I reminded him.

Now he smiled fondly, savoring an old memory, and I felt I had scored some points with him without really trying. Quiet Little Morning had been the star of his stable in 1973 and many thought that the horse had a shot at the Triple Crown. But 1973 was also the year of another horse: Secretariat. Still, the horse had been developing, a steady performer, as game as they came, but he never got to run against the famous "Big Red."

They found QLM dead in his stall one morning, a week before the Derby was run. The reason for his death had never been discovered.

"My pet," he said fondly, then frowned as the fond memory became painful. "But no, Mr. Po, even QLM, as good a horse as he was, was never in the class of Half A Buck."

In the world of horse racing, horses are classified with one word. A "useful" horse is a horse who rarely wins, but usually collects a check for second, third, or fourth; a "good" horse is one who wins, until he comes up against a "great" horse. Obviously Camden felt that Quiet Little Morning had been a "good" horse, but Half A Buck was a "great" horse.

"This animal is a natural champion, Mr. Po, believe me. You seem knowledgeable, you must have seen him run. Don't you agree?"

"He is something special," I said.

"This tragedy we are speaking of now could ruin our dream. No Triple Crown for Wally, myself—or for Half A Buck."

"How long has Half A Buck been missing, Mr. Camden? And why didn't you at least notify Howard Biel?"

They exchanged looks again and Camden nodded, sitting back in his chair. He was turning the conversation over to Briscoe once more, having exhausted himself.

"It's not Half A Buck that's missing, Mr. Po," Briscoe told me.

"What?"

"It's not Half A Buck—"

I was suddenly annoyed.

"For Chrissake, then what's the big deal?"

"Explain it to him," Camden said, his voice so soft we almost didn't hear it.

"It's not Half A Buck that's missing," Briscoe said again, "but his lead pony, Candi."

"His lead pony?"

"Do you know why Half A Buck was unraced as a two-year-old?"

"I've wondered. . . ."

"He was too unruly, too stubborn, more so than any other two-year-old I've ever trained. We couldn't even get him to walk through the post parade. He'd toss his head, run off, kick. He's bitten his fair share of boys, I'll tell you, and I even carry some scars myself. The horse had so much spirit, so much raw speed and power for a colt, yet we thought we'd never be able to race him."

"Then along came Candi," I said.

"That's right."

"This is beginning to sound like some sort of equine love story."

"More like friendship," Briscoe corrected me. "Half A Buck took to Candi the way he had never taken to any other animal or human before. Do you know Jorge Pimentel?"

"Half A Buck's rider."

Briscoe nodded.

"He's ridden Half A Buck in all his victories and they get along fine —as long as Candi is around."

"How long has she been gone?"

"Three days."

"How was she taken?"

"Nobody knows. She was there, and then she was gone. Nobody saw anything, she just disappeared."

Horses don't just disappear, I thought. Not by themselves.

"Can I see her stall?"

Briscoe looked at Camden, who had his eyes closed and might have drifted off, and then said, "Of course."

Briscoe was about fifty now and at one time had been the youngest trainer in the business. He had been forced to retire as a rider early after an injury.

He led me to the stable where Half A Buck had his stall. I recognized the colt by the distinctive blaze on his face. Wide between his eyes and then tapering down, it was almost like an inverted triangle.

"Candi was kept in this stall right next to Half A Buck."

"These doors always kept locked?" I asked, referring not only to the stall doors but to the main stable doors as well.

"Not always, no. Hell, we don't always lock the doors, we don't always have guards. Who expected someone to steal a horse?"

"That used to be a serious crime."

"Sure, but this ain't the Old West. And if they were going to steal a horse, why Candi? Why not Half A Buck himself?"

"Obviously someone figured out how important Candi was to Half A Buck's racing career. Look, Wally, it's plain that someone doesn't want your horse to run in the Derby, but they don't want to come right out and steal a top thoroughbread. They don't want that kind of heat, so they did the next best thing. They took Candi, and that's the end of Half A Buck's career."

He looked at me, stunned by something that had apparently just come to him. "Do you think it's one of the other owners or trainers? It's probably that bastard Hopkins—"

"If you jump to that kind of conclusion you might be sorry, Briscoe," I said. "Let me look into this before you fly off the handle. Mr. Biel will guarantee to keep it out of the papers until it's absolutely necessary."

"I'll have to check with the old man," he said, speaking of Camden with affection in his tone.

"I'm sure he'll agree. Who's usually in charge of Candi's maintenance?"

"Well, the old man's granddaughter usually exercises her. As far as feeding, cooling down and the like, that would be Billy Wainwright."

We walked around the stall, kicking up hay, not really accomplishing anything, just moving while we talked.

"That name rings a bell."

"It should. He was almost as hot as Cauthen a few years ago. For an apprentice, he had unbelievable savvy."

"He had a spill, didn't he?"

"Yep, messed up his right leg, but that healed. What didn't was his head. He had everything—Shoemaker's hands, Velasquez's judge of pace, he was a natural lightweight. What he could have used was Angel Cordero's guts."

"He was afraid to get back up on a horse?"

Briscoe nodded and said, "Under racing conditions, yes. We took him on because I knew how he felt."

"But you weren't afraid," I pointed out. "Your injury was legit."

"Sure, but I still knew how he felt about losing his career."

We started back to the house and I asked for Pimentel and Wainwright's addresses, as well as where I could find Camden's granddaughter.

"I'll get you Jorge and Billy's addresses when we get inside. As for

Sue, she should be along any minute if she's not here already. She's picking up the old man."

"What's her story? Likes to hang around horses?"

"That was when she was a kid. Now she likes to ride them. Actually, she's a jockey, an apprentice. She wants to be Half A Buck's rider, but we couldn't take the chance with him. Pimentel rides him and no one else."

"How'd she take that?"

"In stride, I guess."

"Is she any good?"

"For a girl," he said. He seemed to consider that, then added, "No, that's not fair. She's got the makings. But she lacks patience. She wants the top mounts now, but she just has to wait."

When we got back inside, the old man opened his eyes and looked at us.

"I'll call Howard," he said right away, "and apologize for not phoning him earlier."

I said, "If I may, sir, I'd like to ask you what you thought you were doing for these past three days."

"We thought there might be a ransom demand of some kind. We didn't want to jeopardize our chance of getting the horse back safely."

"You might have done just that," I said, but before we could pursue the point we heard a car pull up out front. Since no call had come from the gate, I assumed it was Camden's granddaughter.

When she came through the front door I confess to being a little stunned. I had expected a skinny teenager with freckles and a long pony tail—possibly blonde. What I got was a seemingly very mature, self-possessed twenty-two-year-old woman with long auburn hair and sparkling green eyes. She was lean, perhaps too tall for a jockey, but she didn't weigh much, which would have helped, and she had the right curves in the right places. I had been accurate about one thing, though. She did have freckles, across the bridge of her nose. I found myself wondering if she had any on her back.

"Ready, Grandfather?" she asked. I noticed that she pointedly ignored Briscoe.

"Just about, my dear. Mr. Po, allow me to introduce my granddaughter, Susan King. My dear, Mr. Po is a private investigator working for Howard Biel. He's going to help us find Candi."

She looked surprised at the news, but recovered and approached me, sticking out her hand. She had the firm grip of a jockey.

"I hope you can find her, Mr. Po. The Derby is only a couple weeks away."

The old man started to struggle to his feet and I made a move to go and help but Briscoe put his hand on my arm and shook his head. Susan quickly moved to her grandfather's side and helped him up.

She turned to me with her arm around Camden and said, "Good luck, Mr. Po. Maybe we'll see each other again."

"I would like to talk to you, Miss King—about Candi."

"Fine. Wally can give you my number. Call me."

When they left, Briscoe avoided any conversation about Sue King. He got me the addresses and phone numbers I needed and we went over the rest of the people employed on the farm who might have had access to the horses. I took their addresses as well.

I told him to wish me luck and he told me to keep my head down in the stretch. I settled for that and left.

I talked to most of the other farm employees and then went to see Billy Wainwright. A lot of the others lived in New Jersey, but the address Briscoe had given me for Wainwright was in Manhattan, in the Village, a long way from the farm.

When I told him who I was and why I was there he opened his door wide to me.

"I sure hope you find her in time, Mr. Po. It would be a damn shame if Half A Buck didn't get to run in the Derby."

"You feel as confident about the horse's chances as his connections do?"

"Definitely. There's not a three-year-old around who can touch him."

He couldn't have been more than five feet tall and he would have been in his prime if he were still riding. He had an unruly mop of black hair that kept falling down across his eyes and a weak chin. His grip, however, was as firm as Briscoe's. "What did you see that day, Billy? The day Candi disappeared?"

"Well, let me think." He sat on the bed to do that. I decided not to wade through the mountain of dirty clothes on my right to find a chair and remained standing.

"I can't think of anything unusual, Mr. Po. Sue exercised Candi, and when I went to feed her she was gone."

"How long after Sue returned with her did you discover her missing?"

He shrugged. "Couldn't have been more than a half an hour."

"You mean someone spirited a fifteen-hundred-pound animal off that farm in half an hour and nobody saw them?"

"Gee, it sure looks that way."

"Did Sue take her out and bring her back at the same time every day?"

"Like clockwork."

That's what a lot of the others had told me.

I thanked him and told him I'd be in touch again if I had any more questions.

I went to see Pimentel, the jockey, next. He was sitting out a five-day suspension for a riding infraction, so I found him home. He was renting a room from a family in Elmont, Long Island, right near Belmont Park.

Pimentel was a veteran jockey, one of the good ones, mentioned in the same breath with Cordero, Pincay, Shoemaker, Maple, and Velasquez.

Pimentel was also about five feet tall, about thirty-three, with a wispy mustache and a heavy Spanish accent. He was in a T-shirt when we talked, and I could plainly see the hard biceps of his arms. Wading through his accent, I found out that he had been at the farm the day but had not seen anything out of the ordinary.

That had to mean that Candi had been stolen in a very ordinary manner.

I decided to call Sue King and invite her to dinner, combining business with pleasure.

She accepted.

I liked her. We had dinner, we chatted, we got along very well, which was a shame. It would have been easier if I'd been able to dislike her.

After dinner I invited her to my apartment and she accepted without hesitation. When we reached there, I opened the door and allowed her to precede me, which gave me an unobstructed view of her bare back—bare because of the kind of dress she was wearing—and she did indeed have freckles on her back.

"Well I'll be damned," I said as I closed the door behind us.

"What?" she asked, turning.

"Your back. You've got freckles on it."

"Don't rub it in."

"I'm not," I said. "I like freckles."

"Do you like me?" she asked, moving closer.

"Very much."

"Good," she said. She-tilted her head up and kissed me. Instead of kissing her back—which I wanted to do—I pushed her away gently and walked past her into my loft.

"What's wrong, Hank?"

"It's this thing with Candi, Sue."

"Is it rough? Can't you find her?"

"Well, it's true I don't know exactly where she is—but I know who took her." She had been moving toward me at that point and now she stopped and even took a step back, looking surprised.

"You do?"

"Yes, Sue, I do. You took her."

She couldn't decide how to act. I think it was because she liked me, too. However ultimately, she reacted the way you would have expected.

"That's silly," she said. "Why would I take her?"

"Well, let's take this one step at a time," I suggested. "Let's start with the how."

I sat, and invited her to do the same.

"Everyone I interviewed told me the same thing: Nothing out of the ordinary happened the day Candi disappeared. But they were wrong. You took Candi out for her exercise ride, same as always; that was ordinary. However, you never brought her back, and that wasn't ordinary. It wasn't ordinary, but nobody noticed. Why? Because you always take her out and you always bring her back. It's the kind of thing that everyone takes for granted, and you counted on that. Even when they didn't see you come back with her, they would simply assume that you had—maybe while they were doing something else—and that's why it worked. That's why everyone thought that Candi had just disappeared."

She didn't deny it. I guess she realized that it would be a waste of time and effort.

"Where is Candi, Sue?"

"She safe, Hank. In an abandoned barn near the farm. I would never have hurt her. You don't know me long, but I think you know that much."

"You're right, I do know that. I even know why you did it. All evening you've been talking about being a jockey, a champion jockey. You saw Half A Buck as a fast ticket to achieving your goal, only your grandfather and Wally Briscoe wouldn't go along. Were you getting back at him?"

She stood up and began to pace.

"No, not back at him. I thought I could prove that I could handle Half A Buck without Candi around. I thought if I could do that they'd let me ride him."

"How did you plan to do that?"

She stopped pacing and faced me.

"I don't know, Hank! I really don't! I hadn't—I didn't—oh, damn!" She paused and took a deep breath, composing herself. "It was stupid, I admit. I acted without really thinking it through. But you were right, I knew I could get away with taking Candi because it was all routine."

"And then?"

"And then I got scared. I started wondering how I could bring her back without admitting I'd taken her. And then I thought maybe if I pretended to find her, they'd let me ride Half A Buck out of gratitude. Oh, it was just a crazy thing to do!" She covered her face with her hands and I stayed where I was.

Finally, she looked at me and said, "I'll go with you when you tell him."

"No."

"What do you mean, no?" she asked. "You're not going to tell him?"

"No. You are. Bring Candi back, Sue, and explain to your grandfather just the way it happened."

"Do you think he'll understand?"

"You know that better than I do, but it's really not important. The important thing is for you to get her back and hope you haven't retarded Half A Buck's preparations for the Derby by taking her."

"Oh God," she said, covering her mouth with her hands. "I hope I haven't done that."

"He's a great horse, Sue," I said. "I don't think four days will matter."

"I hope you're right. You know, when I met you this afternoon I was afraid. But later I thought maybe it was for the best. Maybe you'd find out, and you did."

"Yes, I did."

"Will you do something for me?"

"Of course," I said. "What?"

"Will you be there? When I tell him? You know, for moral support?"

She wasn't a bad person, this girl with the sparkling green eyes and freckles. She hadn't really done it to hurt anyone; she had done it as a possible means to a dream, and it had turned into a nightmare instead. She was a girl with a dream and she was in a hurry to realize it.

Who among us isn't?

Besides, I liked her.

"I'll be there."

The Nickel Derby

Kentucky Derby time is a special time of year for anyone involved in thoroughbred horse racing. The air crackles with excitement and tension as the big day approaches. My involvement with the Derby is usually as a non-betting spectator, but this year it had suddenly become a more substantial part of my life.

My boss, J. Howard Biel, chairman of the New York State Racing Club, had phoned me at home that morning, something which has customarily come to mean bad—or "serious"—news.

Invariably, every year there is a "Big Horse" from the East Coast, and a "Big Horse" from the West Coast. The Kentucky Derby is usually the first meeting between these two special thoroughbreds. This year, the East Coast horse was a big, strapping colt named Dreamland, and the West Coast entry was a sleek, rather smallish bundle of energy called Runamuck. So imposing were the credentials of these two horses that to date only five other horses had been named to run against them in the Derby. Of those, however, one had been felled by injury and another by illness, cutting the total field to five. This had caused this year's Run for the Roses to be dubbed by the media as "The Nickel Derby."

Arriving at Howard's office after his phone summons and accepting his offer of some of that mud he calls coffee, I took a seat while he started to tell me about it. "I've had a meeting with officials from both California and Kentucky."

"About what?"

"There have been some threats against Dreamland and his camp."

"What sort of threats?"

"They've ranged from kidnapping to actually killing the horse."

"And the people on his camp?"

"They've been threatened with bodily harm but no death threats as of yet."

"Well, that's all a real shame, Howard. But why would that cause you to have a meeting with the racing officials of two other states and then call me?"

He hesitated, then said, "Because they don't have a team of special investigators, and I do."

He did have a team of investigators, for which he had fought long and hard with the Board of Directors of the NYSRC. They had finally agreed to give him a grant to hire not the twenty people he'd requested, but four. Take it or leave it, they told him, and he had taken it.

He took it and promptly contacted me because I had done some work for him before. I accepted the job and helped find the three other people.

"Such as we are," I replied now.

"A poor lot, but mine own," he said, spreading his hands.

"So they want to borrow a man, is that it?"

"That's about the size of it. You'd be in charge of security for the animal while he's in California as well as when he's taken to Kentucky." He leaned forward and added, "Henry, if this horse were stolen or harmed, it would be a serious blow to all of thoroughbred racing. That's why I've decided it's important for us to work with these people."

"You mean you've decided that I should work with them."

He smiled grimly and said, "Yes, that's exactly what I mean."

"What about Runamuck?"

"No threats, no calls. Thank God."

"All right, Howard." I stood up. "I'll get going."

"I appreciate this, Henry," he said, opening his top drawer. He withdrew a brown envelope and held it out. "Here's your ticket, and some expense money."

"Think you know me pretty well, huh?" I asked, taking the envelope. "I'll need some background info on the people I'll be dealing with."

He reached down and brought an attaché case out from behind his desk. "It's been prepared."

"Boy," I said, taking that, too, "I really like being unpredictable."

"Good luck, Henry."

"I'll keep in touch."

□ □ □

On the plane, I went through the material in the attaché case. It told me a little about the people in the Dreamland camp: Donald McCoy, his rider, who had ridden him in all of his previous races; his owner, Mrs. Emily Nixon, who had taken the stable over from her father when he died ten years ago and had not had a Derby winner since; and his trainer, Lew Hale, who had been hired by Mrs. Nixon at the time she took over the stable.

It sounded like there could be some pressure on Hale to come through with a Derby winner, so I decided he'd be a good place to start.

When I landed at LAX, I took a cab to a hotel, changed into some California duds, and then took another cab to the racetrack, where I sought and found Lew Hale.

It was early, and workouts were just concluding. I approached Hale as he was looking over a two-year-old filly that was being galloped around the track and introduced myself.

"Oh, you're the investigator from New York," he said, holding out his hand. "Glad to have you aboard, Mr. Po."

Deeply lined, be it from constant exposure to the weather, or otherwise, his face had character. His eyes were gray and his nose prominent. His mouth was what made him look ugly, though. His lips were heavy, and twisted, so that he looked as if he had just sucked a lemon. He was taller than me by some four inches, which put him at least at six-two. He was in good shape for a man in his late fifties—hell, he was in good shape for a man my own age.

"I don't mind telling you, I've been plenty worried since those threats started."

"How long has that been?"

He thought a moment, then said, "A couple of weeks, I guess. First there was a note saying that Dreamland would never make it to the Derby."

"That sounds more like an opinion than a threat," I pointed out.

"Which was why we didn't react to it."

"Did you keep it?"

"I'm sorry, no. I threw it out. I never realized it was a threat until I got the phone call."

"Where did you receive the phone call?"

"Here, at the track."

"What time of day?"

"Early, before the day's racing began."

"Was the caller a man or a woman?"

"Oh, now that's hard to say. It could have been a woman with a deep voice—"

"Or a man with a fairly high one," I finished for him.

"I'm afraid so. It sounded sort of muffled, as if the person had their hand over the phone."

"What did they say?"

"That Dreamland was going to take a ride, but that it wouldn't be to Kentucky."

"How many other calls did you get after that?"

"Two. The last one said that Dreamland would be dead before he could reach the finish line."

"What about the threats against you and his jock?"

"I don't scare, Mr. Po, but he sure did."

"What?"

"No, you wouldn't know about that yet," he said. "He quit yesterday. He got a call and wouldn't even tell me what was said. He just wanted out, and I let him go. I don't need a gutless jock."

"In what way were you threatened?"

"They told me I'd be dead if Dreamland won the Derby. Bullshit!"

"I wonder if I could see where you keep the colt now?"

"Of course. Just let me finish watching Miss Emily work."

"The filly?" I asked.

"Yeah."

"She looks like a beauty."

"The lady knows horse flesh," he admitted.

"Mrs. Nixon?"

He nodded. "She bid on the filly herself and went for more bucks than I would have. But then, it's her money and I guess she knows what she's doing."

We watched the filly work until, apparently satisfied, Hale said, "Come on, let's go and see Dreamy. He's impressive as all hell just standing in his stall."

We walked out to a parking lot and got into a Chevy that was covered with dust. We drove into the stable area on a dirt road. Hale stopped the car in front of one of the larger stables and we got out. I could see a uniformed guard standing outside one of the stalls, so it wasn't hard to figure out where Dreamland was.

"I've had a guard on him day and night for three days now, since the last call," Hale explained.

When we reached the stall, the guard nodded at Hale but made no attempt to stop me or have me identify myself.

"This is Mr. Po," Hale told him. "He's from New York, and he will be in charge of security from now on."

"Yes, sir," the guard replied, and he nodded at me now that we'd been introduced. "Are you private, or track security?" I asked the guard.

"Private, sir."

Hale said, "He's actually from the same company the track uses, but he's not assigned to the track permanently. Mrs. Nixon hired his company and they send us our own guards."

"Do you want to see my ID?" I asked the uniformed man.

"Uh, that won't be necessary, sir," he answered.

"Yes, it will," I said, taking out my ID and showing it to him. "I don't care whose company a stranger is in," I added, "I want his ID checked. Understand?"

The guard compressed his lips at the scolding and said, "Yes, sir, I understand." I stepped past him, leaned on the stall door and peered in. Hale had been right; Dreamland was impressive. He picked up his head and looked me straight in the eye, wondering who the interloper was.

"Well, hello, your majesty," I greeted him.

"You get that feeling too, huh?" Hale asked. "He's regal-looking as all hell, eh?"

"That he is," I agreed.

"And he runs like all hell, too."

"How many shifts do you have the guards working on?"

"Three."

"When are you flying to Kentucky?"

"Day after tomorrow."

"Okay, until that time I want two guards on every shift. One here, and one moving about."

"I'll arrange it."

"It'll cost more."

"Lady Emily doesn't care about the cost," he assured me.

"Is that a nickname?"

"One of the milder ones," he answered, "and they're usually used behind her back."

"Has McCoy been around today?" I asked.

"Not today," he said. He turned his attention to the horse and said,

"See you later, Dreamy." Dreamland gave him a sideways glance and then raised his head up high, as if ignoring us.

"Not very friendly," I commented.

"And that may be his only idiosyncrasy. But the way he runs, who cares? Come on, let's go to my office. If you can't locate McCoy around here, you might find him at home, licking his wounds."

"Why wouldn't I find him around here?" I asked. "He didn't quit riding altogether, did he?"

"When he quit me, he might as well have."

Hale gave me McCoy's address and phone number, and then I spent the better part of an hour trying to locate him on the track. When the day's racing began and I still hadn't found him, I gave up. None of the trainers I spoke to would admit that McCoy had been blackballed, but none of them were using him as a rider.

When I left the track, I grabbed a cab and gave the driver McCoy's home address, which turned to be an apartment building in a middle class neighborhood. Asking the driver to wait, I went into the lobby and rang McCoy's bell, but received no answer. I returned to the cab and had him take me back to my hotel, where I'd plan out my next move.

I checked in at the desk to see if there were any messages, not really expecting any, but when you're staying at a hotel you tend to do that. To my surprise, there was a message in my box. I controlled my curiosity until I got to my room. Once inside, I opened the envelope and took out a neatly typewritten note.

I read: "Mrs. Emily Nixon requests that you dine with her tonight. A car will come by your hotel to pick you up at seven sharp."

No signature.

It was some hell of a "request," but since I wanted to talk to the lady anyway, I wouldn't argue.

I read the note again, then put it down on a writing desk. Before showering, I dialed McCoy's number but got no answer. I showered, then tried again, still getting no response. I wanted very much to talk to McCoy and find out from him why he withdrew from a mount that very likely would have made him a lot of money. Hale had told me his version, but Hale—and Emily Nixon—were management; and management always had their own idea about how things should be.

I got dressed and was ready when "Lady Emily's" driver knocked on the door.

1 didn't expect to find anyone else in the car, since I thought that the vehicle was being sent specifically to take me somewhere, but there she was. When I stuck my head in, the first thing I saw were a pair of shapely legs. The second thing I saw was the face of an extremely handsome woman, which at the moment was wearing an amused smile.

"Good evening, Mr. Po," she said.

"Mrs. Nixon."

"Please, step all the way in and take a seat."

When I stepped in, the driver slammed the door behind me, got behind the wheel and got under way.

"Let me say how grateful I am that you agreed to come to California and help us with our problem."

"I'm happy to be of help, Mrs. Nixon."

She had violet eyes that were very bright and intelligent. She appeared to be in her early forties but was exceptionally attractive and radiated youthful vitality.

"I hope you like expensive food, Mr. Po," she said. "It's the only kind I ever eat."

"I only indulge when someone else is paying, Mrs. Nixon."

"Then you're in luck, aren't you?"

We spoke idly of racing until we reached our destination, an extremely expensive-looking Italian restaurant on Wilshire. When we entered we received the preferential treatment a woman of her station deserved—and craved—and were shown to "her" table.

After we had ordered dinner and had drinks in our hands, she said, "Well, what will your first step be in finding the man who has been making all these ghastly threats against us?"

"I think I should explain," I replied, "that my primary concern is not in finding the person making the threats, but to make sure that no harm comes to Dreamland or any of the people around him."

"I see," she said. "I'm afraid I misunderstood then. I was under the impression you were a special 'investigator' for the New York State Racing Club."

"I am," I assured her.

"Oh? Then what is it that a special investigator does?" she asked. "Investigate, no?"

"Under normal circumstances, yes," I said, trying not to lose my temper with her. "But not in this instance, I'm afraid."

"What have you done, then, to assure Dreamland's safety?" she asked. Her tone was considerably colder than it had been to that point.

I explained that I had been to the track and had increased the security around Dreamland's stall. I also told her that I had spoken to Lew Hale, and was looking for McCoy.

"I don't want to talk about McCoy," she said vehemently. "How dare he do that to me!"

"You're talking about withdrawing from the mount?"

"Of course! What else?" she shot back. "I cannot believe—" She stopped herself in midsentence, closed he eyes and said, "I do not want to talk about that little man."

"What about Hale?"

"Hale is fired if Dreamy doesn't win the Derby," she said. "I've given him long enough."

"Ten years, isn't it?"

"Yes, ever since my father died. My father, George Gregg, had two Derby winners and three other horses who finished in the money. I have not had a horse accomplish any of that."

"Lew Hale seems fairly confident," I observed.

"We are all confident," she agreed, "but confidence does not win horse races." Dinner came and I asked if she minded talking while we ate.

"Well, well, a gentleman," she said. "How nice. No, of course I don't mind. Thank you for asking."

As we cut into our food, I asked, "Will you be going to Kentucky with Dreamy?"

"No, but I'll be there later in the week, the day before the race," she answered. "I don't want to miss the Derby Eve festivities."

"Mrs. Nixon, about the threats. The notes, the calls—"

"One call," she said. "I received only one call."

"I understood there were more. And at least one note."

"The other calls and the note were received by Lew Hale."

"Did you see the note?"

"No, I did not. He told me about it, but said he threw it away."

"What about the call you did get?"

"A voice—"

"Male or female?"

That stopped her, as it had Hale, and she had to think about it. "The voice was rather deep. I did not get the impression that I was speaking to a woman."

I put a lot of stock into her "impression"—or lack of one. I reasoned that a woman would know instinctively if she were speaking to another woman.

"Go on," I said.

"The voice said that if I made the trip to Kentucky, I'd be lucky as all hell to make it back."

This time I was the one who was stopped for a moment. Then I said, "Was that verbatim?"

"What?" she asked, hesitating over a forkful of linguini.

"The message you got on the phone, the way you gave it to me just now—was that word for word?"

She thought a moment, then said, "Yes. That's the way I remember it. Why?"

"Nothing," I said, not wanting to voice my thoughts at that moment. It would take more than what I was thinking to build a case. I went on, "How much contact have you had with Lew Hale over your ten-year association?"

"Actually, not all that much. Outside of the winner's circle—when we get there—I don't think I see him more than two or three times a year."

"Isn't that unusual?"

"Perhaps. But unlike my father I do not like the way horses smell. I don't spend that much time around the stables, and if I'm at the track it's either in the clubhouse or my private box."

"I see."

She put her fork down and said, "Why are you asking all these questions about the threats if you don't intend to investigate them?"

I was caught.

"Curiosity," I pleaded, "an investigator's curiosity. A few questions can't hurt, and if I *can* find something out, I naturally will. But security is still my prime concern. I'll be satisfied just to see Dreamland run in the Derby."

"And win?" she asked.

I put my right hand out, palm down, and wiggled it back and forth a few times. "I'm like that about who wins, although I am an Easterner at heart," I confessed.

There was less tension between us after that, and at times I thought she might even be coming on to me. But I feigned ignorance.

When her driver arrived, we got up to leave and I asked if she minded if I made a phone call. She said she'd wait for me in the car.

I found a pay phone and dialed Don McCoy's number again and this time got a busy signal. I hung up, dialed again, got the same thing. On a hunch, I called the operator and had her check the line. She informed me there was no ongoing conversation and said the phone was either out of order or off the hook.

When I got back to Mrs. Nixon's car, I said, "Would you take me by Don McCoy's apartment?"

She compressed her lips and I thought she was going to refuse, but instead she said, "I'll have Arthur take me home, and then drive you over there."

"Thank you."

We dropped her at "one of" her residences, a ritzy apartment house near Beverly Hills, and then her driver took me to McCoy's less ostentatious residence. "Mrs. Nixon instructed me to wait if you wanted," Arthur told me.

"I appreciate that," I said, "but I'll find my way back. Thanks."

He touched the tip of his cap, then drove off.

I went into the lobby of McCoy's building and rang his bell. There was no answer. I tried the oldest trick in the official Private Eye Handbook. I pushed a few of the other buttons and was buzzed in. With access to the elevators now, I rode up to McCoy's floor—the fifth —and found his apartment. I knocked and rang his buzzer and when I still didn't get an answer, I used my lock picks to get in.

The apartment was lit by a small lamp in the living room. On the desk next to the lamp was the phone, its receiver hanging by the cord, dangling just above the floor.

I went from room to room—there were only three—and finally found what I wasn't looking for in the bathroom.

Don McCoy was in the tub, but he wasn't taking a bath.

He was dead.

"How did you get in?" Lieutenant Taylor of the LAPD Homicide Squad asked me.

"The door was open," I lied.

"Is that so? If I searched you right now, Mr. Po, I wouldn't just happen to come up with a dandy little set of lock picks, would I?"

"You might," I admitted. "But that still wouldn't mean that I didn't find the door open."

He had to concede me that point, and he did so grudgingly.

After getting over the shock of finding McCoy in the tub, with his blood running down the drain, I called for the police. A squad car had responded first. The uniform had taken one look at the tub and put in a call for Homicide, Forensics, and the M.E.

Homicide was Lieutenant Bryce Taylor, who reminded me a little of my sometime friend, sometime adversary on the NYPD, Detective James Diver. Taylor had a ruddy complexion and salt-and-pepper hair, and he also had a spare tire around his middle-aged middle. It didn't look so bad on him, though, because he was tall enough to carry it. Actually, at six-six or so, he was tall enough to carry almost anything.

The medical examiner, a Doctor Zetnor, came out of the bathroom and Taylor asked, "What can you tell me, Doc?"

Zetnor, a small, neat, precise-looking man of indeterminable ancestry—and his name didn't help—said, "He was shot twice, at close range. Either bullet looks like it could've done the trick, but I'll know more after I go inside."

"Report on my desk in the morning?" Taylor asked.

"As soon as I can," Zetnor promised. He supervised the removal of the body, and followed it out.

"You toss the place?" Taylor asked, turning to me. Before I could speak, he added, "Don't dummy up on me, Po. I won't come down on you if you level with me, but you're out of town talent. If you hold out on me I could cause you a lot of heartache."

He was tough but didn't come on as tough as he could have, so I decided to level. "I did look around," I said. "Just for something to do while I waited."

"What did you come up with that we'll eventually come up with anyway?"

"A note," I said.

"What kind of note?"

I explained to him my reason for being in town, and told him that McCoy had received threats that had caused him to withdraw from the mount of Dreamland.

"Horses," he said, shaking his head. "You know, even my wife makes a bet at Kentucky Derby time. Waste of money. Where's the note?"

"Top drawer of his dresser."

"Not in your pocket?"

"Lieutenant," I scolded.

"Sorry," he said, touching his forehead, "I don't know what came over me. Come on."

I followed him into the bedroom.

"You dust this dresser yet?" he asked one of the forensics men.

"Yes, sir."

He opened the drawer, looked around and came up with an envelope. "This it?" he asked me.

"That's it."

"Looks like a letter," he said. It was addressed to McCoy, with a stamp and a postmark, the date of which was earlier that week. He opened it, scanned it, and said, "Reads like a note."

"Read it out loud," I told him.

"What?"

"Humor me. I think I may be able to help you wrap this one up quick."

"I'm all for that," he said, and proceeded to read out loud.

When he'd finished, I said, "Let's check that note for prints, and I think I can tell you whose to check it against."

"If there are any prints," he said. "People who make death threats aren't usually that helpful."

"Why don't you give me a ride to my hotel," I suggested, "and I'll tell you a story about a man and a slip of the tongue."

"All right, but you better have something worth the cab fare."

He drove me to my hotel, listened to what I had to say, and agreed to pick me up the next day. He admitted that I might have something, however slim a hook I was hanging it on.

"What did you get?" I asked as I got in his car the next morning.

"Enough to keep me going along," he said. "The man owes a bundle, his job is in danger, and we already had his prints on file from an old gambling bust. They matched the ones taken from the note."

"All right," I said. "Let me go in to talk to him first. Maybe I can get him to say something that will make your case easier."

"Okay," he said. "Here's the note."

"We going alone?"

"I'm short handed on my squad. That's the only reason I responded myself last night." He started the car, then added, "I'll have a unit meet us at the track."

"Quietly," I suggested.

"Natch."

□ □ □

I found Lew Hale watching the workouts and persuaded him to accompany me to his office. I told him I had some news about McCoy, and about the man making the threats. "Man?" he asked me on the way. "So you've determined that it was a man?"

"Oh, yes," I said. "I'm dead sure it was a man."

When we got to his office, he sat down behind his desk and said, "Well, what about McCoy and the guy making the threats? You don't mean it was him, do you?"

I shook my head. "No, it wasn't him. McCoy's dead. According to the M.E.'s report, he was killed night before last."

"That's too bad," Hale said. "He was gutless, but that's not a reason for a man to have to die."

"My thoughts exactly, Mr. Hale," I said. "And yet, you did kill him."

"Me?" he replied in surprise. "Are you crazy?"

"And there must have been more of a reason than the fact he was gutless."

"Have you got any proof of what you're saying?" he demanded.

"I think I do," I replied.

"Well, you'd better be sure as all hell that you do!"

"That's what first put me onto you, Hale," I told him. "That phrase you keep using. Most people say 'sure as hell' or 'fast as hell,' but you always add the word 'all.' You said Dreamland was 'impressive as all hell,' remember?"

"And that makes me guilty of murder?"

"Not necessarily, but that's what made me start to think you might be guilty of fabricating and making threats."

"Fabricating? Didn't Mrs. Nixon tell you she got a call—"

"She did. She told me that the caller said she'd be 'lucky as all hell' to make it back from Kentucky."

"So?" he demanded, looking uncomfortable.

"And then there's this," I said, taking the envelope and note from my pocket.

"Now what's that?"

"A note Don McCoy received earlier this week, which probably caused him to withdraw from his mount on Dreamland. The note says he would be 'deader than all hell' if he rode Dreamland in the Derby."

"I don't say—"

"Yes, you do, Hale. You don't notice it because it's become habit with you. But I noticed it right away. It didn't dawn on Mrs. Nixon because she didn't spend enough time around you that she would notice."

"This is ridiculous," he sputtered. "You have to have more proof than—"

"You owe a lot of money," I said, cutting him off. "Gambling debts. You stood to make plenty if Dreamland lost, but if he lost you also stood to lose your job."

"You're saying that I wanted him to run and lose, and that I didn't want him to run at all. You should make up your—"

"And then there are your prints on this piece of paper," I said.

"Prints?"

"Fingerprints. You probably had no way of knowing that McCoy would keep the note, and—not being a true criminal—it probably never occurred to you to wear gloves when you wrote it. Your prints are on file with the police because of an old gambling arrest, aren't they?"

He made a quick move, opening his top drawer and pulling out a thirty-eight.

"All right," he said, "all right." He was nervous, flexing his fingers around the gun, making me nervous. "I didn't mean to kill McCoy."

"Tell me about it," I said, sensing that he needed little prodding to do so.

"You were right, there were two ways I could go. I could allow Dreamland to run, hoping that he'd win and save my job, but that wouldn't pay my debts. Of course if he ran and lost, without my job I wouldn't be able to make any payments at all."

"Let me guess. First you scared McCoy, then you offered him a deal."

Hale nodded. "To pull the horse, throw the race. I'd make a bundle and the people I owe money to would make a bundle, too."

"What happened?"

"McCoy got irate, the little fool," he hissed. "He said he'd rather be scared off than bought off. When I showed him the gun, he jumped me. We struggled and it went off."

"Why were there no calls or threats for the past four days?" I asked.

"The people I owe found out what I was trying to do," he explained. "They said that keeping the horse from running so he wouldn't lose and cost me my job was small thinking. They said I'd lose my job anyway, sooner or later. They made me see that the only way to get square with them—and even make some money for myself—was to make sure Dreamland ran and lost. So I changed my plans." He flexed his fingers around the gun some more. "Now I've got to change my plans again."

"Did you find a jockey that could be bought?"

"There are enough of them," he said. "I'll give one of them the mount . . . but first I've got to take care of you."

"You're not going to kill me, Hale," I said. "Look at how nervous you are. You killed McCoy by accident. I don't think you can kill me in cold blood."

A drop of perspiration rolled down his cheek to the corner of his mouth, where he licked it off.

"Besides," I went on, "the police are right outside listening to everything. Kill me and you'll be a lot worse off than you already are." I raised my voice and said, "Lieutenant?"

The door opened and Taylor walked in, followed by two uniformed cops.

I took a step toward Hale, holding out my hand. "Let me have the gun, Hale. It's all over."

He hesitated long enough to scare me a little, but finally handed over the weapon.

"Okay," Taylor told his men, "take him out and read him his rights."

As they led the trainer from the office, Taylor walked over and relieved me of the thirty-eight.

"I guess he could look on the bright side," I said.

"What's that?"

"Maybe in prison he'll be safe from the people he owes money to."

"Maybe," the tall cop said, shaking his head, as if something were still eating at him.

"What's on your mind, Lieutenant?"

"Oh, nothing much," he said. "This is just the first time I've ever built a case around a slip of the tongue, that's all."

The Girl Who Talked to Horses

The trainer's name was Carlucci and everybody said he had an edge. What was it? Well, they said he was a whiz with horses, but he liked them better than people, and that's why they performed for him.

I don't know how many people believed it, but Anthony Carlucci had been having a hell of a career in New York for the past four years, but if he had an edge it had run out today.

Today Carlucci was lying in a stall at Belmont Park, out on Elmont, Long Island, and he didn't have an edge anymore because he was dead.

When Carlucci's body had been discovered by his assistant trainer that morning, I'd been called in because I was in charge of security for the New York State Racing Club. That is, I was in charge when there was some investigating to be done. There were uniformed guards working the track who worked for another outfit. They didn't have to report to me, but we had an understanding.

So, to get the sequence of events right, the assistant trainer, Dick Dermott, found Carlucci's body when he arrived on the backstretch at 5:30 a.m. He immediately called for a uniformed guard, who then called his boss, who then called me. Being the fair-minded man I am, since we were all up I figured I might as well call my boss and wake him up, too.

"This better be good," J. Howard Biel said when I identified myself on the phone.

"Murder," I said.

"Murder?"

"Well," I said, "somebody's dead, let's put it that way. I don't know if it's murder, but—"

"Who's dead?"

"Apparently," I said, breaking it to him gently, "Anthony Carlucci."

"What?"

He had a right to be upset. One of the hottest young trainers to come down the pike had chosen the Belmont/Aqueduct/Saratoga/Staten Island Downs circuit to ply his trade. That was good, that was a feather in the NYSRC's hat. Having him turn up dead was . . . well, bad.

Biel agreed to meet me at the track, but I arrived before he did and identified myself to the guard on duty. His name tag identified him by his last name, Mattingly.

"Anybody call the cops yet?" I asked.

"I don't know," Mattingly said. "I called my boss, and he told me to stand guard and not let anyone in until you got here."

"Okay," I said. There was nobody else around. "Where's Mr. Dermott? You didn't let him leave, did you?"

"No, sir," the guard said. "He's in Mr. Carlucci's office."

"Good."

"Do you want me to get him, Mr Po?"

"No, no," I said, "leave him there. I'll take a look at the body first and then talk to Dermott. Since we don't know if the police have been called, if they do show up let them in, all right?"

"Yes, sir."

"Also, Mr. Biel is on his way, so let him through, too."

"Yes, sir."

That settled, I went into the barn to take a look at Anthony Carlucci. He was lying on the floor of one of the stalls, and had obviously been kicked to death by a horse. His head was bleeding, and the blood had soaked into the straw and dirt around him. I went into the stall and bent over him, but there was nothing for me to do. I didn't touch him, or move him. I got out of there, feeling slightly sick. It's not every day you see somebody's brains scattered about.

Outside I asked the guard, "Who moved the horse?"

"Mr. Dermott."

"What horse was it?"

"I'm not sure, sir," the man said, "but it might have been Tobasco Boy."

That didn't surprise me. Tobasco Boy was the crown jewel of Carlucci's barn. He was supposed to run in the Kentucky Derby in three weeks. Last year's two-year-old champ, he was going into the Derby undefeated in five starts last year, and three starts as a three-year-old.

As brilliant as the horse was on the track, though, his comportment off the track was legendarily bad. He had taken a piece out of more people—his trainer, assistant trainer, groom, hot walker—than any other horse, and he made the newspapers for it. It would come as no surprise to a reader of the racing newspapers that he had stomped someone to death.

The question I had was: What was Carlucci doing alone in the stall of such a notorious horse?

"I'm going into the office to talk to Mr. Dermott now. Watch for the cops, and Mr. Biel."

"Yes, sir."

I walked to the end of the shed row and found Anthony Carlucci's office. I knocked and entered and found Dick Dermott sitting behind his boss's desk, like he belonged there.

There were photos on the walls, as well as various pieces of racing equipment, like whips and bridles, and, on one wall, a saddle. The office smelled of leather, and the creams used to soften and preserve it.

"Mr. Dermott?" I asked, even though I recognized him. I didn't know if he knew me, though.

"That's right."

He was in his mid-thirties, a bit younger than Carlucci, who I thought I recalled as being in his early forties. They were considered a good team, each a fine trainer in his own right, but the barn was Carlucci's and so was the reputation.

"My name is Henry Po," I said, "I work for the Board—"

"I know who you are, Mr. Po," Dermott said, cutting off my introduction. "I've seen you on the grounds. Are the police here?"

"No," I said. "Did you call them?"

The man looked surprised. "No, I thought you had."

"I will, if I can use that phone," I said, "but afterward I'd like to ask you some questions."

"Shouldn't we wait for the police?" Dermott asked.

"We could," I said, "and we will, but we might as well talk while we're waiting, don't you think?"

"I don't know," Dermott said. I found his eyes and his state of mind remarkably clear for someone who had found his colleague, and for all I knew his friend, dead. This had never happened to me before, but I was suddenly very certain that he had something to do with Anthony Carlucci's death.

□   □   □

"Mr. Po?"

"Yes?"

"You wanted to use the phone?"

"Oh, yes, thank you."

That was when I knew I was staring at him, and maybe he did, too, because he was watching me as I dialed nine-one-one and reported the incident.

"It'll be a while before detectives get here," I said, as I hung up. "First they'll send a uniformed patrol, and then they'll send for a supervisor, and finally they'll call for the detectives."

"I see," Dermott said, "then this is going to go on for a while."

"Yes."

"I'd better let my people know."

His people? They were his people, already?

"Your staff, you mean?"

"Yes."

"Can you do that by phone?"

"Why?"

"Well . . . I really can't let you leave the area, Mr. Dermott. After all, you did find the body, and . . ."

"And I'm a suspect?" Dermott asked. "Is that what you mean?"

Suddenly, I felt like Columbo, playing cat-and-mouse games with a famous guest star, only I wasn't a brilliant-yet-rumpled cop, and Dermott was not a famous star.

"I thought it was an accident," I said. "At least, it looks like an accident."

Dermott surprised me by shaking his head, violently. "It couldn't be."

"Why not?"

"Tony would never have gone into Tobasco Boy's stall alone. I'm sure you're aware of the horse's violent nature."

"I've read about it, yes."

"Then you understand," Dermott said. "We agreed that no one would ever try to handle him alone."

"Who usually handled the horse?"

"His groom, and his hot walker."

"Who are they?"

"Oh, sorry," Dermott said. "The groom's name is Hennessy, and the hot walker is Amanda Ellis."

I didn't know either one of them, but then, there was no reason I should. I did spend time at the various tracks, but there was no way I could know the personnel of each stable, unless they had been there as long as I had, and Carlucci's Canyon Valley Stable had only been in New York four years.

"The police will want to talk to them."

"They're probably around," Dermott said. "They're usually here even before me and Tony."

There was only one guard outside, and I needed him to keep people out of the stable. I didn't have anyone to send looking for Hennessy or Ellis.

As if on cue, there was a knock at the door.

"May I?" I asked.

"Please."

I walked to the door and opened it. There was a girl standing there, about five-five, slender and attractive, wearing a sleeveless T-shirt, exposing the powerful forearms and upper arms of someone who worked with horses for a living. She was not muscle-bound, but well-toned, like Linda Hamilton was in *The Terminator II*. When your job was controlling an animal who weighed over a thousand pounds, you tended to be in shape. It was the case with jockeys, exercise riders, hot walkers and grooms.

Also, if you watch racing on television you've probably noticed how many of the people who hold these jobs—especially the hot walkers— are women, and attractive young women. I don't mean that they could be models, but they're usually wearing T-shirts and jeans, and they're almost always in fabulous shape, as this woman was. She appeared to be in her early twenties.

"What's going on?" she demanded. "Who are you? Why can't I get into the stable? Where are—"

I held up my hand and said, "I can answer your questions, miss, but they have to come one at a time."

"Amanda?"

She looked past me to Dermott, who had called her name. "Dick? What's going on?"

"Mr. Po, that's Amanda Ellis. Would you let her in please?"

"Of course," I said, backing away. "Miss Ellis?"

She came in, giving me a sideways glance, and walked right to the desk. "Dick?"

"There's been an accident," Dermott said, without standing up. I thought he looked extremely comfortable behind the desk.

"What kind of accident?" she asked. "One of the horses?"

"Not exactly," Dermott said. "It's Tony. He's dead."

"What?" Her back was to me, so I couldn't see her face, but she lifted her hands to her mouth.

"Tobasco Boy stomped him to death this morning."

"What?" This time her tone was more strident. "What will they do to him?"

Dermott shook his head and shrugged helplessly.

"I don't know," he said. "This is Mr. Po. He works for the Board—"

She turned quickly to stare at me. She was not the most beautiful woman I had ever seen, but at that moment she was certainly the most attractive. She was magnificent, muscles tense, nostrils flaring. Why did I think she was more concerned about the horse than the poor, dead trainer?

I answered honestly.

"I have no idea what will happen to the horse," I said, "if he did, in fact, stomp Mr. Carlucci to death."

"If?" she asked. She turned on Dermott. "You said he did it."

"Mr. Dermott," I said, "found Mr. Carlucci in the stall this morning, dead."

Dermott nodded. "Tobasco Boy's stall, and the horse was standing over him."

"So then you don't know for sure that Toby did it?" she asked.

"Toby?" I asked.

"My nickname for Tobasco Boy."

"We don't know for sure that the horse did it," I said, "no. The police are on their way, Miss Ellis. They'll want to talk to you."

"About what?"

"About the horse, about Mr. Carlucci—"

"Does Sam know?"

"Sam?"

"Hennessy," Dermott said. "I told you about him."

"The groom."

"Does he know?"

"Not yet."

"Someone has to tell him."

"Why don't you do that, if you don't mind?" I asked.

"No," she said, "I don't mind. I—I'd like to tell him."

"Fine," I said, "you can also tell him the police will want to talk to him, too."

"Are you some sort of a detective?" she asked.

"As a matter of fact, I am," I said. "I have a private detective's license, but I work primarily for the racing board. I report directly to Howard Biel."

She looked impressed. "Does he know about this?"

"Yes," I said, "in fact, it's a toss-up as to who will get here first, him or the police."

"I'll want to talk to him."

"About what?"

"Toby—Tobasco Boy," she said. "If he did it he'll need someone to plead his case, won't he?"

"Probably," I said, "but who will plead Tony Carlucci's?"

She and Dermott exchanged a glance and then she left, promising to get Hennessy and stay around.

"Why do I get the feeling she and Carlucci didn't get along?"

"They didn't."

"Why not?"

Dermott shrugged. "Who knows?"

I turned and faced him squarely. "I think you do." In fact, I thought he knew a lot more than he was saying.

"All right," he said, "Tony was something of a chauvinist. He treated Amanda like he'd treat a girl, woman . . . do you know what I mean?"

"I think I do."

"He'd pat her on the ass, send her on menial errands, like getting coffee, you know. She finally had enough one day and told him off. Since then . . ." He shrugged.

"Why'd she stay?" I asked. "Why didn't he fire her?"

"For the same reason."

"Which was?"

"She was the only one who could handle Tobasco Boy."

"I thought nobody could handle him."

"Except Amanda," Dermott said. "She's uncanny with horses. She—well, this will sound silly . . ."

"Go ahead."

"She claims that the horses talk to her."

"I'm sorry?"

"She says that she can communicate with the horses," Dermott explained. "It sounds odd, I know, but she gets along with them like no one I've ever seen. Often she's able to figure out what's wrong with them when they're not training right in the morning, or not running right in the afternoon."

"How?"

"She says that . . . they tell her."

"And you believed her?" I asked. "You and Carlucci?"

"We didn't care," he said. "She worked wonders with them and we didn't care if she was goddamned Doctor Doolittle, as long as she was right."

"Great," I said, "maybe she can get Tobasco Boy to tell us what happened here this morning."

"Who knows?" Dermott asked. "Maybe she can, at that."

The next few hours were hectic, and confused. Howard Biel arrived just ahead of the police. As I'd predicted, we ended up with cops, supervisors and then plainclothes detectives. Not only that, but the man who was in charge of the uniformed guards at the track, Patrick Lukas, also arrived, ready to kick some ass. He regarded the "incident" as a black mark against him and his crew.

The detective in charge of the case was a man named Zeke Tomachek,, a tall, gray-bearded, dignified-looking man who stood over six feet tall, but seemed to stoop a bit to hide it.

Biel had a talk with Tomachek first thing and managed to arrange for me to remain on the scene as his representative.

"Henry," he said to me, "I have to go to my office and make some calls. I've got to try to keep the lid on this. Keep an eye on things, all right?"

"All right, Howard."

Tomachek asked that Carlucci's "employees," Dermott, Hennessy and Amanda Ellis, wait in the office to be questioned. Dermott agreed to do so but complained about being called Carlucci's employee.

"I'm sorry," Tomachek said, "I'm not up on my racetrack terminology. What is it you do, Mr. Dermott?"

"I'm the assistant trainer."

"Very well," Tomachek said, "I'll refer to you that way from now on."

"Thank you."

As Dermott walked away, Tomachek asked me, "Who paid his salary?"

"Carlucci."

He nodded. "That's what I thought: He worked for the guy."

"Right."

"Then why does it upset him to hear it?"

"Because he liked to think he worked with Carlucci, not for him."

"Hmm," Tomachek said, "looks to me like somebody's not satisfied with his lot in life."

Tomachek also had an altercation with Lukas about his men. The detective wanted the private security people off the premises—except for me.

"My men belong here, Detective," Lukas complained.

Lukas was ex-military. You could tell it by looking at him. He might also have been an ex-mercenary. His demeanor exhibited all of the worst attributes of both.

In other words, he was an asshole.

"Mr. Lukas," Tomachek said, "I've asked you nicely to remove yourself and your men from the scene. They are free to maintain their posts in another area of the track, but I want them—and you—gone from here."

"But—"

"Please leave willingly; don't make me have you removed." They stared at each other and, in the end, Lukas blinked. He and his men were gone by the time the coroner and his men arrived, or else we would have really had a crowd. I never heard the coroner's name. They only called him "Doctor." Tomachek and I entered the stable area with the coroner and watched while he examined Carlucci's body.

"What do you say, Doctor?" Tomachek asked.

The doctor—in his fifties, with steel-gray hair and goatee—crouched next to the body and shook his head.

"What a mess."

"Is that your professional opinion?" Tomachek asked.

The man ignored Tomachek's attempt at humor, the first indication that he had no sense of humor—or maybe he just didn't have one when it came to death.

"This man has been bludgeoned about the head, very possibly beaten to death. I won't say more until the autopsy."

"Just tell me this, Doctor," Tomachek said. "Did the horse do it?"

The doctor stood up and scowled. "How could I possibly say that with a certainty?"

"Then just tell me if it could have done it. I just want to know if I can rule it out or not."

"Of course you can't rule it out," the doctor said, "not until I've autopsied the body—and if I can get out of here, I can do that."

"All right," Tomachek said, wearily, "take him away." He turned to me and asked, "I don't suppose there's someplace we can get some coffee."

"There's a backstretch cafe," I said. "I can have somebody—wait, you chased all the track security away."

"I'll have an officer get it," Tomachek said, "Just give him directions—"

"All right."

"—and tell him what you want."

He brought a man over and I did as he asked, asking for a black coffee for myself.

We watched as the coroner's men bagged the body and removed it. That left the stall empty, except of blood. The coroner's people had also picked up whatever minute pieces of bone and brain matter might have been left behind.

"Where's the horse?" Tomachek asked me.

"He's in a stall farther down."

"Who moved him?"

"Dermott."

"I thought one person couldn't handle him?"

"The first guard on the scene, Mattingly, helped him. He, uh, just followed Dermott's instructions and they got Tobasco Boy moved."

"I don't know anything about racing," Tomachek said. "Is this a good horse?"

"One of the best in training."

"Too bad."

"Why?"

"If he did it," Tomachek said, "what will happen to him?"

"I'm not sure."

"If it was a dog they'd put him to sleep."

"A thoroughbred is not a dog," I said. "There are investors, and insurance premiums . . ."

"Hmm," Tomachek said, "insurance . . ."

We walked into the stall together.

"Did you examine him?" Tomachek asked.

"I didn't touch him," I said. "I just wanted to be sure he was dead."

He started moving bloody straw around with his foot, whether idly or with purpose, I didn't know, but I saw something. "Wait," I said, "don't move."

"What?" he asked, freezing.

"Just back away a minute."

He did. I stepped outside the stall and looked around until I found a pitchfork. I came back in the stall and used the tool to clear away the straw.

"See?"

He stepped forward and looked down.

"I see," he said, and we both stared at the twin marks in the ground that could only have been made by the boot heels of a man being dragged.

"Look here," I said, pointing to the front of the stall. "There were marks, but they were wiped out."

"We've got a murder here," Tomachek said.

"And the killer missed the heel marks that were hidden by the straw."

"Now the question is," Tomachek said, "was he dead when he was dragged in, or was he unconscious and helpless while the horse stomped him to death?"

"Maybe," I said, "we should ask the horse."

Naturally, I had to explain that.

Tomachek didn't know whether or not to take me seriously. Frankly, I didn't know either.

"Do you believe this stuff?" he asked.

"I don't know," I said, "but Dermott believes it, and that may be what's important."

"What do you mean?"

Tomachek and I were inside, while everyone else was outside. I decided to tell him what I'd been thinking.

"Have you had many feelings like this in the past?" he asked when I was done.

"No."

"Worked on many murders?"

"No."

He regarded me curiously.

"Why should I go along with this?"

I shrugged. "What have you got to lose?" I asked.

"Okay," he said, "then tell me how you see it."

"I see it done all of a sudden," I said. "It's too sloppy to have been planned. Those heel marks showing that he'd been dragged into the stall, that's amateur stuff."

"So you're saying it's a crime of passion?" Tomachek asked. "He was killed by someone he knew?"

"I'm just telling you what I feel," I said, "and what I think. I think that horse stomped an already-dead man. Maybe the coroner can tell the difference between a hoof print and some other kind of blow, but maybe he hasn't got enough skill to be able to. If this happened the way I think then the murder weapon is still around."

Tomachek regarded me for a few more moments and then said, "I'll have a thorough search done. Meanwhile, what do you want to do?"

"I want to talk to Amanda Ellis."

"What if she's the murderer?"

"Then she'll jump at the chance to implicate someone else, won't she?"

"Maybe."

"Again," I asked, "what have you got to lose? Maybe you've got a chance to solve this thing before another hour goes by. What'll that do to your statistics?"

I was talking about the statistic that said if a murder wasn't solved in the first forty-eight hours—or twenty-four, or seventy-two, whatever it was—then it wouldn't be solved at all.

"It would knock it to hell," Tomachek said. "Okay, I'm gonna go along with you on this, only because I don't have any feeling at all for the people, and you seem to."

I didn't bother telling him that I had only just met these people about an hour ago myself—but he was right about one thing. I had a feeling, and he didn't.

"I'll get the girl and have her brought in here," Tomachek said.

"Thanks."

While he went to arrange for the search and to have Amanda Ellis join me, I studied Tobasco Boy in his new stall. He stood very still, seemingly totally relaxed, and stared at me balefully.

"What have you got to say about all this, Toby?" I asked. "Are you getting a bum rap here?"

He didn't bother answering me. Maybe he'd tell Amanda Ellis.

When Amanda Ellis appeared she approached me tentatively. "Miss Ellis," I said. "Would you like to see Tobasco Boy?"

She brightened and quickened her step. "Yes, I would."

"Here he is."

I stepped aside as she approached the stall and reached her hand out to him. He came over to her immediately and nuzzled her hand.

"That's amazing," I said. "That horse is supposed to be as ornery as—"

"He's not ornery with me," she said.

"Because you can communicate with him?"

She turned and looked at me. "You're not like the others."

"In what way?"

"You refer to the horse as `him' and not `it,' like most of the others do."

"Like Dermott?"

She snorted. "Him, especially. I suppose he told you about me talking to the animals?"

"He mentioned it."

"Did he make the Doctor Doolittle reference?"

"He did."

"Asshole."

"Can you talk to the horses?"

"I don't exactly talk to them," she said, "but they are able to make their feelings known to me. There is a woman, though, out in California who says she can actually talk back and forth with the horses."

"How do the people around here feel about what you can do?"

"Most of them don't believe it," she said, "but they do listen when I tell them when a change of diet, or training regimen, might improve the horse's performance."

"And then it does?"

"Most of the time, yes."

"Amanda—may I call you Amanda?"

"Sure."

"Can you tell if Tobasco Boy stomped Mr. Carlucci?"

"I can look at his hooves."

"Would you do that for me?" I asked. "You're not afraid to go into the stall with him, are you?"

"Of course not."

She opened the door, slipped in and closed it behind her. She talked gently to the horse while lifting his hooves and examining them, then rubbed his neck lovingly and came back out.

"Well?"

"He's got blood on his hooves."

"He could have walked in the blood, though," I said. "He didn't have to stomp Carlucci to get the blood on him."

"You don't believe he did it?"

"No, I don't," I said. "Even if he did stomp the man, I think he was already dead."

"Who do you think killed him?"

"I was hoping you'd be able to tell me that."

"Me? How?"

"By asking the horse."

"What are you talking about?" she demanded, annoyed. "I just told you I can't really talk to the horses."

"But there are people who think you can," I said.

She frowned. "What are you asking me to do?"

When Detective Tomachek returned he was shaking his head.

"What?"

"No murder weapon," he said, "but we'll keep looking."

"It's got to be here."

"If it happened like you figure," Tomachek reminded me, "on the spur of the moment." He looked at Amanda. "Is Miss Ellis being helpful?"

"Very."

Tomachek gave her a long look.

"Am I under suspicion?" she asked him.

"At this point," he said, "everyone is. That's standard procedure."

"I'd like to talk to the others now, Detective," I said.

Tomachek showed me a warning finger. "I'm only going to give you so much leeway, Mr. Po," he said. "If your plan is not working I'm going to call it quits."

"Fine," I said "if that happens it will fall to you, anyway. I'll be out of it."

"Agreed."

We left the stable and went to Carlucci's office, where a uniformed policeman was at his post outside the door. "Are they inside?" Tomachek asked.

"Yes, sir."

Tomachek knocked, then entered. Dermott was still behind the desk. Another man who I assumed to be Sam Hennessy was sitting in another chair, shoulders slumped. He must have been a jockey at one time, given his size and makeup. He looked to be in his late forties.

"It's about time," Dermott said. "How long are we going to be kept here? We've got work to do, you know."

"What sort of work, Mr. Dermott?" I asked.

Dermott looked from me to Tomachek in some confusion, then settled on me. "We've got a stable to run," he said. "The horses have to be tended to."

"You expect to continue to run the stable?"

"The owners will expect it," he said, "and who else will do it?"

"Well, I'd expect at least one day of mourning . . ." I said, letting it trail off.

"Don't think for one minute that we won't mourn Tony, Mr. Po," Dermott said, "but as a trainer, not as a person."

"He wasn't a nice man, then?"

Hennessy snorted.

"Mr. Hennessy, is it?"

"That's right."

"You didn't like Mr. Carlucci?"

"Nobody did," Hennessy said, "not even the horses. I'm not surprised one of them killed him."

"Oh, Mr. Carlucci wasn't killed by the horse, Mr. Hennessy."

The smaller man looked confused, and tossed Dermott a long glance, which I found interesting.

"What do you mean?" he asked. "Mr. Dermott said—"

"Mr. Dermott said a lot of things," I said, looking at the assistant trainer.

"What are you talking about?" Dermott demanded. He looked at Tomachek. "Aren't you in charge?"

"Mr. Po has the floor right now, Mr. Dermott."

"You claim you found Carlucci in the stall," I said to Dermott. "You didn't."

"How dare you—"

"He was dragged into the stall," I continued. "The softer ground inside the stall still shows the drag marks made by his heels. You neglected to wipe out the marks beneath the straw."

This time it was Dermott who threw Hennessy a look. Things were becoming clearer.

"Let's get right to it, Mr. Dermott," I said. "On top of everything else, you're a bad actor."

"What . . . what do you mean, everything else?"

"The coroner's report will show that Mr. Carlucci was not killed by blows from the horse, but that he was already dead when the horse stomped him. You killed him, then put him in the stall and agitated the horse so he would stomp the dead body. Then you hid the murder weapon, which will be found, eventually."

"You can't prove any of this."

"No," I said, "I can't, but the horse can."

Now Dermott looked confused and, for the first time, shaken. "What?"

"Yes," I said, "you were right about Miss Ellis being able to communicate with the horses."

"What?" he said, again.

"The horse didn't do it, Mr. Dermott," I said. "He told Miss Ellis he didn't do it."

Dermott stared at Amanda for a few moments and she kept quiet. I'd asked her to play along, and she was, silently. "That's impossible."

"No, it's not," I said. "Every living thing can communicate, Mr. Dermott. Maybe the horse doesn't talk to Miss Ellis, but he communicates with her, and what he communicated was that he didn't kill Carlucci—you did."

Dermott looked at Tomachek for help. "This is preposterous," he said. "You can't honestly believe—"

"Mr. Dermott," Tomachek said, playing his part, "I think we better go downtown."

"Am I under arrest?"

"I think we'll just hold onto you until we get the coroner's report," Tomachek said. "At that time I'd say yes, you will be under arrest."

"But, I didn't—"

"Yes?"

Dermott looked at Hennessy, who was looking around the room, as if seeking an avenue of escape.

"What's wrong, Mr. Hennessy?" I asked.

"Huh? Nothin's wrong. I just . . ."

"Do you believe that Mr. Dermott killed Carlucci?" I asked.

"I—I don't know—I—"

"What was your part, Hennessy?"

"What?"

"Did you kill him, or just help drag him into the stall?" I asked.

"Po—" Tomachek said. He was confused now, but the looks

Hennessy and Dermott had been passing back and forth were—for me, anyway—remarkably easy to read.

"They both did it, Tomachek," I said. "Both of them."

They looked at each other again.

"I didn't—" Hennessy finally said.

"Shut up!" Dermott shouted.

"Hennessy?" I said. "You want to wait until Dermott goes downtown and gives you up?"

"I didn't kill him!" Hennessy shouted. "He did. He got into an argument and . . . and hit him."

"He wasn't dead!" Dermott said. "I—I hit him, but it was your idea to put him into the stall with the horse, your idea to let Tobasco Boy finish him." Dermott looked at us. "He helped me drag him into the stall." Then he looked at Hennessy again. "You were suppose to clean away the heel marks!"

"I did!"

"Not good enough," I said. "Detective?"

Tomachek went to the door, opened it and called in the uniformed officer. "I'm going to need your cuffs," he said.

Later, Amanda Ellis came with me to Howard Biel's office. She was upset, and I told her we'd talk, but I had to check in with my boss first. She stayed in the outer office while I went inside.

"So who killed him?" Biel asked, after I relayed the story to him. "Was it them? Or the horse? Did the horse stomp a dead man?"

"They killed him, all right," I said. "Whether or not he was dead when they dragged him in there, they're responsible for his death."

"But if the horse—"

"If the horse did it he was their weapon, Howard," I said. "Their other weapon, aside from the one Dermott hit him with, which still hasn't been found. To tell you the truth. I don't think they even know if he was dead when they dragged him into the stall. The coroner will have to come up with that answer."

Biel frowned. "What do we do with the horse?" he asked. "Can we let it continue to race if it killed a man?"

"Howard," I said, "even if he did put the finishing touches on Carlucci, how can you blame the animal?"

"I'll have to talk to some people—think about this very carefully."

"I've got Amanda Ellis outside," I said. "She's real upset, and I told her we'd talk a while."

"Tell me something."

"What?"

"Did you ever suspect her?"

I hesitated, then said, "Briefly."

"What changed your mind?"

"Oh, I still think she could have killed Carlucci," I said. "She didn't like him, and maybe hated him."

"So why . . ."

"The horse," I said.

"What about it?"

"She loves him, Howard," I said. "Even if she'd killed Carlucci, or been in on it with Dermott and Hennessy, she never would have tried to frame Tobasco Boy for it."

The Goodly Race

1

They call them the "goodly race." I was told the term came from an old Irish poem, but nobody has been able to tell me the name of the poem or the poet. In any case they say the phrase was used to describe horses in Ireland, and I say it's as good as any and better than most. I've been around people and horses a lot the past few years, and I have to tell you I like horses better.

Even as I struggled to find my way through Dublin Airport I still couldn't believe I was there. It actually looked the same as any American airport, but the sounds—now, they were different. Have you spent much time in airports? There are always announcements being made over the PA system—"So-and-so meet your party at . . ." and "So-and-so please dial . . . " At Dublin Airport, though, even the announcements had a musical sound to them. The conversations going on around me, whether in Irish or "English," were more like songs.

All of the airport facilities were there as well. A baggage claims area, a bank, a post office, a tourist information booth, shops, restaurants, bars, a hairdresser, "car-hire" counters—there was even a church and a nursery. The difference between these facilities and their American counterparts is that most of these were manned—or "womanned"—by people with manners. Some of them were downright pleasant. A guy from New York could find this hard to get used to.

Yesterday morning I was called into J. Howard Biel's office. Biel is the chairman of the New York State Racing Club, which operates Aqueduct, Belmont, Staten Island Downs, and Saratoga. I'm a special investigator working, along with three others, for him. Recently, however, he had bestowed on me the title of Head of Security. It doesn't mean much. I don't run security for the track. There's a company with uniformed men that does that. I still basically do what I did

before: investigate "special" problems for the NYSRC. The only difference is I now make a little more money than the other investigators,
and they have to report to me.

Of course, the fact that there were only two of us now, because the
other two got better offers, sort of watered down the honor. The other
investigator is a woman named Shukey Long, who claimed that my
newfound title had also earned me this trip to Ireland—a trip I neither
knew about nor wanted yesterday afternoon.

"Ah, Henry," Biel said when I entered his office at Staten Island
Downs. "Thanks for being so prompt. Come on in."

"I'm always prompt, Howard," I said. "It's one of my many sterling
qualities."

"Most of which I am well aware of," Howard replied, "only I wasn't
aware that promptness was one of them."

"Okay," I said, sitting down in front of his desk, "so sometimes I'm
late."

"Sometimes," he said, nodding and rubbing his hands together.

"Since I'm on time today, what's on your mind?"

"Ireland."

"I didn't know you were Irish."

"I'm not."

"Then why is it on your mind?"

"Because I'd like you to go there."

"Business or pleasure?" Maybe he was offering me an all-expenses-
paid vacation.

"A little of both," he said.

"You'll have to explain that to me, Howard," I said. "It's too convo-
luted a prospect for me to handle alone."

"I'd like you to go there and do a favor for me," Biel said, "and then
take a few days to enjoy the Irish countryside. You know, they say
there's magic in the ground there."

"Why do I get the feeling there's bullshit in the air here?"

"You wound me."

"Uh-huh. What's the favor?"

"Dublin has two central racecourses, Leopardstown and Phoenix
Park."

"What about the Curragh?" That was the only Irish racetrack—or
"course," as they call it there—that I knew, because one of our American horses—Fourstars Allstar—went there a few years ago to win a big
race. I think it was the 5,000 Guineas.

"There are several other courses within easy drive of Dublin, and the Curragh is one of them. We, however, are concerned with Leopardstown."

"Why are we concerned with Leopardstown?"

"Because I have a friend—my opposite number there—who is having some problems and he needs the services of an outside investigator."

"Outside," I said. "Yeah, I guess bringing me in from the U.S. to Ireland would qualify me as an outside investigator."

"This would be a favor to me, Henry," Howard went on, undaunted, "but my friend, Seamus Kilkenny, insists on paying you. I told him that would have to be between you and him."

I frowned.

"Howard, why would I want to be paid for doing you a favor?"

So I didn't particularly want to go to Ireland. So what? Howard Biel only asks me for a favor once or twice a month! It doesn't hurt to have him constantly in my debt.

So I ended up in Dublin. During the cab ride from the airport, the thing that struck me about Dublin was its doors. It seemed that every building had a different door—different style, different shape and, most striking of all, different color. I had never been so fascinated by doors.

There were several ways I could have traveled from the airport—car rental, bicycle rental, bus—but I chose a cab. It was the most expensive, but my expenses were being covered by Seamus Kilkenny.

My accommodations had already been arranged by Kilkenny: a hotel called the Clarence. I found out later that the area was called Temple Bar, south of the Liffey—the Liffey being a river. Temple Bar was one of Dublin's hot restaurant and bar areas.

The hotel itself was pretty big, located on Wellington Quay and actually overlooking the River Liffey. The Clarence was a middle-range accommodation, so my guess was that Seamus Kilkenny had some bucks.

I got a room halfway up, facing front so that I overlooked Wellington Quay and the river. Off to the left—west of me—was a bridge I later found out was called Grattan Bridge. Several blocks to the east was Ha'penny Bridge.

As I was checking in, the desk clerk, as pleasant and polite as everyone at the airport had been, handed me a message slip. I waited until I was in my room to read it. I was craning my neck to see the Ha'penny Bridge as I unfolded it. "Meet me at the Ha'penny Bridge Inn at 7 p.m." It was signed simply "Kilkenny."

I looked at my watch. It was four, which gave me three hours to wander around and get the feel of the area, maybe even have something to eat. I didn't know whether I'd be eating with Kilkenny or just drinking, so I thought a snack would be in order.

I also could have rested, but I really wasn't that tired. Coming to Ireland hadn't been my idea, and I might never have gone there without Howard Biel asking me to do him a favor. I had somehow gotten into my late thirties without ever having left the United States. Now that I had, though, I was kind of excited about it, and I wanted to see as much as I could.

There was a map of the area in the room. I took that with me when I left, because I didn't want to get lost and be late meeting Kilkenny.

2

Okay, so I was a little late, maybe ten minutes. I had stopped in several pubs and was surprised to find the people friendly and curious. When they found out I was from America, they had all kinds of questions to ask, and they'd go out of their way to make me feel welcome. I don't think I bought myself one drink, and in one pub they took the time to teach me how to throw darts properly.

And the pubs themselves were an education. The frontages on all of the buildings were different and again so were the doors. I had never before found myself so concerned with architecture. I walked and walked, enjoying the ever-changing scenery from building to building. When I finally looked at my watch, it was 6:55. When I reached the Ha'penny it was 7:10.

I was about to enter when I saw there was some commotion across the street, by the Ha'penny Bridge. I considered crossing to see what it was, but I was late so I went inside.

I looked around for a man of Kilkenny's description, which had been given me by Biel. He said Kilkenny was built like a six-foot fire hydrant. I didn't see anyone who fit that description.

I ordered a pint of Guinness. Actually, I didn't say a pint, but just ordering Guinness or Harp in Ireland will get you a pint.

I sat down to sip my drink and realized that in all my pub-hopping I hadn't had any food. I also realized, as I sipped my Guinness, that it was either my fourth or fifth of the day.

By 7:20 Kilkenny hadn't shown up, and now there were police cars and an ambulance across the way. I was feeling uncomfortable, and then a man came walking in who was apparently fairly well-known in the pub. He was wearing a white shirt, a vest, a tweed jacket, a black cap, corduroy pants, and Wellingtons. There were other men in the place dressed similarly. It seemed to be the uniform of the pub or the area.

"Sean, what the hell is goin' on by the Ha'penny, do ya know?" someone yelled.

"Sure, I know," Sean replied. He was a wizened little man who, if I had seen him on the streets of New York, would have brought to mind the word snitch.

"Well, will ya be tellin' the likes of us?" someone else asked.

"Fished a feller out of the river, they did," Sean said.

"Anybody we'd know?"

"Nobody I know," Sean said, "but it's a big feller, he is, or so I hear. 'Ave ya got a pint for me, now?"

I didn't wait to see whether they had a pint for him. I was out the door and crossing the street to the bridge. The uncomfortable feeling I had in my stomach had grown into something downright painful.

3

In Ireland the police are called the Garda. To me, though, they were still the police. The detective inspector whose desk I sat in front of was roughly the equivalent of Detective Hocus at home in New York, a hard-working cop with more cases than he could handle.

I'd met him at the foot of the Ha'penny Bridge, where in a sprinkling rain they had dragged Seamus Kilkenny's body from the water. He had a bump on his head, so he had fallen and hit his head, or been hit from behind and dumped in.

It had taken me several minutes to get the local police to let me speak to someone in authority, and that turned out to be Detective Inspector Jack Donnelly.

We spoke briefly by the bridge, and I told him I was waiting to meet someone who was late.

"And you're afraid this poor feller might turn out to be him?"

"It's a possibility, I guess." I didn't bother telling him about the feeling in the pit of my stomach.

"Come have a look, then."

"It might not help," I said, as we walked to where the body lay with a blanket draped over it. "We were meeting for the first time."

"Did ya have a description?"

"Just that he was a big man."

"And his name?"

"Seamus Kilkenny."

When we reached the body, he had the blanket removed and we both looked down at a man who was broad in the shoulders and must have stood six-two when he was upright. From the angle of the body I couldn't see the wound on the back of his head, for which I was grateful.

"Inspector?" a uniformed man said.

"Yes."

He handed the detective a wallet.

"Where was it?"

"In the dead man's pocket."

"Thank you."

I waited while he looked inside the wallet and came up with several pieces of ID belonging to Seamus Kilkenny.

"Would you be comin' back to the station with me, sir?" the detective asked politely.

And there we were.

I was waiting for the inspector to finish his telephone conversation, during which he must have said, "Don'tcha know?" six or seven times. I'd also heard the phrase countless times during the day in the pubs.

He was dressed simply in a white shirt, black pants, and a dark gray sports coat. The shirt had slightly frayed cuffs and collar, and the jacket was also slightly frayed around the cuffs.

Jack Donnelly hung up the phone and stared across the desk at me. He was a round-faced man carrying about twenty extra pounds here and there, which made him look lumpy. His hair was mousy gray and thinning, and he occasionally ran a hand through it, to no avail. It would never look anything but windblown.

"Now I was askin' ya . . . what?"

I reached across the desk and handed him my ID and passport. "Ah, yes," he said, accepting it. "Thank you."

He studied my papers and then looked at me again.

"A private inquiry agent from America, eh?"

"We usually say private investigator."

"And you had business with this feller Kilkenny?"

"I was meeting with him as a favor to a friend of his in America."

"And what were you meetin' him for?" When he said "for" it sounded like "far."

"I don't know."

"Your friend who you're doin' the favor for, he didn't tell ya?"

"No," I answered. "He said Kilkenny would fill me in when we met."

"And now ya can't be filled in, can ya?" Donnelly asked, handing me back my papers.

"I guess not."

"Will you be leavin' us, then?"

"Hmm? Oh, you mean going back home? Well, I didn't know how long I'd be here, so my ticket is open-ended. I guess I could leave, but . . ."

"But what?"

"Your city is very beautiful," I said, "and the people are friendly, and I'm from New York."

Donnelly grinned. "I know what you mean, sir, but you know, if you stay even a few days you might not want to go back to New York City, don'tcha know?"

"I think that's a chance I'll take."

"Before you leave, can you tell what business Mr. Kilkenny was in?"

"Thoroughbred horse racing."

"Ah, a trainer, was he?"

"No, he worked at the track. In fact, I think he ran the track."

"And which track would this be?"

"Leopardstown."

"Ah, yes," Donnelly said. "I haven't been there meself. Been to the Curragh once or twice, though. Beautiful track. You might want to go and see it."

"You're right, I might." I hadn't bothered to fill him in on my real job in New York. It didn't seem necessary.

Until he asked me his next question.

"And your friend, the one you'd be doin' the favor for, who is he and what does he do?"

I explained who J. Howard Biel was and what I did for him.

"So Mr. Kilkenny's problem had to do with racin'?"

I decided to be vague. "I don't know."

"Well, if your Mr. Biel runs a . . . track, is it?"

"Yes."

"—track in New York, and Mr. Kilkenny runs our Leopardstown course here, it would seem logical that the problem had to do with racin', don'tcha know?"

"It would seem logical, I agree, but I'm afraid I can't confirm it for you."

"I suppose I'll finally make a visit to Leopardstown, then, huh?"

"I guess you'll have to," I said. "Is that all?"

"I think so," Donnelly said with a frown. He nodded and added, "Yes, for now. Where are you stayin'?"

"The Clarence."

"I'll have someone run ya back."

"I'd appreciate it. I'd also appreciate knowing if you find out anything while I'm still here, Inspector."

Donnelly smiled and said, "I will try to keep you informed, Mr. Po."

I said, "Thank you," even though I had the feeling that keeping me informed would not be on his list of priorities.

4

By the time I returned to my hotel, I still wasn't quite sure what I was going to do. I went up to my room, put the key in the lock, opened the door, and stopped when I saw the man sitting in the chair by the window.

"You don't look surprised to see me," he said.

"I'm not." I entered and closed the door. "Seamus Kilkenny, I presume."

"That's right. How did you know the body by the bridge wasn't mine?"

"The way Howard Biel described you," I said. "The dead man was tall and broad in the shoulders. Not exactly what you'd call built like a six-foot fire hydrant."

Kilkenny was a tall man, but he was thick, like a hydrant. Not at all like the dead man.

"Bein' built like this is hell on gettin' suits," he said, "but it helped me today. Just before the other feller hit me from behind, I sensed something and started to turn. The blow struck me on the back of the shoulder, where I'm well padded."

"And you killed him."

He nodded.

"We struggled and he fell into the river. I saw him hit his head on the way down."

I stared at Kilkenny for a few minutes, wondering what the hell I was doing there.

"Why didn't you wait for the police?" I asked.

"Somebody is tryin' to kill me, Mr. Po," Kilkenny said. "I was not about to stand around and give them another chance at me, don'tcha know?"

"Them?"

"Whoever it is."

"You don't know who's trying to kill you?"

"No, I don't."

I studied Kilkenny. This was Howard Biel's friend, the man I had come over here to help. As far as the police were concerned, he was dead, but how long would that last? Once they checked the cadaver's fingerprints, that would be the end of that.

Or would it?

According to what Biel told me, Kilkenny had money, and had been the racing secretary—or whatever its equivalent was—for the past seven years. The man sitting in my room, looking around nervously, did not fit that description. But then, I was used to seeing Howard Biel in his office, or at some thoroughbred racing function. How would he look sitting nervously in a hotel room?

"So is this what we were going to talk about at the Ha'penny Inn, Mr. Kilkenny? That someone is trying to kill you?"

"Not exactly," he said. "This is the first attempt on my life, but it just shows how the situation is escalatin'."

I waited, but when he did not continue I asked, "From what to what?"

"There has been some horse dopin' goin' on at Irish tracks, Mr. Po."

"How long has it been going on?"

"It came to my attention a few weeks ago when a horse died in its stall at Leopardstown after a race."

"And the autopsy revealed drugs in its system?"

"Yes."

"That must have been a big headline in the papers here."

"No, it wasn't."

"Why not?"

"It was not revealed to the public that the horse's death was drug induced."

"What was the reason for that?"

Kilkenny fidgeted in his chair. "I was told to keep it quiet."

"Somebody told you to keep the lid on it?"

He nodded.

"Who?"

"I can't say."

"Can you tell me why?"

"The trainer is a very big name here, as is the owner."

"And between them they had enough clout to keep it quiet."

"That's right."

"But you know about it."

"Yes."

I sat down on the bed.

"You're telling me they'd kill you to keep you quiet?"

"No," Kilkenny said, "I'm telling you that's the problem I was havin' here."

"That's the reason you needed an outside investigator?"

He nodded again.

"I was thinkin' I wanted to find out if they've done it before," he said. Kilkenny clasped his hands, placing them between his knees so that his shoulders were hunched. "I love horses, Mr. Po," he said, and then he quoted, "'The Goodly Race.' There's no better name for them. I love the animals, and the game. When someone starts contaminatin' it, no matter how big they are . . ."

"Let me get this straight, Mr. Kilkenny," I said. "There's no doubt that this high-profile trainer and owner doped that horse?"

"No doubt."

"And if you spoke up, they'd be ruined."

"Their reputations would be damaged," Kilkenny said. "I don't know that they'd be ruined, but they'd get some dirt on them, to be sure."

I thought about that for a while. Racing was a big business all over the world, a rich man's business. Jenny Craig owned horses, Burt Bacharach, princes, sheikhs, and kings. Would someone kill to keep their reputation intact? To keep some dirt off their name?

Oh yeah.

But there was still something wrong, something that smelled.

"What is it?" Kilkenny asked. He must have sensed something, or seen a look on my face.

"I think we should go to the police."

"No."

"Why not? You're in the right here, Mr. Kilkenny."

"I think you should go home, Mr. Po, and let me handle this."

Something dawned on me then. "You didn't want me here at all, did you, Mr. Kilkenny?"

"No."

"Biel forced me on you."

"He didn't even tell me you were comin' until you were in the air."

"And you already had your plan in play, didn't you?"

"My plan?"

"Who was the dead man, Mr. Kilkenny?" I asked. "The owner or the trainer?"

He didn't answer.

"They'll find out the body is not you soon enough. They won't be fooled for very long by the wallet."

He unclasped his hands, put his hand inside his jacket, and came out with the gun. I could be excused for not noticing it. It was a small automatic, and not at all visible while he was seated.

"This isn't the way, Kilkenny."

"What have you figured out?" he asked.

"The dead man did not fall into the water during a struggle," I said. "He had your wallet in his pocket. You could only have put it there if you overpowered him, and then tossed him in the river. You arranged to meet him there, didn't you? You planned to kill him."

"He's scum, Mr. Po," Kilkenny said, not bothering to deny it. "Pure scum."

I'd been thinking wrong all along. It wasn't the trainer and owner who would kill to keep their names from being dirtied, it was Kilkenny who would kill to keep the "game" and "the goodly race" from receiving a black eye.

In other words, a fanatic.

"He killed that horse sure as if he'd shot it," Kilkenny explained. "The animal's heart just exploded. It's a wonder it didn't happen on the track, durin' the race. It's happened before, you know. At the Breeder's Cup in America?"

I remembered a race during which a horse's heart literally "exploded," killing it along with the animal that fell over it and had to be put down.

"I never heard anything about drugs in that case."

"It doesn't matter," he said. "It's goin' on all over the world."

"`And they dared to do it at your track, huh?"

"They think they can get away with anything."

"And what about you? How do you expect to get away with this? Why'd you put your wallet in his pocket?"

"They'll notify my wife, and she will go to the morgue and identify my body."

"You've convinced her to go along with you, huh?"

He laughed.

"She loves horses more than I do, Mr. Po. In fact, it was her idea, and I readily agreed."

"Kilkenny," I said, "this is murder. You can't—"

"They murdered that animal!"

"And what about me?" I asked. "Are you going to murder me as well? I never harmed an animal."

"You're a danger to me, lad," he said. "I'm sorry for ya, but you are."

He raised the gun as if to fire, and I tensed, getting ready to leap at him in the hopes that I'd get to him before the bullet got to me. There was no need, though. At that moment the door to my room flew open as if kicked, and then the man who kicked it rushed in with two other policemen, one of whom was Detective Inspector Jack Donnelly.

5

"How did you know he was here?" I asked Jack Donnelly, after the other two policemen had led Seamus Kilkenny from the room.

"I didn't, for sure," Donnelly said. "I was just playin' a hunch. I didn't think you'd come all this way from America for nothin', so I made sure I'd be able to hear what was goin' on in your room."

"You bugged my room?" I asked. "You don't need a court order for that kind of thing in your country?"

"Ah, well, I didn't really bug your room." He walked over to the telephone, which I noticed now was just slightly ajar, enough to keep the line open.

"We were in the room next door," he said, hanging up the phone. "I had one of my men make the connection."

I shook my head.

"What if he wasn't here?"

"Then maybe he would have gotten away with it long enough to make good his escape." Donnelly shrugged. "As I said, it was just a hunch. I thought you knew somethin'."

"Did you hear enough to know that I didn't?"

"Oh, yes," Donnelly said. "I won't be detainin' you, Mr. Po. You can leave anytime you want."

I had wanted to see some of Ireland, but now I couldn't wait to leave.

"Well, thanks for saving my life, Inspector."

Donnelly smiled and said, "It's my job, sir," and headed for the door.

"Donnelly."

He turned.

"What would have happened if I went to make a call and assumed a maid had knocked the phone ajar?"

He shrugged.

"Any number of things might have happened, Mr. Po, but they didn't. I guess you were lucky you didn't want to make a call."

As he left the room, I went to the phone. I wanted to make a call now, that was for sure. I wanted Howard Biel to know what he had sent me into by trying to force a friend to take his help. If this had taught me anything, it was that being helpful was not always a good thing.

Or a goodly thing.

Green Legs and Glam

1

I was not in New Orleans specifically to ogle naked women, but I figured what the hell? Where was the harm? I was actually in the Big Easy as a favor to my boss, J. Howard Biel, the chairman of the New York State Racing Club. He had asked me if I would help out a friend of his who had a problem. Requests like these were not outside of my job description. Recently, one of them had taken me to Ireland for a few days. I figured why turn down an all-expenses-paid trip to New Orleans, the French Quarter, and the Fairgrounds Race Track.

The Fairgrounds was where Biel's friend hung his hat. Not the big magilla Biel was in New York, his friend, Andrew Cone, was still the number-two man at the Louisiana track.

Cone had handled all the travel arrangements and had booked me into a hotel right in the Quarter, on Bourbon Street, called the Bourbon Orleans. When I arrived at 2 p.m., there was a message waiting for me at the desk. I waited until I got to my room before reading it.

"Enjoy what the Quarter has to offer," it said, "and meet me at the Blue Orleans Gentlemen's Club at 1 a.m."

It was signed, "With thanks, A. C."

I assumed by "Gentlemen's Club" we were referring to a strip joint. I wondered about the lateness of the meeting, but Cone was footing the bills, so I decided to keep the appointment.

Oh, did I mention it was Saint Patrick's Eve? March 17 was never a big holiday for me. I wasn't one of those people who suddenly became one-quarter Irish when Saint Paddy's Day rolled around, so it didn't bother me to be away from New York and miss the parade.

Since the meeting was for one in the morning, it would actually take place on Saint Patrick's Day. I spent the rest of the evening walking around the Quarter and—as Cone had suggested—taking advantage of what it had to offer. That meant great food and music and an interesting few hours spent in Jackson Square, getting sketched, read—tarot and palm—and fed.

I went back to my hotel after a late dinner to take a two-hour nap before meeting Cone at the Blue Orleans. I left a wake-up call because I was pretty groggy after the flight and spending the day walking around.

Now, I had spent a short time walking down Bourbon Street because it was so famous and I had never been there before, but that had been during the day. I left my hotel at 12:30 a.m. to give myself plenty of time to find the club, but I needn't have bothered. At midnight Bourbon Street was like no street I had ever seen before, even in New York.

It was closed to vehicles, so people were walking in the center of the street as well as on the sidewalks. There were gentlemen's clubs everywhere, each with a unique way of advertising itself. One had a girl on a swing moving in and out of a window, apparently naked, but to be sure one had to go inside—and pay the cover charge. All you could see from outside was a pair of excellent bare legs and maybe—if she swung out too far—the hint of a bare bottom.

Some of the clubs had one or two girls loitering just inside the doors, so that as you passed you got a glimpse of a nice set of boobs or an excellent derriere. Other clubs had girls dancing in the windows, but the windows were opaque, so that all you saw was a very shapely silhouette dancing and touching herself.

Music emanated from all these clubs, as well as the regular bars and jazz clubs along the street. There were vendors open late still selling the traditional New Orleans hotdog called "a Lucky Dog." On almost every corner there was a daiquiri shop selling the icy drink in all flavors, and people strolled and sucked them up through straws while they stepped in and out of the gift shops. Amazingly—at least, amazing to me—each of the daiquiri shops and a lot of the gift shops had their own ATM machines. I had never seen so many bank machines on one street before; but then they were necessary, because everyone you saw on that street was either buying or selling something.

I found the Blue Orleans Gentlemen's Club with no problem. It was one of the ones that had a naked girl or two right at the front door. As I entered I immediately had a nude girl on each arm, pressing a bare boob against me. I had a B-cup on one side and a D-cup on the other.

Being a D-cup fan, I gave her most of my attention.

"You here to see me, honey?" she asked. "I'm Alicia."

"I'm here to see you," I said, "and to meet a friend."

"I can be very friendly," she said, rubbing her boob up and down my arm. It was very firm and warm and the sensation was anything but unpleasant. Both girls were wearing that patented "stripper scent" that most strippers seem to wear. They must all buy it from the same central location. It's very sweet and heady and stays with you a long time after you've left the place.

Okay, yeah, this wasn't my first time in a strip—excuse me—a gentlemen's club.

"Would you like me to come to your table later and show you?" she asked.

"I won't leave here until you do."

"You want to sit down in front or in the back?"

"What's the advantage of down front?"

Now she wiggled both boobs at me, the magic of silicone keeping them from jiggling uncontrollably, and said, "Well, a bird's-eye view, for one."

"And for another?"

"You never know when a naked girl will plop herself down in your lap."

"Well," I said, "my friend and I are going to be discussing some business, so I guess you better put me in the back."

She pouted at me and said, "I'll have to come find you, then."

"You do that."

She brightened and said, "I'll show you to your table and then I'll know where you are."

"Sounds like a plan."

Somewhere along the line the B-cup had disentangled herself. Guess I hadn't noticed.

What can I say? I'm a boob man.

2

By 2:30 I was starting to wonder if Cone was going to show, and I was considering moving down front. I was still working on my first five-dollar beer, which had been dyed green for Saint Patrick's Day.

"There you are!" Alicia said, running up to me.

"I saw you up there," I said. She had been up on one of the stages doing her thing a little while ago. Her thing was to be noticed, and she did it very well.

She sat down next to me and said, "Your friend stood you up?"

"Maybe," I said. "It's been over an hour, but I guess I'll give him a little more time."

"How about a lap dance while you wait?" she asked. She leaned over so that her stripper smell was very strong in my nostrils and put her hand on my arm. "For twenty bucks I slide into your lap and wiggle all around!"

Having her think she had to explain a lap dance to me made me realize how young she probably was. I started to feel like a dirty old man.

"Wow," I said, "I'm tempted, but I better put it off until a little later."

I had given her a five-dollar bill just for showing me to the table, and now I slipped her another so she wouldn't forget about me.

"Gents," the announcer said into the microphone, "put your hands together and give a nice Saint Patrick's Day welcome to . . . Glam!"

The lights went down, a spotlight hit the center stage, and a girl. stepped into it. She had green hair, and green legs, and her name was Glam. All of a sudden I was reminded of Dr. Seuss—but that didn't last long. Once she started moving she was nothing like the Cat in the Hat, at all!

She was different from the other girls. For one thing, as the spot hit her she was already naked, except for the green stockings, or leggings, whatever they were. The other girls all strutted on stage with little outfits on and proceeded to move around in some parody of a dance, stripping the outfit off little by little. This girl had the body and the moves of a trained dancer so she was actually more of an entertainer than a stripper, since she had nothing to strip off.

Her body was lean and muscular, her breasts small but solid. When she moved you could see the muscles in her calves and thighs rippling, when she turned the muscles in her buttocks were evident. While she danced to Joe Cocker singing "You Can Leave Your Hat On," everything else in the place stopped.

Then the music stopped and the spot went off, and when it came back on she was gone.

There was a collective sigh from the spectators, me included. We all knew we'd just seen something special.

At this point I realized Alicia had not left, but had remained seated there during Glam's number.

"Is she the headliner?" I asked.

"Hmph," Alicia said, "she thinks she is."

"How long has she been dancing here?"

"Only a week, and already she's got her own dressing room."

Well, I thought, somebody else thinks she's the headliner, too—like maybe the boss?

"And what about the green wig and stockings? Does she always wear that?"

"No," Alicia said, "that's for Saint Patrick's Day. Who is she kidding? She's not even Irish."

At this point I saw a man come in the front door, accosted by a B-cup and another girl, probably a C. He shook them off and spoke to a man who came walking over. Unmistakably, there was a handoff between them, but some people passed into my line of sight at the crucial moment and I couldn't tell which way it went.

"I'll be back later to see if you want that dance," Alicia said, and went stalking off, obviously upset that I had enjoyed Glam's number. She didn't know that if she was a bit older, she'd still be more my preferred body type.

I looked for the customer involved in the handoff and was surprised to see him coming toward me.

"Henry Po?" he asked, as he reached the table.

"That's right," I said, standing up.

"Andy Cone." He extended his hand and I shook it. He was younger than I had expected, maybe because Biel—who was in his sixties—had described him as being a friend. This man was closer to my age, somewhere in the mid to late thirties. "Sorry I'm late. I got caught up in something."

"That's okay," I said. "I've been entertained."

"I thought you might, that's why I had you meet me here," Cone said. "I come here a lot. Who showed you to your table?"

"A girl named Alicia."

"Ah," he said, his eyes lighting up, "nice."

"A little young," I said, for some reason.

"Maybe," he said. "Look, I hate to do this, but how about having another beer on me. I have to go in the back and talk to one of the girls, but then I'll come out and join you."

I shrugged and said, "It's your party, and your dime."

"Great," Cone said. "Thanks for being understanding."

Actually, I didn't understand at all, but the girls were naked and the beer was green and . . . well, none of that mattered. I was feeling pretty relaxed and mellow, at the moment. The pulse of Bourbon Street was dancing in my head and in my veins, it seemed. I'd never been anyplace like it, and I liked it; so I was quite willing to sit there and wait. Having nothing to do was a luxury for me.

Cone disappeared, somehow managing to get backstage. A waitress came over, topless and pert, and I ordered another beer.

3

The beer hadn't arrived when Cone reappeared, moving a lot faster than when he had disappeared. He looked at me and stopped, fidgeting, appearing to be in a quandary over whether to come over to me or head for the door. Suddenly, there was a scream from somewhere in the back and Cone froze, unable to even fidget.

Nobody seemed to know what to do. Patrons looked around, torn between the girl on the stage and the scream. Even the girl on stage seemed unsure. I sighed. Nothing was going to get done unless I did it. So much for relaxing.

I got up and rushed over to Cone, grabbed his arm.

"What happened?"

"I didn't . . ." he stammered, "I didn't know . . ."

"Take me there."

"What?"

"Take me into the back!" I probably wouldn't get back there without him. "Come on." I pushed him in the direction he had come. He led me to a curtained doorway I couldn't see from my table. A man was blocking it, obviously a bouncer.

"Hold it!" he said.

"Police," I said, not knowing the penalty in New Orleans for impersonating a cop, and not wanting to know.

"Oh," he said, "okay. What's goin' on?"

"That's what I'm gonna find out," I said, and pushed Cone ahead of me again.

We went through the curtain into a hall, and from there I didn't need Cone anymore. There was a small crowd in front of a door at the end of the hall. I didn't need him, but I pulled him along anyway.

When we reached the door the crowd parted, probably something in my eyes or the way I was moving.

"Stay here," I said to Cone.

"But—"

"Don't make me have to find you." I turned and went into a small dressing room.

She was on the floor, arms and green legs askew, her green wig half on and half off, revealing red hair underneath. She wasn't naked anymore, wearing what looked like a silk dressing gown that was half on and half off. Her red pubic thatch was peeking up at me. There was blood under her head, soaked into the wig and spreading. The bullet had entered dead center in her forehead. The bloody puddle beneath her stood out in stark contrast to her pale skin.

There was a man in the room, wearing a cheap suit, a cheap hairpiece, and a frightened look.

"I don't know what to do," he said to me. I guess I looked as if I did. He was sweating so bad I could smell him.

"Who are you?" I asked.

"The manager."

"How many bouncers you got working?"

"Five"

"How many ways in and out?"

"Three."

"Block them," I said, "nobody in and nobody out."

"Okay," he said, glad to finally have something to do.

"And call nine-one-one."

"The police?" he asked, looking frightened again.

"They usually get called to the scene of a homicide."

He reached for a phone on a dressing table.

"Not from here," I shouted. "Go to your office and call them."

"But . . . I pay, I'm protected."

"Not against murder, friend."

4

Uniforms arrived first, then detectives. It was the same in every state, I guess.

They got the back hallway cleared out, probably putting everyone in the club. The music had been stopped a long time, and the girls had probably all covered up. There were two detectives, and they were in the dressing room with me and the dead girl.

"From what I've been told, you're the only one who knew what to do," one of them said.

"Somebody had to do something."

"Why you?" he asked. "I mean, how did you know what to do?"

I took out my wallet and handed him my ID.

"Private?"

"That's right."

"From New York."

That wasn't a question. It was on my ID. He handed it back. "The manager says you made him call us."

"That's right. He told me he was protected. I assumed that a little protection money didn't include murder."

He impressed me by not denying anything, but simply saying, "You assumed right."

He looked at his partner, who nodded. They were the same age, forties; and had all the signs of having worked together a long time. The nod was one of the signs. They had communicated without saying a word, and had come to a decision.

"Mr. Po," the first man said, "my name's Detective LaSalle, this is my partner, Detective Batiste."

Batiste and I exchanged a nod. I had the feeling I had just gone up several notches in their estimation. With most cops, when they see your PI ticket, you go down; but I had known what to do in this situation, and that worked for me.

"Quick thinking to keep everyone inside," LaSalle said. "Now just tell me one other thing."

"What's that?"

"Who killed her?"

"I wish I knew," I said. "She was . . . special."

"How do you know that?" he snapped.

"I saw her dance," I said. "She was different from all the others."

"You don't know how different," LaSalle said, looking down at her. No one from the Medical Examiner's office had arrived, so they hadn't moved her. "She was one of ours."

"A snitch?"

He shook his head and looked at me with tremendous sadness in his eyes.

"A cop," I said.

He nodded. "She was working undercover."

"One of the girls said she came in a week ago."

"That's right," LaSalle said.

"And she already had her own dressing room."

"She has—had—dance background. That was why they sent her in here."

"Too bad."

"About what?"

"If she hadn't had the dance background, hadn't distinguished herself from the others, she might have shared a dressing room and not been alone."

He nodded. "I see what you mean."

"What was she working on?" I asked.

"Somebody is selling drugs from inside the club," LaSalle said. "It was thought that all that was needed was somebody on the inside who would keep their eyes on something other than the girls. That's why they sent in a woman."

I frowned, thinking back to what I had seen in the club.

"You didn't hear a shot?" LaSalle asked.

"No," I said, "just the scream of the girl who found her."

"Must have been suppressed, then," LaSalle said.

"The murder was planned," Batiste said.

"Somebody sniffed her out," LaSalle said. "She was a good cop, but somebody spotted her."

"One of the other girls, maybe," I said. "Even if she had her own dressing room they still saw more of her than anyone else."

"This is not the way a woman kills," LaSalle said.

I shrugged. "A woman may have fingered her."

LaSalle looked down at Glam again. Each time he did the pain in his eyes was evident. Batiste's glances at her were more dispassionate. "I want this guy," LaSalle said.

I looked at Batiste, who stared back at me without expression, and yet I felt as if he'd passed me something.

"Look, Detective," I said, "I'm not from here, and I don't mean to try and do your job, but . . . if I could have a minute to leave the room?"

"If you can do anything to give me the killer," LaSalle said, "you can leave the state and come back."

"No," I said, "just the room."

"Go."

As I left he was still sitting, his shoulders slumped, and I thought I saw his partner put his hand on his shoulder.

5

I went out into the club and looked around. There was still a bouncer standing at the front door and one that I could see at a side door. In each case a uniformed policeman had joined him. Since there were three ways out, I assumed that there was also a bouncer and a cop on the third door.

I found Andrew Cone seated at the table I had been sitting at, with three other people, none of whom seemed to know each other. The police had simply made everyone sit down, so that most of the seats were taken.

"Cone," I said, "come with me for a minute."

"What for?" He looked frightened.

"Just come on."

He stood up, and I walked him over into a corner where we could talk alone.

"Tell me what happened in the back," I said.

"Did you tell them—"

"I didn't tell them anything," I said, "and if you answer all my questions I might not. Why did you go into the back?"

"I—I'm having a thing with one of the girls. I went in the back to see her."

"And what happened?"

"I—I saw the new girl's dressing room door open and I saw green legs on the floor. I walked over and took a look. She was on the floor . . . there was blood . . . I wanted to get out."

"Why?"

"I . . ." He stopped, as if answering that question was harder than the others.

"Is it because you have drugs on you that you're afraid would be found in a search?"

His eyes widened and he looked around to see if anyone had heard me.

"No one can hear us," I said, keeping my voice low. "When you walked in I happened to be looking at the door." That was when I found out how young and dumb Alicia was, and I lost interest in her, D cups or not. If not for that I might not have seen what I did. "I saw a hand-off when you walked in, but I didn't see what was exchanged. Were you selling, or buying?"

He didn't answer right away.

"Come on, Andrew," I said, "you can answer me or the cops."

"Buying," he said, quickly in a barely audible voice. "I was buying."

"So the bouncer is the one selling drugs out of the club?"

"That's right."

"Which one?" I asked him. The sale had taken place at the door, but that didn't mean that the bouncer on that door was the one. As it turned out, he was.

"That one," Cone said, and pointed at the man.

The bouncer must have been watching us. Maybe Cone was the last person he had sold drugs to, maybe the only one in the club he had made a sale to. In any case, when Andrew Cone pointed him out the man bolted for the door.

"Stop him!" I shouted to the cop who had been standing with him. "Stop that man!"

Too late. The cop was too slow and the bouncer was out the door. I took off after him, ran out the door myself before the cop could intercept me.

Out into the combination of people and sounds and lights and music that was Bourbon Street after midnight.

6

The bouncers in the club all wore the same thing, black pants and a black T-shirt with the club's logo on it which—luckily—was yellow. As I ran out the door onto the street I looked both ways and spotted the yellow logo hightailing it up Bourbon Street. I took off after him, and then we were both dodging two-way traffic of people who were having a good time, moving slowly, men and women trying to stop us to throw beads on us or flash us. The bouncer literally ran over three or four people, knocking them to the ground, scattering green daiquiris onto the street, forcing me to try to avoid them and in the process knocking one or two people down. The only difference is that although neither of us stopped, I tried to toss apologies over my shoulder.

The bouncer stayed on Bourbon Street, probably figuring to lose himself in the people, rather than turning off on a side street. However, he was knocking so many people over that he was leaving a trail behind him. Neither one of us was making much progress, me in catching him or him in getting away. He risked a look over his shoulder once or twice and saw me chasing. I didn't know if there were cops running behind me or not, and I didn't take a look, not wanting to risk taking my eyes off him.

Finally, he decided he wasn't getting anywhere and turned down a side street. When I reached it I saw that it was Orleans Street. Now we were away from people and running down a darker street. I could still see him ahead of me and hear his feet pounding. With fewer people to avoid, he was able to pick up speed, but so was I. He ran one block and turned right at the corner, trying to lose me. As I turned the corner I saw him make a quick left and duck into Pirate's Alley, a street I had been on earlier in the day.

I had been to the Faulkner House bookstore and I knew that the alley would give out onto Jackson Square. In the afternoon the square was teeming with as much life as Bourbon Street was at night. At this time of night it would be empty. I had to keep him in sight to see which way he would go when he reached the square.

As luck would have it we were now running on a cobblestoned street, something the bouncer was probably not used to. Truth be told, neither was I, but I didn't stumble and fall and he did. It happened in every movie, and it happens in real life. Sometimes you're just running too fast for your feet to keep up with, or you simply trip. He did one of those things and went down flat on his belly.

I could hear him slide as he hit the cobblestones, then the sound his hands and feet made as he scrambled to get up. He had just gotten his balance when I hit him, tackling him low around the knees. He was a lot bigger than me, and I still didn't know if I had help behind me. I took him at the knees because it's easier to fight a man who is bigger than you if you take him off his feet.

We went down together. His hands and knees must have been smarting from his first fall, and I heard the wind go out of him as he hit this second time.

I scrambled this time, trying to get on top of him so I could keep him down. I got into his back and as I did he heaved himself up and me with him. He was big and strong, and if I was alone in this alley with him I was going to be in trouble.

Luckily, that was not the case.

As he tossed me off and tried to get to his feet two uniformed cops hit him and took him down for a third and final time.

7

"So you saw an exchange take place at the door, but you didn't see what was exchanged," LaSalle asked me, about half an hour later, "or who the exchange was made with."

"Right."

"And you figured drug buy?"

"What can I say?" I asked. "I have an extremely suspicious mind."

He stared at me, not sure whether I was telling the whole truth or not. I was trying to keep Andrew Cone out of it, because I believed what he had told me. He'd simply chosen the wrong night to make a drug buy and to have a meeting with me to discuss whatever problem it was he needed help with. I didn't know what that problem was, or if it had anything to do with drugs, but I knew I wasn't going to hang around to find out. If LaSalle would let me I was going to be on the first plane home the next day.

"So you went out into the club to see if he was still there?"

"Right."

"One of my boys said you talked to someone else."

"Right," I said. "I came here to meet someone, and I wanted to check in with him when I had the chance. Then I started toward the bouncer, and he took off."

"Why would you figure he was the killer?"

"Well, if it was a drug buy, it fit in with what you told me about Glam and what she was doing here."

"And how did you come to see this buy?"

"I told you," I said. "I just happened to be looking at the door."

"With all these naked girls here you were looking at the door?" he asked, doubtfully.

"Like I said," I replied, "I was waiting for someone."

"Yeah," the detective said, "you did say that. I'm going to need his name by the way."

I gave it to him. I figured they'd question Cone, but not search him. What happened while they were questioning him would depend on how guilty he felt. That was his problem, not mine.

At that moment the M.E.'s men came out of the back carrying the body of the dead cop. We both waited until they had passed and gone out the front door. Batiste was gone, having taken the bouncer to wherever they'd take him to question him and book him.

LaSalle looked back at me.

"How do you figure the bouncer got back there to kill her?"

"He works here, he's got access. According to the manager there are five bouncers working and three ways out. Put one on each door, and one on the door to the dressing rooms, and you got one guy who can float. He was probably the floater when he went back and killed her. Check with the bouncer who was on that door and see if he went back there."

"We did," LaSalle said. "He says the guy went back there only for a minute and came right out again."

"Then it fits."

"There were girls going in and out, too."

"Like you said," I reminded him, "not a woman's crime."

"I wonder how he made her."

I thought about Alicia, and how jealous she seemed of Glam. Some of the other girls probably felt the same way. I wondered if one of them had made her for the killer, maybe even innocently.

His cell phone rang then, and he plucked it from his belt and answered it by saying his name. He listened, nodded, grunted, said, "Thanks," and hung up.

A uniformed cop came over with a gun in a plastic bag. Also in the bag was a suppressor.

"Where'd you find it?"

"In a garbage bag in the back. Had to go through a bunch. The bags had all been tied off, but whoever had the gun was able to shove the gun and suppressor through a hole without untying it."

"Good. Get it down to the lab. We should be able to get some prints off it."

"And they'll match those of the bouncer," I said, helpfully.

As the uniformed cop walked away LaSalle said, "Yeah, they will. That was my partner on the phone. The guy confessed. He did it. He killed her."

"All right," I said. "You got him."

"You got him, Mr. Po," LaSalle said, and I was surprised to see that he was close to tears. "And I'm very grateful."

"Detective . . ." I said, then decided not to ask.

"You got a right to know," he said. "She and I, we were . . . well, close."

"I'm sorry."

"Yeah," he said. "Listen, if you'll come down and make a statement tomorrow, I don't think we'll have to detain you in town any longer."

"Thanks. I'll be down first thing."

He handed me his card with the address of the police station I was to go to, then turned to walk away.

"Can I ask," I said, and he turned around, "what her real name was?"

"Shannon," he said, "her name was Detective Shannon O'Brien."

"So she was Irish, after all?"

"Oh yeah," he said, "she was definitely Irish. She loved Saint Paddy's Day."

Neither one of us appreciated the irony.

Cowards Die Many Times

1

"Whatta we got?" Detective Sam McKeever asked the uniformed policeman as he entered the second-story hotel room.

"This fella says he left the game to take a piss, and when he got back everybody was dead."

"That so?" McKeever said. He looked down at the man in question, who was sitting on a sagging sofa. Across the room five men were strewn about a poker table, two slumped over it, two on the floor by it, and one underneath. There were cards and poker chips and cash all over the place. And blood.

"Come on, I asked is that so?" McKeever said, kicking the man in the shin.

"Lay off, McKeever." The seated man raised his head and looked up at the policeman.

"Oh shit, Val?"

"That's right," Val O'Farrell said, "it's me."

"You know this joker?" the policeman asked.

"Did he identify himself to you?" McKeever asked.

"Said his name was O'Farrell," the young patrolman said. "Didn't mean nothin' to me."

"He used to be one of us," McKeever said.

"A cop?"

"A dick," McKeever said. "I said one of 'us,'" McKeever repeated, which clearly meant not one of "you." "Now he's private."

"Well," the cop said, "he's still the only one left standin' outta this group."

"Go downstairs and wait for the meat wagon," McKeever said. "I'll talk to him."

"Whatever you say."

As the cop reached the door McKeever called out, "Where's your partner?"

"Talkin' to the neighbors, to see if anybody heard anything."

"Shit," McKeever said. "Okay, go ahead." As the younger man left McKeever said, "They're hirin' babies, and they all think they're dicks."

"I feel for you, Sam," O'Farrell said.

McKeever looked down at the private detective. Usually a natty dresser O'Farrell was without his jacket and tie, and his white shirt looked soiled around the collar and cuffs.

"How long was this game goin' on?" he asked.

" 'Bout forty hours," O'Farrell said.

"Ain't you a little long in the tooth for two-day poker games, Val?" McKeever asked.

"I'm the same age as you, you sheeny bastard."

"That's what I mean," McKeever said. "I'm too old for two-day poker games."

O'Farrell was in his forties, had left the police force in 1919 to go private. In three years he had become one of the most sought-after private detectives in New York. Tonight, however, he'd been sought after by a little guy named Kevin Allison, who had knocked on the door of the hotel room and asked to speak to him. It was while he was downstairs in the lobby talking to Kevin that he heard the shots from the second floor and rushed back up. When he entered the room and saw that everyone was dead, he'd gone back down to the lobby, but Kevin was gone. He didn't know why Kevin had lured him out of the room, but it had saved his life, and he wasn't ready to throw the man to the dogs—or the cops.

"I didn't see anything, Sam," O'Farrell said.

"How were you doin' in the game?" McKeever asked.

"I was winning."

"Big?"

"Not that big."

"Who were the other players?"

"Sam—"

"Val, you know Turico's gonna be here any minute," McKeever said, "and he's gonna be pissed as it is, bein' called out at midnight. The quicker you answer my questions, the quicker you get out of here."

There was very little love lost between O'Farrell and Lieutenant Turico. Their relationship had not been good when O'Farrell was on the force, and if anything, it had gotten worse since he left. So he needed to cooperate with McKeever and get out of there so he could go looking for Kevin Allison.

"So who were the other players?" McKeever asked, again. O'Farrell told him, and answered other questions. . . .

He'd just taken a hand with a full house, queens over threes, beating Tex Fitzgerald's hand of jacks full over eights. Two full houses in a six-handed game of draw poker, and they had each drawn three cards. O'Farrell had been dealt the threes, kept 'em, and drew the three queens.

"Bad beat," Eric Monahan had said to Tex.

"Shut up," Tex had replied, bitterly. He was losing badly all night, and with good hands. O'Farrell knew how that felt. He didn't mind losing on a night when the cards weren't coming, but losing with hands like jacks full was brutal.

There was a knock at the door as the deal passed to Mike Pappas. The man hosting the game, Del Manning, got up and answered the door. He cracked it, spoke to someone, then turned to the table and said, "O'Farrell, it's for you."

"Deal me out," O'Farrell had said, before Pappas could deal. The Greek nodded and dealt by him.

"Come right back," the fifth man, Lenny Davis said. "You got most of my money."

"I'll be back," O'Farrell said. "Who is it?" he asked Del as they passed.

"I don't know 'im," Manning said. "He said it was important. I figured you knew him, since he knew where to find you."

"I'll be right back," he said again.

"You better," Manning said. "You got everybody's money, and you're killin' Tex."

O'Farrell didn't know Tex well. In fact, the only players at the table he knew at all were Manning and the Greek, Mike Pappas.

When he got to the door he saw Kevin Allison standing outside, nervously shifting from one foot to another. He recognized him, but they weren't friends. He wondered how the ex-pug had been able to find him.

"You looking for me?" he'd asked.

"Yeah," Allison said. "I need to talk to yuh . . . downstairs."

O'Farrell stepped out into the hall, pulling the door closed behind him.

"What's wrong with right here?"

"Gotta be downstairs," Allison said, nervously. "It's, uh, too light up here. Please, Mr. O'Farrell."

O'Farrell stared at the man a few moments, then asked, "How did you know where I was?"

A lot was going to hinge on the man's answer, because there were only two people who knew where he was and what he was doing. Allison was going to have to come up with one of those names.

"How'd you know where I was. Allison?"

"I talked to Dorothy," he replied. "She told me."

Dorothy was a girl O'Farrell had been seeing for a few weeks. Hers was one of those names. Later, he'd find out from Dorothy how she happened to talk to Allison. At that moment he wanted to get this over with so he could get back to the game before his cards cooled off.

"All right," he said. "Let's go downstairs."

Since they were only on the second floor they took the stairs rather than the elevator. When they reached the lobby Allison took off across it like he was being chased, not running, but almost.

"Hey," O'Farrell had called, "wait up—" and that was when he heard the shots. Allison took off out the front door, leaving the detective with two options. He could chase the man, or run back upstairs and see what was going on.

He went back up and found the bodies.

He managed to get out of the hotel before Turico showed up. He hadn't said a word to McKeever about Kevin Allison. That was the only thing he'd held back. He wasn't prepared to throw the man to the wolves until he found out his whole story. He stuck to his own story about going down the hall to take a piss. He heard the shots, he said—which was about right—and came running back to find everybody dead.

Allison was an ex-pug. His fighting weight had been bantam, and he'd gone by the name "Kid Alley." There were a few places O'Farrell knew he could look for the ex-boxer, but there was also someone he knew who knew more about where the ex-pugilists hung out.

He went downstairs and around the corner to where he had parked his Twin Six Packard Roadster. He sat in the front seat for a few moments, going over the evening's events in his mind. While he thought he sought to make himself more presentable, using the rear view mirror. He combed his hair with his fingers, buttoned his collar, rolled down the sleeves of his white shirt and buttoned the cuffs, then donned the jacket of his linen suit. He left his tie in the pocket of the jacket, where he'd deposited it during the ninth hour of play. He'd been forced by McKeever to leave his winnings on the table. It would have been a small price to pay for having his life spared, but after two days of playing fairly even, he had eventually gotten to the point where he was well ahead. By the time Turico got through picking the place clean he knew his winnings would be gone.

When he felt a bit more presentable he started the engine.

2

Dorothy LeMay was—for want of a better word—a songstress. O'Farrell never really thought of her as a singer because she didn't have that great a voice. She got her jobs singing in clubs because of her great looks. Long, wavy blond hair and a willowy but top-heavy figure got her all the jobs she wanted, as long as it was a man doing the hiring and her dress was cut low enough. The really nice thing about Dorothy was that she knew all this and was okay with it. She had no illusions about being a great singer, she just wanted to do it for a living.

He'd met her at a night club where she was singing, invited her to have a drink with him after her set. It had been a quiet night, not too many people left in the place by the time she was done. They'd talked until somebody kicked them out of the place, and then she'd gone to his apartment with him. Ever since then they'd been seeing each other three or four times a week.

Now she was singing in a dive called The Martini Pit.

"Good evening, Mr. O'Farrell," Cory, the red-headed hat check girl, greeted him. She was a cute little thing, short but full-bodied, with a deep, shadowy cleavage he knew got her plenty of tips. If it hadn't been for Dorothy, O'Farrell would have taken their flirtatiousness to another level—but flirt they did.

"Hello, kid," he said, handing her his fedora. "You're looking as lovely as usual tonight."

She put his hat on a shelf, turned back and handed him his check, gave him a look he flattered himself she didn't give to many other men.

"You look a little tired," she said. "Handsome, but tired."

"Well, thanks for the first," he said. "As for the second, it's been a rough night." Two nights, actually. "Dorothy is here, I take it?"

"She sure is," Cory said. "I think she's in her dressing room, changing for her next set."

"Maybe I can catch her before she goes on, then," he said. "See you later."

With one last look at the shadowy place between her breasts he presented himself to Leo, the maitre d'.

"Evenin', Mr. O," the big man said. Leo doubled as the bouncer, since Miles DeKay, the half-owner of The Martini Pit, was too cheap to pay to have one of each. Since O'Farrell wanted to go back to Dorothy's dressing room to see her, he was going to have to get past Leo.

"You need a table tonight?" the big man asked. "I can get you right up front."

O'Farrell was usually able to sit up front because the Pit was hardly ever more than half full. He wondered how the two owners kept the place going.

"Thanks, Leo," he said, "but all I need is a few minutes of Dorothy's time in her dressing room. Can we work that out?"

"For you? Sure, Mr. O. Follow me."

As he followed in the big man's wake he checked out the postage stamp-sized tables. Those that were inhabited were taken by couples ranging from their forties to their sixties. The Martini Pit was not the kind of place that appealed to the younger set. Those clubs were further downtown, or up in Harlem, like Jack Johnson's Club Deluxe (which would, three years later, become the Cotton Club).

Leo showed O'Farrell down the long, cramped hallway to Dorothy's closet-sized dressing room. She never complained about it and was happy that she had a bathroom of her own. The big man knocked on the door and said, "Mr. O'Farrell to see you, Miss LeMay."

After a moment the door opened and Dorothy graced Leo with a wide, beautiful smile.

"Thank you, Leo. Let the gentleman in, please."

"Yes, ma'am."

Leo stepped aside and said, "There ya go, Mr. O."

"Thanks, Leo."

O'Farrell went past the door and closed it behind him. Dorothy came into his arms and said, "Kiss me quickly, before I put my lipstick on."

He kissed her and held her tightly. Every time she was in his arms he realized why he enjoyed her company. It wasn't only because she felt good and smelled good, but it was in the way that she hugged him so warmly and lovingly. He'd never received a halfhearted hug from her. Even now, when she was minutes from going on, she hugged him tightly.

She kissed him once more—soundly enough to arouse him—and then pushed him away.

"You'll have to talk to me while I finish getting ready," she said. "What brings you here? I thought you were at a poker game."

"I was," he told her, "and that's why I'm here."

She moved in and out of the bathroom while he explained what had happened. When he got to the part about the shooting she backed up and stared at him through the doorway.

"Oh my God," she said. "You could have been killed."

"Yes," he said, "but I wasn't."

"Why?"

"That's what I want to find out. Did you talk to a fella named Allison?" he asked. "Kevin Allison?"

"A nervous little man with a flat nose?"

"That's him. He got that nose in the ring."

"Yeah, I spoke to him. He took a chance with Big Leo, trying to get by him to see me in my dressing room. He was so insistent I told Leo to let him by."

"What did you tell Allison?"

She moved into the doorway now, bringing her hair brush with her.

"Now don't be angry with me," she said, "but I told him where you would be playing poker."

"I'm not angry," he said. "Just tell me why you told him?"

"He was very anxious to find you," she explained. "He said it was a matter of life and death. He was shaking and sweating so much that I believed him." She let her hands drop to her sides and stared at him. "I had no idea he was talking about your life."

"He was," O'Farrell said, "and he saved it by luring me out of that room."

"Why would he do that?" she asked.

"I don't know."

"Are you friends?"

"I hardly know him."

"Then why—"

"I'm going to ask him," O'Farrell said, interrupting her, "as soon as I can find him."

"How are you gonna do that?"

"By looking. What time did he come by the club?"

"It must have been . . . it was between my first and second set, and I went on at ten . . . must have been ten thirty, when I came off."

"He didn't come to the hotel until almost eleven," O'Farrell said, mostly to himself. "It doesn't take that long to get from the club to the hotel." The club was on Twenty-Third and Eighth, while the hotel was on Nineteenth Street and Broadway. It was a walk, and not a long one.

"Maybe . . ." she said.

"Maybe what?"

Still brushing her hair she said, "Maybe he was scared. Maybe it took him that long to decide to actually do it."

"Maybe."

"You said there was five other men in the game?" she asked, moving back into the bathroom.

"That's right."

"I wonder . . ." she said, and the rest was unintelligible.

"What?" he said. "What did you say?"

She backed up again so she could see him, and so he could hear her.

"I said, I wonder which one the killer wanted to kill? I mean, it couldn't have been all of them, could it?"

He stared at her for a moment, then looked away and said to himself, "That's the question, isn't it?"

He walked to his Twin Six, got in and decided to drive home. He needed to take a shower and have something to eat before he started out again. He decided he shouldn't be asking only why Kid Alley had lured him out of that room, but who in that room someone had wanted to kill so badly that they were willing to kill four other men as well.

3

The next morning he drove down to the offices of the *New York Telegraph,* on Williams Street near Park Row, where most of the newspapers had their offices, to see his friend Bat Masterson.

He parked his Twin Six around the corner and entered the building. It was ten in the morning, and the newsroom was buzzing. He found Bat Masterson sitting at his desk, staring at his typewriter. Over the years he had made his way from lawman, gunman and gambler to columnist for the paper, and eventually to the position he now held, vice president.

"This sonofabitchin' thing," Bat said.

"Good morning to you, too."

Bat looked up and said, "You look like crap."

"A two-day poker game and almost getting killed will do that to you," O'Farrell said.

"Well," the Old West legend said, "that sounds more interesting than what I'm working on. Give."

O'Farrell gave the story to Bat, who listened intently and silently until the end.

"So you're lookin' for this ex-pug Kid Alley."

"And you know all the fighters in town."

"You came to the right place," Bat said, standing up. "I was just about to throw this infernal machine out the window. Let's go."

"Where?"

"I happen to know someone who knows someone . . ."

They tried Perry's first. It was ostensibly a drug store right next to the newspaper building, but in point of fact it was a speakeasy called The Pot of Glue frequented by the journalists and writers in the area. As luck would have it, Damon Runyon was there, sitting with the rewrite man from the *New York World* named James M. Cain.

"Do you know why the postman always rings twice?" Cain asked O'Farrell as he entered.

"No, but—"

"You will," Cain said. "You'll read it, after I've finished writing it."

Cain went past him and left, heading back to his typewriter in the *World* offices.

"What was that about?"

"Don't know," Runyon said. "He was also askin' what we knew about double indemnity. He's writing a couple of things. Some fiction. You look like hell, Val. Have some Brown Ruin, fellows."

Runyon didn't drink the stuff himself but wasn't above pushing it.

"God, no," O'Farrell said. "I have more respect for my stomach than that."

Bat also refused.

"What brings you here, then?" Runyon asked. "And looking less than spiffy."

"We're looking for Kevin Allison," Bat said. "I thought I remembered you doin' a story on him a few years ago."

"'Kid Alley'?" Runyon asked. "What do you want with a washed up pug like him?"

"I think he saved my life," O'Farrelll said.

"You think?"

"I can't explain it now," O'Farrell said. "I just have to find him. Any ideas?"

"A couple of gyms, maybe," Runyon said.

"He's not fighting again, is he?"

"No," the writer said, "but he likes to hang around it."

"Any one in particular?" O'Farrell asked.

"Three or four, probably," Runyon said, and reeled them off. "But there's something else you should know."

"What?"

"I hear the Kid's running with Arnold Rothstein."

"See?" Bat said. "I knew that was the kind of thing we'd get from this guy."

"What the hell would Rothstein want with a broken down ex-pug like Allison?"

Rothstein, largely believed to be the man behind the 1919 Black Sox scandal, had of late begun running liquor into the U.S. from Great Britain. He did most of his business from a table at Lindy's, on Broadway and Forty-Ninth Street.

"Rothstein is always planning and scheming," Runyon warned. "He must have something planned where he thinks the Kid could be of use to him. You don't want to cross him."

"Rothstein and I already crossed swords once or twice while I was a cop," O'Farrell said, "but thanks for the warning."

"Is there a story in this?" Runyon asked, as O'Farrell turned to leave.

"Maybe," O'Farrell said, "probably, but not one with a sports connection."

"Call me first, Val," Runyon said. "A story's a story, you know?"

"What do I look like?" Bat asked. "Chopped liver?"

"There might be enough story to go around," O'Farrell said. "I'll keep in touch. Thanks."

O'Farrell and Bat checked out a couple of the gyms suggested by

Damon Runyon but with no luck. O'Farrell thought that Kid Alley might be lying low, but why? Because he'd drawn O'Farrell out of the hotel room, thereby saving his life? Or was he more involved in the massacre of everyone else at the poker game? O'Farrell didn't even know Allison well, which confused him even more. Why would the man risk himself to get the detective out of the room?

O'Farrell replayed the scene in his head. . . .

It was obvious that Allison never had anything to tell him. As soon as they hit the lobby the ex-pug took off for the door. He knew what was going to happen upstairs. The big question was, why had he lured O'Farrell from the room?

O'Farrell decided to go home and freshen up before he continued looking for Kid Alley.

"You go on," Bat said. "I have a few ideas about where to look. I'll be in touch."

4

O'Farrell had just stepped from his shower when someone knocked on his door. He wrapped a towel around his waist and answered it.

"Puttin' on weight, Val," Detective Sam McKeever said. "Didn't notice it when you were dressed. Must be those expensive suits."

"What's on your mind, Sam?" O'Farrell asked, backing away and letting the policeman enter.

"I tried to keep you out of it as long as I could, but it ain't possible, anymore," McKeever said. "The lieutenant wants me to bring you in for questioning."

"By lieutenant you mean Mike Turico?"

"You know that's who I mean."

"Do I have time to get dressed?"

"Yeah, but I'm gonna watch you," McKeever said. "I don't want you makin' me look bad by goin' out a window."

"You think I'd do that to you, Sam?"

McKeever put a cigar into his mouth, went about lighting it. "Only 'cause you've done it before."

"Not this time," O'Farrell said. "You have my word."

McKeever frowned. "Leave the door open so we can talk."

O'Farrell went into the bedroom, and began to dress. The shower had freshened him, but his eyes still felt sticky with lack of sleep. McKeever's cigar smoke wafted in from the other room.

"You find out anything since this mornin'?" McKeever asked.

"No," O'Farrell said. In point if fact it had taken him most of the day simply to decide he was asking the wrong questions.

"That's too bad," the detective said. "Turico thinks you know what happened. He's gonna grill you."

"He's tried that before," O'Farrell said.

"You might wanna call a shyster before you go down," McKeever said. "I can give you the time to do that."

"That's okay," O'Farrell said. "I can handle Turico."

"Suit yourself."

When O'Farrell came out he was wearing one of his best suits.

"Oh, Val . . ."

"What?"

"That suit costs more than . . . seein' you in that is gonna drive Mike up a wall."

O'Farrell smiled and said, "That's the general idea, Sam. Come on."

McKeever escorted O'Farrell into Lieutenant Mike Turico's office. Turico remained seated behind his desk and said, "That's all, McKeever."

"But it's my case—"

"I'm not takin' your case, Sam," Turico said. "I just wanna talk with O'Farrell alone."

McKeever hesitated, then nodded and backed out, closing the door behind him.

"You think that suit impresses me?"

"Mike," O'Farrell said, taking a seat across from the man, "to tell you the truth, I never really gave it any thought."

"The truth?" Turico laughed. "When have you ever told the truth?"

"You're my age, Mike," O'Farrell said. "You ever think about retirement?"

"No," Turico said, with a frown, "why?"

"You're getting too cynical."

"Cram it," Turico said. "Ya know, I should can your friend McKeever's ass for lettin' you walk away from the scene last night."

"Why?" O'Farrell said. "I just missed being a victim."

"You're the only one who survived the game," Turico said. "That makes you the number one suspect, in my book."

"Come on, Mike," O'Farrell said. "I was seen in the lobby when the shots were being fired."

"Yeah, but how did you know to go down to the lobby at that moment?"

"Didn't Sam tell you? I was taking a piss when—"

"Yeah, yeah, I heard. Look, O'Farrell, I actually asked you here to get your help."

O'Farrell bit back a smart remark. Antagonizing Turico since he'd left the force had become a hobby of his—mostly because it was so easy. This time, though, the lieutenant seemed serious.

"What can I do?"

"Tell me about the other players," Turico said. "Help us figure out who the target was."

Farrell didn't see any harm in that.

O'Farrell gave Turico what he wanted—the names of the other players—and then went back home. As he entered the telephone rang.

"Val?"

"Bat? Where are you?"

"I'll give you the address," Bat said. "I think you better meet me here."

"What's goin' on?"

"We'll talk when you get here," Bat said. "And hurry. You wanna beat the police here."

"Bat—" he started, but the Old West legend had hung up.

At one time a haven for German immigrants, Alphabet City was now inhabited by the Jews, Italians and Irish. Little more than a slum, it didn't surprise O'Farrell that Bat may have found Kid Alley living here.

He found the building he wanted on Avenue B and walked up the three flights to the apartment number Bat had given him. The door was closed so he knocked. He heard footsteps on the wooden floor and then the door swung open.

"Come on in," Bat said. "Your man is in the bedroom."

O'Farrell didn't like the way he said it, so he almost expected to find Kid Alley dead in the bedroom. What he didn't expect to find was the man's brains all over the bed sheets and wall. The ex-pug was lying face down on the bed, and you didn't have to be a doctor to know he was dead. He backed out of the room.

"Needless to say I found him like that," Bat said.

"Have you looked around?"

"Sure," Bat said. "I didn't find nothin' to tell us why he would've saved your life. But it looks like he did it at the cost of his own."

"My hero," O'Farrell said.

"What now?" Bat asked.

"If I was still a cop," O'Farrell said, "I'd start looking into the lives of all the dead poker players."

"Didn't you know 'em already?" Bat asked.

"I knew some of them," O'Farrell said, "but I didn't know everything about them."

"That sounds like a big job."

"It is," O'Farrell said. "That's why I'm going to leave it to McKeever and Turico."

"So then what are we gonna do?" Bat asked.

"We?"

Bat shrugged.

"I got some free time."

"You got any suggestions?"

"You're the detective," Bat said, "but I know what I'd do."

"I'm open to suggestions."

"Cheesecake," Bat said, "at Lindy's."

And by that he meant Arnold Rothstein.

"That is," Bat added, "if you really want to pursue this any further. Allison is dead, after all."

O'Farrell took off his hat and scratched his head.

"I owe him," he said.

"Okay, then." Bat said. "Cheesecake it is."

"You comin'?" O'Farrell asked.

"You kiddin'? I wouldn't miss is."

5

Arnold Rothstein was easy to find even in a busy Lindy's. He was the one surrounded by bodyguards. O'Farrell and Bat Masterson crossed the floor under the wary eye of those guards.

"Boss," one of them said as the two men reached them.

"Well, well," the well-dressed Arnold Rothstein said, looking up from his cheesecake, "two of New York's more famous people. Make way, boys, for Val O'Farrell and the great Bat Masterson."

O'Farrell could see the bodyguards react to Bat's name. They made their living with guns, and even Bat Masterson in his sixties was a man to be respected.

"What brings you bents to my table?" Rothstein asked. "Have a seat, please."

O'Farrell and Bat sat—Bat, from old habits, so that he could see most of the room. O'Farrell was wondering if the old legend was heeled, and he was sure others were wondering the same.

"I understand you know an ex-fighter named Kevin Allison," O'Farrell said.

Rothstein wiped his mouth with a cloth napkin and looked up at one of his men—he was fairly young, maybe late twenties, a big guy with broad shoulders who dressed like he used his boss's tailor.

"We know this guy?"

"We use him as a runner, sometimes," one of them said.

Rothstein looked back at O'Farrell and Bat, shrugged and said, "I don't know the guy. Lenny?"

"Don't know 'im real good," Lenny said. "Like I said, he runs errands and stuff."

"This is Lenny Green," Rothstein said. "I'm groomin' him, I just don't know for what, yet."

O'Farrell looked at Green, who stared back with no expression.

"What's your interest in a busted-up ex-pug?" Rothstein asked.

"He's dead," Bat said.

"That's too bad," Rothstein said. "He got family? We'll send flowers."

"No family," Bat said. "From what I know of him he lived alone."

"Too bad," Rothstein said. He looked at one of his men. "Make sure we pick up the body. I'll pay for a funeral."

"I'll take care of it," Lenny Green said.

"That's big of you," O'Farrell said.

"Hey, he worked for me," Rothstein said. His brown eyes sparkled in his pale face. Others had often commented on Rothstein's "happy" eyes, his dominant feature, and O'Farrell could see that they were correct. "I take care of my own."

"You wouldn't have any idea how he was killed, would you, Mr. Rothstein?" O'Farrell asked.

O'Farrell saw that he had played it right. If he'd said, "Arnold" or "Rothstein" the man might have bristled, been reluctant to answer, but he used the more respectful "Mr." and Rothstein appreciated the deference.

"I just heard he was dead from you fellas, Mr. O'Farrell," Rothstein said. "How would I know that?"

"He was shot in the head."

"Executed," Rothstein said.

"Yes."

"Not by me or mine," Rothstein said, and O'Farrell believed him. "I don't kill my own men, even a straggler like Kevin."

His reference to the dead man as "Kevin" showed that he had, indeed, known him, and O'Farrell did not think it was an accident.

"Who would kill him, then?" Bat asked.

"A rival?" Rothstein asked.

"Who would that be?' O'Farrell asked.

"Too many to mention, I'm afraid," Rothstein said. "I'll have to look into it myself. Or have Lenny do it. Can I help you with anything else?"

"Yes," O'Farrell said. "Do you know any of these men." He reeled off the names of the men he'd been playing poker with. Lenny leaned down and said something in Rothstein's ear.

"I recognize the names," Rothstein admitted.

"From where?"

"The newspaper," Rothstein sad. "Seems all of those men were wiped out during a poker game a night or two ago."

"I was in that game, too."

"And you lived?"

"Only because Kevin Alison got me out of the room before the shooting started."

"Ah," Rothstein said, "now I see. Kevin saved your life, and you don't know why. So you feel you owe him, even now that he's dead."

"Maybe more because he's dead," O'Farrell said.

"You're an honorable man, Mr, O'Farrell," Rothstein said. "I always knew that about you. And I value that."

O'Farrell didn't have anything to say to that.

"So," Rothstein said, sitting back, "you came looking for my help."

"Well, first," O'Farrell, said, "I wanted to satisfy myself that you did or didn't have him killed."

"And you've done that?"

"Yes."

"And what have you decided?"

"You didn't kill him."

"Why'd you decide that?"

"Well, you just told me you didn't," O'Farrell said.

"You're willing to take my word for that?"

"Sure."

"Why?"

"Because you're a man who values honor."

"But, you only have my word for that, too."

"I'm a good judge of people," O'Farrell said. "If you were lying to me I'd know it."

"You know," Rothstein said, completely disregarding the fact he'd claimed not to know Kid Alley well, "I always thought the Kid had a yellow streak in him, figured it kept him from being a winner."

"You couldn't tell by me that he had any coward in him," O'Farrell said.

"Who's that quote from?" Rothstein asked, looking at his men, who all shrugged. "You know, 'A coward dies many times. . . .'"

More shrugs.

"Well, he only died once," O'Farrell said, standing up. He didn't bother telling Rothstein he was trying to quote Shakespeare. "That was enough."

"Look," Rothstein said, as Bat stood, "I'll keep my ear to the ground. I come up with anything I'll let you know."

"We'd appreciate it," O'Farrell said.

"Hey, old man," Rothstein said to Bat. "You still got it, huh? Got my boys shakin' on their shoes."

"I'm not shakin'," Lenny said.

Bat smiled slowly.

"I'm just an old man who sits at a desk all day."

"Yeah," Rothstein said, his happy eyes getting even happier with his smile, "right."

6

On Broadway, outside the restaurant, Bat asked, "If not Rothstein, then who?"

"Who what?" O'Farrell asked. "Who killed all those poker players, or who killed Kevin Allison?"

"Allison," Bat said. "Seems to me that's the murder we have to solve. We do that, then we might be able to solve the other one."

"Since we haven't told the police about Allison yet," O'Farrell said, "we have a head start."

"We didn't tell the police, but we told Rothstein."

"He won't talk to the police," O'Farrell said.

"He talked to us."

"That's because you're the great Bat Masterson."

"Ah," Bat said, "you mean he respects his elders?"

"Did you think he was kiddin' in there?" O'Farrell asked. "You're still Bat Masterson. Sometimes I think you forget that."

"Maybe I forget who Bat Masterson is," Bat said, "but I always know who I am."

The distinction escaped O'Farrell, and he had too many other questions in his head to pursue this one.

"I don't believe a rival of Rothstein's would strike at him by hittin' one of his runners," O'Farrell said.

"Then Rothstein is not gonna be any help at all."

"And the Kid had no family that we know of," O'Farrell said. "What about friends? Other fighters? Ex-fighters? And could he have had a girl?"

"All possibilities," Bat said. "I can check the gyms again."

O'Farrell didn't answer right away. Something had occurred to him and he was trying it on.

"Val?"

"Huh? Oh, sure, check the gyms."

"And what just occurred to you?"

"I don't know," O'Farrell replied, "just somethin' that doesn't wash. I'm just gonna do some checking."

"Okay," Bat said.

"You want a ride?"

"I can walk from here," Bat said. "It'll do me some good."

It was late in the day, but still too early to find Dorothy at the club. He parked his Twin Six in front of her building on the Upper East Side. It was not where the swells lived, but it was a lifetime away from where Kevin Allison had died.

She answered the door swaddled in a white terrycloth robe.

"This is a nice surprise," she said, "but it would have been better earlier. I just got out of the shower."

He entered her apartment and closed the door. She smelled of bath soap.

"I'm here to talk, Dorothy."

"Oh? About what?"

Her robe was wet and was clinging to her. He tried to keep his mind on business.

"Kevin Allison."

"Who?"

"You know," he said, "the man you sent to the hotel to get me out?"

"I sent—no, I told you, he came to me and asked where you were. Said it was an emergency."

"Yeah, you told me that," O'Farrell said, "but why did he come to you?"

"Why did he—well, I don't know." She reached up to take her wet hair off her neck, held it above her head. The movement made the robe gape, showing her breasts and nipples.

"How long have we been seeing each other, Dorothy?" he asked. "Three months?"

"I suppose—"

"You're a lot younger than I am," he said. "I've often wondered why you approached me at the club."

"You're an attractive man, Val—"

"Maybe I am," he agreed, "but not to a lot of girls your age. What are you, twenty-eight? Nine?"

"Twenty-eight."

"Almost twenty years younger than me," he said. "I was flattered— have been flattered all along, but now . . ."

"Now what?"

"Now I'm suspicious," he said. "You knew where that poker game was because you coaxed me into telling you." While they were in bed, he recalled.

"What are you saying?"

"I'm saying you could have set that game up to be hit," he replied.

"And I . . . what? Arranged to meet you three months ago so I could set this up?"

"A hit like that would have to be set up in advance," O'Farrell said. "I want to know if I'm the boob who got all those men killed."

"If I set it up why would I have you pulled out?"

"Maybe you really do like me."

Suddenly she came real close to him. The robe was half off, now.

"Baby, I do like you," she said, "you know that." Her damp breasts pressed against him.

"I think I do know that, baby." He placed his hands on her hips and gently pushed her away from him. "It just doesn't make sense to me that Kevin Allison would come to you out of nowhere, looking for me."

"So it had to be a set-up?"

"Yes."

"And you think I set it up?"

"I think you helped," he said. "What I don't know is who you helped. That's what you're gonna tell me now."

O'Farrell parked the Twin Six around the corner from his destination and walked. As he reached the Majestic Apartment Building on the corner of Seventy-Second and Central Park West, he saw Bat Masterson stepping down from a street car across the way. He hurried across to his friend.

"What are you doin' here?" he asked.

"Maybe the same thing you are," Bat said. "I got a name from Joey Pounds."

"Joey Pounds?"

"Somebody we both forgot about," Bat said. "Kid Alley's only living family—his old manager. Found him at a gym in Times Square."

"What's the name?"

Bat told him.

"Pounds said that the Kid was afraid of this guy, and didn't like him. He likes him for killin' the kid. I was just gonna rattle his cage, some."

"I got the same name from Dorothy."

"Your Dorothy?"

"As it turns out, not my Dorothy," O'Farrell said, "but I'll explain that later. Why don't we do this together?"

"I wouldn't have it any other way."

"You heeled, old man?"

"I anticipated the need," Bat said, patting his side. The way Bat's jacket was hanging O'Farrell figured he'd simply slipped the pistol into his pocket.

"Let's go."

As they started to cross the street, a horse-drawn cart impeded their progress. While they waited for it to pass, standing in the center of the street, the front door of the Majestic opened and four men came out. One of them was the man they were looking for, and he spotted them and immediately surmised their goal.

"Kill them!" he shouted to his companions, and drew his own gun.

The New York street erupted in a hail of lead.

Bat's old Peacemaker was out first, proving that what Arnold Rothstein had said at Lindy's was the truth—he did still have it. His first shot put one man down on the ground for good.

O'Farrell's Colt was in his hand just after Bat's. He fired two shots, one of which clipped a man's shoulder, the second a window in front of the Majestic.

Men were scrambling for cover now, including O'Farrell, but he noticed that Bat stood his ground and continued to fire, despite the fact that lead was flying all around him. He caught another man through the neck as he was trying to duck behind a roadster.

The man O'Farrell had hit in the shoulder had staggered and gone down to one knee. As he brought himself up and prepared to fire, O'Farrell shot him again, this time in the chest.

Lenny Green had been firing his gun since he first shouted at his men to kill O'Farrell and Masterson. Now he was crawling along the ground, looking for cover, as O'Farrell and Bat moved from the middle of the street to the front of the Majestic.

Onlookers had gathered and were watching with interest.

Lenny Green was cowering on the ground, empty gun hanging from his hand by the trigger guard.

"We're gonna have to explain this," O'Farrell said.

"They started shootin' first," Bat pointed out.

O'Farrell looked around.

"We'll need a couple of witnesses."

"You want me to pick them out?"

"You tell them who you are they'll say anything you want."

"You're probably right." Bat looked down at Lenny Green.

"He's not goin' anywhere."

Bat ejected the spent shells from his gun, the casings making pinging noises as they hit the sidewalk. He loaded live rounds, holstered the weapon and went to find the witnesses. Old habits died very hard.

O'Farrell reached down and snatched the empty gun from Lenny Green's hand.

"Your boss know you set up the hit at the poker game."

"No."

"Want me to tell him?"

"Hell, no."

"Then you'll talk to the police when they get here," O'Farrell said. "That is, unless I kill you myself. Why'd you pick on me? Send Dorothy after me?"

Green smirked and O'Farrell almost pistol-whipped the expression off his face.

"I knew you were a regular in that game, but I never knew where the game was," Green said. "A couple of those boys needed killing."

"A couple?" O'Farrell asked. "So you killed them all?"

"If I only killed the two I wanted, Rothstein would've known it was me. Or suspected. I couldn't take that chance."

"What'd you have against those two?"

Green shrugged. "They were in my way."

Spoken like a man on the way up, O'Farrell thought, who not only wanted to step over people, but leave them dead in his wake.

"If it wasn't for that stupid broad sending that broken-down pug to get you out, I would have gotten away with it."

Knowing that Dorothy had sent Kid Alley to save his life was small consolation for being made a fool of. Did cuckhold apply? No matter, it felt like it.

Also realizing that it was Lenny Green who either killed or had Kid Alley killed, O'Farrell tried to not shoot him in the head while he waited for the police to arrive.

Author's note

Many of the characters in this story are actual historical figures. The obvious ones are, of course, Bat Masterson, Damon Runyon, James M. Cain, and Arnold Rothstein. However, Val O'Farrell is also a historical figure. Little is actually known about him save that he was a New York City policeman during the time Bat Masterson was in New York, and he left to become a private detective. What little information I do have on him came from the book Bat Masterson *by Robert DeArment.*

The presence of James M. Cain in this story is capricious on my part. When I started the story, Bat Masterson was not to be a factor, so it was set in 1923. In its present form it is set in 1921, only a couple of months before Bat died. Cain and Masterson would not have met but for my poetic license. Cain spent only a short time in New York between Baltimore and Hollywood, so I had a small window to work with..

Below are the last words Bat Masterson typed before he died sitting at his typewriter at his desk at the Morning Telegraph:

"There are those who argue that everything breaks even in this old dump of a world of ours. I suppose these ginks who argue that way hold that because the rich man gets ice in the summer and the poor man gets it in the winter things are breaking even for both. Maybe so, but I'll swear I can't see it that way."

The Majestic Apartment building did and still does exist. Meyer Lansky, Lucky Luciano, and Frank Costello all lived there at one time or another.

So Beautiful, So Dead

1

Val O'Farrell looked down at the dead girl with a gut-wrenching sadness. So beautiful, so dead.

"What a body, huh? Why would anyone want to cancel the ticket of a babe like that? And pluggin' her in the head, too. Jeez, how you gonna figure that?"

O'Farrell turned to look at Detective Sam McKeever.

"What?" McKeever asked. "She's a babe. Hey, she's lyin' there naked under a sheet, what am I supposed to do, not look?"

"No," O'Farrell said, "she's used to bein' looked at."

"Like most beautiful young dames, huh?"

"This one more than some," O'Farrell said. "She's supposed to be one of the contestants at that new beauty pageant out in Jersey."

"Yeah? No kiddin'?" McKeever said. "I heard they was gonna let them wear these new skin-tight bathing suit things."

"Tight and skimpy."

"You seen 'em?"

"Not yet."

During the beauty pageant in Washington, D.C., last year, the contestants had worn long stockings and tunic bathing suits. However, Atlantic City's first contest was going to be something really different and special because the censors had seen fit to lift their bans on bare knees and skin-tight suits. It remained to be seen if the idea would fly.

"Hey," McKeever said, "you better get out of here before the boss shows up. You ain't a cop no more, you know."

"Oh, I know."

O'Farrell had retired from the force two years ago, in 1919, and had opened his own detective agency. He'd been on the "inside" so often while on the job that he catered to a pretty high-class clientele these days. He'd gone from being the best-dressed cop in town to the best-dressed shamus.

"How'd you know to come up here, anyway?" McKeever asked.

"I was supposed to pick her up and take her out to Jersey."

"You knew her?"

"Yeah."

"Maybe you better tell me about it, Val," McKeever said, folding his arms, and O'Farrell did. He laid it out for the detective just as it had happened. . . .

2

Vincent Balducci had come into his office two days before with flash and confidence bordering on arrogance. Most of the flash came from the sparks he was wearing in a couple of rings.

"I've got a job for you, Mr. O'Farrell," he'd said, after introducing himself. He said his name like O'Farrell was supposed to know who he was. He did, but he didn't tip his hand.

"How did you get my name, Mr. Balducci?"

"You were referred to me by a mutual acquaintance," Balducci said. "His name is not important. He said you used to be a cop, an honest cop—or as honest as they get around here. He said you were thorough and you wouldn't gouge me on your fee just because I'm rich." Balducci looked around O'Farrell's well-furnished office. "I'm thinkin' the last part is probably right."

"All the parts are right, Mr. Balducci," O'Farrell said. "Why don't we get to the point of the visit?" O'Farrell motioned him to his visitor's chair.

"All right." Vincent Balducci sat down. He laid his coat over his lap. O'Farrell noticed it had a velvet collar. He laid a matching hat atop it. His hair was dark—too dark to be natural—and shiny, combed straight back. "Yes, why don't we. Do you know who I am?"

"I read the newspaper," O'Farrell said. The *New York Times* regularly carried stories on Vincent Balducci, a millionaire "philanthropist." What that generally meant to O'Farrell was that the man had a lot of money and didn't know what to do with it.

"That will save us some time, then," Balducci said.

That was when Balducci told O'Farrell about Georgie Taylor. He was married, he said, but it was a loveless, sexless marriage that was entered into for convenience. Naturally he needed a friend outside his marriage. When he met Georgie he knew she was the one.

"But she's younger, right?" O'Farrell asked.

"Well, yes," Balducci said, "quite a bit younger. I am sixty-five and she is, uh, twenty-five."

"You look good," O'Farrell said. "I had you pegged for fifty-five."

"Thank you," Balducci said, "I try to keep myself in shape."

And he did a fine job. Except for his obviously dyed hair and some lines on his face he did look younger than he was. He was tall, fit, and he moved like a younger man. O'Farrell sneaked a look at his own growing paunch. He was more than fifteen years younger than the millionaire, but they probably looked the same age. He decided not to think about that.

"Lots of married men have dames on the side, Mr. Balducci," he said. "Where do I come in?"

"Have you heard about this beauty pageant in Atlantic City this weekend?"

"I heard something about it," O'Farrell said. "Is that the one with the new bathing suits?"

"Yes," Balducci said. "One of the major sponsors is the Atlantic City Businessman's League, of which I am a member."

O'Farrell was starting to get the drift, but he let the man go on.

"I've entered Georgie in the pageant."

"You didn't guarantee she'd win, did you?" O'Farrell asked. "You're not going to tell me that the fix is in, are you?"

"No," Balducci said, "that part is not your concern."

So maybe the fix *was* in. But okay, the client is always right. That wasn't his concern.

"Fine."

"Georgie is very beautiful, and talented, and she has a big career ahead of her."

O'Farrell almost asked, "As what?" but bit his tongue.

"But I think she might be in danger."

"From who?"

"Well . . . an old boyfriend, other contestants . . . my wife . . ."

"Does your wife know about Georgie?"

"Not exactly. She knows that I have . . . friends on the side, but she doesn't know about Georgie specifically."

"All right," O'Farrell said, "go on."

"The contest kicks off with a gala event at the Atlantic City Yacht

Club on Friday. Among others, my wife will be there. I want you to escort Georgie."

"Be her date?"

"As it were, yes—and protect her."

"We've never met—"

"I will take you to her apartment on Beekman Place for an introduction," Balducci said. "After that it will be up to the two of you to plan your Friday evening."

"Mr. Balducci," O'Farrell said, "today is already Wednesday and I haven't got a thing to wear."

"On top of a thousand-dollar free," Balducci said, taking the comment completely serious, "I will buy you a new wardrobe and pay all other expenses for the night. I would send you to my tailor, but there's no time, so you can simply shop in the best men's stores available."

O'Farrell was a man who enjoyed good clothes. He knew where to shop. Even while still in the employ of the New York City Police Department he used to dress better than any other detective—regardless of rank—leading to speculation that he was on the take. It was only the fact that everyone knew how scrupulously honest he was that undercut the speculation.

"All right," O'Farrell said. "When and where do I meet the young lady?"

"Tonight, if you're free," Balducci said. He leaned forward and placed a slip of paper on the desk. "Come to that address and 8 p.m. I'll make the introductions."

O'Farrell picked up the paper, glanced at it, then put it in his shirt pocket.

"I'll need an advance."

"Of course," Balducci said. He took a wad of cash out of his pocket. No checks, no paper trail.

"Five hundred now? And a hundred for clothes?"

"Better make it two for clothes," O'Farrell said.

Balducci didn't hesitate. He peeled off seven hundred-dollar bills and placed them on O'Farrell's desk.

"Will that do?"

"That's fine." O'Farrell left the cash where it was.

"I'll see you tonight, then."

"I have some more questions."

Balducci stood up. He shot his cuffs and looked at his watch. "I'll answer the rest of your questions tonight. Right now I have another appointment."

O'Farrell walked his new client to the door.

"Eight o'clock, then," Balducci said, and left.

After Balducci was gone O'Farrell picked up the hundred-dollar bills and rubbed them together. He turned and looked out his second-floor window down to Fifth Avenue, where a chauffeur was holding the back door of a Rolls Royce open for Vincent Balducci. He probably should have asked for more money. A guy who rides in a Rolls and is dizzy for a young dame probably wouldn't have squawked about it.

3

O'Farrell presented himself at the Beekman Place address at 7:55. He paused out front to look up at the building. It was only five stories, but Beekman Place was not an inexpensive address. Each apartment was occupied by money—or, as in this case, paid for by someone with money.

He was wearing one of the new suits he'd bought that afternoon. It was September and the weather was still mild so he'd bought one brown linen and one blue pin-striped. He was wearing the linen. The pin-striped was for the night at the Yacht Club.

The young doorman announced him and he was allowed up to the third floor. When he rang the bell the door was opened by Balducci himself. O'Farrell had expected a butler or a maid.

"Come in," the man said. "Georgie is still getting dressed."

O'Farrell entered and closed the door behind him. He followed Balducci down a short hall until they entered a plushly furnished living room.

"I've made a pitcher of martinis," his host said. "Would you like one?"

"Sure."

"Olive or onion?"

"Olive, please."

Balducci poured out two martinis, put olives in both, and then handed one to O'Farrell.

"I was expecting a servant to answer the door," the detective said. "Maid's night off?"

"No servants," Balducci said. "It's bad enough the doorman knows me and sees me coming here."

O'Farrell understood.

"Ah," Balducci said, looking past him, "here's Georgie now."

O'Farrell turned. He didn't know what he'd expected, but Georgie took his breath away. She was tall and slender with a proud thrust of breasts. Her dark hair was piled high atop her head. Her powder-blue gown was high-necked but left her pale shoulders bare. Since 1919 hems had been rising, and currently it was not unheard of for them to be six inches from the floor—affording a nice view of ankle—but Georgie's gown was full length. It was her eyes that really got O'Farrell. They were violet, the most amazing color he'd ever seen, and they were great big eyes. When she blinked he thought he could feel it inside.

She was pretty enough to be a Zigfeld girl. O'Farrell wondered why Balducci didn't just use his pull to get her that job, rather than put her in some silly pageant?

"Georgie, this is Val O'Farrell, the private detective I hired to protect you."

"To hide me, you mean," she said tightly. She was smoking a cigarette, took a moment to remove a bit of tobacco from her tongue with her thumb and pinky while appraising O'Farrell. Flashes of light on her fingers attested to the fact Balducci didn't mind sharing his love of diamonds. "Well, he's big enough for me to hide behind."

"I just want him to protect you, darling," Balducci said.

O'Farrell suddenly realized how dressed up the two of them were and what it meant. Balducci's suit easily cost five times what his own new suit cost.

"Are you folks going out to dinner?" he asked.

"We all are," Balducci said. "I thought it would be a good opportunity for us to get acquainted."

"Don't let him fool you, Mr. Detective," Georgie said. "He just wants to use you as a beard. That way if anyone sees us together he can say I was your date. He's become an expert at hiding me."

"Georgie . . ."

"Oh, all right," she said, "I'll be a nice girl. Mr. O'Farrell, would you care to join us for dinner?"

"Well, I don't—"

"Please," she said. "Vincent will be paying the bill."

"Well," O'Farrell agreed, "when you put it that way . . ."

□ □ □

The only chink in Georgie Taylor's beautiful armor was her voice. It was high-pitched, almost a whine, and marred what was otherwise a perfect picture. O'Farrell knew nothing about how this beauty pageant was supposed to be run. He wondered if it called for the girls to actually speak?

Dinner was a tense affair at a nearby restaurant that O'Farrell suspected was below Balducci's usual dining standards. Even Georgie had lifted one side of her lips and sniffed when they entered. For his part, O'Farrell found his steak delicious.

For a dinner where they were supposed to be getting acquainted— actually, he and Georgie—Vincent Balducci did most of the talking. O'Farrell spent more time looking at Georgie than listening to his client.

Later, when they returned to the apartment house on Beekman Place, Balducci stopped in the lobby and said, "I'm not coming up."

"Why not?" Georgie asked.

"Because you two need to talk," Balducci said. "I want you to spend some time together and really talk, this time." He turned to face O'Farrell. "Georgie has all the details about the party at the Yacht Club Friday night. I won't see you again until then. I'll have my wife with me, so if we come face to face we will just be meeting. Do you understand?"

"Perfectly."

"My dear," Balducci said. He leaned over to kiss Georgie but she presented him with nothing but a cheek. "I'll see you soon."

"Yes," she said, quietly. Then she looked at O'Farrell. "Well, come on, then."

The building had an elevator, but Georgie preferred to walk, which O'Farrell had discovered on their way down. He, in fact, had a distrust of elevators and had walked up when he first arrived. This was something he had shared with his friend, the great Bat Masterson. Masterson, a legend of the Old West, lived in New York and not only had a column in *the Morning Telegraph* but was a vice president of the newspaper. In his mid-sixties, the old lawman still had more faith in a horse than an elevator, and almost never used a telephone if he didn't have to. O'Farrell liked to think of himself as someone who had been born too late. He should have been with Bat on the streets of Dodge City, with a gun on his hip.

Georgie opened her door with her key and marched right to the sideboard. She was dragging her mink stole behind her and let it drop to the floor. O'Farrell bent, picked it up, and deposited it on a chair.

"I need a drink," she said. "Join me?"

"Why not, but if you don't mind I'll have bourbon."

"A man after my own heart," she said. She poured bourbon over some ice cubes in two glasses and handed him one. She sipped herself, clunked the glass against her teeth and eyed him over the rim.

"After this we could go to the bedroom and fuck our brains out," she offered. "Or we could take the drinks with us and go in now."

"Somehow," O'Farrell said, "I don't think that's what your boyfriend had in mind when he said he wanted us to get better acquainted."

"You don't think so?" she asked, raising her eyebrows. "Why else do you think he sent us up here alone? Come on, I saw the way you were lookin' at me in the restaurant."

"We're supposed to talk about Friday night," he said, "about the beauty pageant."

"Beauty pageant," she said. She held her glass tightly and let her other arm swing loosely about. He didn't remember how many drinks she'd had at dinner, but she certainly seemed drunk now. "What a crock! What a stupid idea. Marching around in bathing suits while a bunch of lecherous old men decide who the winner will be."

"I wasn't aware that the contest would be judged by a panel of old men?"

"Oh, it's not, but you know what I mean." She finished her drink and poured herself another.

"You don't think you can win?"

She turned around quickly, sloshing some bourbon onto her wrist. She took a moment to lick it off, a move O'Farrell found particularly erotic, especially since she kept those violet eyes on him the whole time. He shifted his legs, his position in his chair, but it didn't help.

"Of course I can win," she said. "I've got the looks, don't you think?"

"Oh, definitely."

"I just don't have the voice," she said, candidly. "I'm no dummy, I just sound like one. I know that when the contestants start to speak—to answer questions—my voice is going to be a liability."

O'Farrell was impressed. The girl had no illusions about herself or, apparently, her situation.

"And Vincent doesn't love me," she said. She wiggled the fingers of one hand at him, the light playing off the sparks. "He owns me, like one of these diamonds. It sounds odd. He just wants to have me on his arm to show me off, but then he never takes me out. I can't explain it. All I know is he's not here tonight and I really want it. Whataya say?"

"Look, Georgie—"

She did something with the top of her dress and it fell to her waist. Her breasts were beautiful round orbs with tight pink nipples. She would not have made a good Zigfeld girl, after all. Too big. She stared at him with those big violet eyes and poured the rest of her bourbon over her bare chest.   One ice cube fell to the floor while another disappeared into her dress.

Why not? he thought, coming to his feet. When would he ever get a chance like this again? He had to find out where that second ice cube had gone.

4

They spent the next morning getting acquainted over breakfast because they really didn't do much talking during the night. When O'Farrell asked her about the doorman she told him not to worry. The doorman liked her and wouldn't say a word to Balducci about O'Farrell staying the entire night.

"So who would want to hurt you?" he asked her over steak and eggs at a diner around the corner. He was wearing his linen suit again, but had left the silk tie off this morning, preferring to stow it in his jacket pocket. Georgie was wearing an angora sweater with a pin in the shape of the letter "G" and a skirt with a fashionable six-inch hem. The sweater molded itself to her breasts. Her hair was pulled back in a ponytail. She wasn't wearing as much makeup as the night before and looked much younger. But those eyes . . . made up or not, they popped.

"That's another one of Vincent's fantasies," she said. "Nobody wants to hurt me. I don't need a bodyguard—although I certainly needed you last night, didn't I?" She ran her toe up his leg.

"Just answer the question and stop playing footsy, young lady."

"Ooh, Daddy," she purred, "scold me some more."

Somehow, after spending the night with her, her voice didn't seem quite as whiney or annoying. She certainly had more than enough other qualities to make up for it—although some of those qualities certainly would not be seen by the judges.

"Georgie," O'Farrell said, moving his leg, "be serious."

"I am serious," she said. "Nobody wants to hurt me. Vincent thinks everyone wants what he's got. Well, if no one knows he's got me, what's the problem?"

"Someone must know," O'Farrell said. "Somebody who works for him and knows when to make excuses for him."

"Sure, they know he's got *someone*," she said, "but not who."

"Look," O'Farrell said, "Balducci is paying me to protect you, and that's what I'm going to do."

"And more, I think," she said.

After breakfast O'Farrell walked Georgie back to her building and said he had to go home to change.

"Aren't you afraid someone's gonna attack me?"

"I think what Vincent wants is for me to escort you to the beauty pageant, and protect you," O'Farrell said, "starting with the party at the Yacht Club. So I'll pick you up here—what time is the party?"

"The festivities start at three," she said. "I'm supposed to be there at noon, though."

"Noon?"

"I'm part of the show, after all," she said.

"How many contestants are there?"

"There were supposed to be a lot, but we ended up with just twelve. Some folks—sponsors—are really upset about it."

"Twelve beautiful girls, huh?" O'Farrell said. "All right, then I guess I'll pick you up here at ten. I assume Balducci will supply transportation?"

"He'll have an automobile here to take us over to New Jersey. Probably a Rolls."

O'Farrell made a face. He still preferred horses, but it was a long way to Atlantic City.

"Okay," he said. "I'll see you then."

"What about tomorrow?" she asked. "Don't you want to see me tomorrow?"

"I don't think—"

She came closer to him.

"After everything we did to each other last night you can wait two days to see me?"

"Hey, Georgie," O'Farrell said, "you're the one who said that what we did last night was just sex."

"Well, yes," she said, touching his lapel, "but it was good sex, wasn't it?"

"It was great," he said, "fabulous. You're a wonderful gal, but you belong to my client."

"That didn't seem to bother you last night?"

"Last night I gave in to bourbon and a pair of gorgeous . . . eyes."

She smiled. "You think my . . . eyes are gorgeous?" she asked.

"You know they are." Behind Georgie, O'Farrell could see the doorman watching him. A different one today than last night, but another young man, this one eyeing Georgie appreciatively—not that O'Farrell could blame him.

"You sure this doorman is not on Balducci's payroll?"

"I'm this sure," she said. She slid her hands around his neck and gave him a kiss that could have melted the soles of his shoes. Her tongue fluttered in his mouth and she bit his bottom lip lightly before stepping back and smiling at him.

"Okay," she said, wiggling her fingers at him, "see you the day after tomorrow, lover."

5

But Friday, when he went to pick her up, there was no answer at the door. He went down to ask the doorman if he'd seen Georgie Taylor that morning. This was the same doorman who had watched her kiss him goodbye the other day.

"No, sir," the man said. "I haven't seen her today at all."

O'Farrell studied the man for a moment, then took a ten out of his wallet.

"What's your name?"

"Henry, sir." Henry was a young man in his late twenties. He was eyeing the ten in O'Farrell's hand hungrily.

"Tell me, Henry, has Miss Taylor had any visitors since I was here?"

"No, sir."

"Not Mr. Balducci?"

"Well, yes sir," Henry said. "He came by last night. I didn't know you meant him."

"Did he stay the night?"

"No, sir," Henry said, "He left after a few hours."

"Okay . . . anyone else?"

"No, sir," the doorman said. "She hasn't had anyone else upstairs since you left the other morning—except for Mr. Balducci."

"Did she go out at all since then?"

"Oh, yes sir," Henry said. "I saw her go out yesterday. She did some shopping and came home with a few bags. She stayed in after that—at least, as long as I was on duty."

"How many doormen are there, Henry?"

"Three, sir, but only one other—Leslie—" he said the name with a wry grin, "—has been on duty since you were here. He worked yesterday afternoon and evening as well as the evening you arrived."

"I'd like to find out what he knows, Henry," O'Farrell said.

"I could ask him when I see him."

"No," O'Farrell said, "I'd like to find out as soon as possible. Could you call him? There'd be ten in it for him, and a second ten for you."

The promise of twenty bucks sent Henry to the phone to call Leslie. He asked the second doorman the same questions O'Farrell had asked him, and hung up shaking his head.

"Leslie says he never saw anyone go up to Miss Taylor's apartment, and he never saw her leave."

O'Farrell went over it in his head. So she'd only been out once all day Thursday, didn't go out Wednesday after he left her, or any time Friday morning until now. Balducci was the only person seen going up.

"Is there a back door, Henry?"

"Yes, sir," the doorman said. "It's kept locked. Tenants don't use it, and don't have a key. It's access to an alley where we throw out the trash, sometimes take deliveries."

"So you have a key, in case of deliveries."

"Yes, sir."

"Any deliveries since I left here Wednesday morning?" O'Farrell asked.

"No, sir."

O'Farrell gave Henry the twenty dollars and then took out another twenty.

"Henry, have you got a key to Miss Taylor's apartment?"

"Yes, sir. Do you think something's happened to her?"

"Let's just say I have a bad feeling."

Henry waved away the second twenty and got the key.

□ □ □

"We found her like this," he told McKeever.

"Well, you've got each other to vouch for that," the detective said. "Is there anything you haven't told me?"

There was. He'd left out the part about having sex with his client's girl, and spending the night. He only hoped Henry had left that part out, too.

"No, that's it."

"That pretty much jibes with what the doorman told us. Well, you better scram, Val. The lieutenant's gonna show up soon and he ain't gonna like it if—"

"Too late," the police officer on the door said.

O'Farrell and McKeever both turned in to see Lieutenant Mike Turico enter the room.

"Well, well," Turico said when he saw O'Farrell. "Guess you musta forgot you ain't a cop no more, O'Farrell."

"Hello, Mike."

Turico approached O'Farrell and felt the texture of the wide lapel of the private detective's blue pin-striped suit.

"Turnin' private musta really paid off for you, Val," he said. He looked down at the matching fedora O'Farrell was holding.

"I'm doin' okay, Mike," O'Farrell said. "Thanks for askin'."

"Bet the swells really like you in this outfit." He touched O'Farrell's red silk tie, straightening it. Without looking at McKeever he asked, "Who let him in here?"

"He just walked in, boss," the detective said. "You know how Val is."

"Yeah," Turico said, "I do." He stepped back from O'Farrell, jerked his thumb at the door and said, "Blow."

"Nice to see you again, too, Mike," O'Farrell said. The two had not gotten along when they were both police detectives, and it was no different now. Turico had always resented how O'Farrell got the high profile cases, but O'Farrell had a reputation for getting results, and Turico didn't. Turico had risen to the rank of lieutenant since rank had more to do with who you knew than results.

Turico moved to inspect the body and McKeever followed O'Farrell to the door.

"Sam, sorry to bust in on you like this."

McKeever waved his apology off.

"Forget it. If the boss is gonna chew me out it's gonna be over this or somethin' else. But just between you and me, Val, you got a personal interest in this?"

"My client pays the bills for this place," O'Farrell said. "I met the girl. I liked her."

"Ah," McKeever said, "the sugar daddy. You got an idea where I can find him?"

"You can get his address from the manager of the building," O'Farrell said. "I don't have it on me. And he's got an office downtown somewhere. If the manager can't help you, let me know."

"McKeever," Lieutenant Turico yelled, "get your ass over here."

"Gotta go, Val. You gonna look into this?"

"I'm not sure, Sam."

"Well, let me know, huh?" McKeever said. "Turico might be here, but this is my case."

"I'll stay in touch." As he went out past the uniformed policeman he patted his arm and said, "See you, Ed."

Did he have a personal interest? Goddamn right, he did.

6

O'Farrell was still dressed for the Yacht Club party when he approached Bat Masterson at his desk at the *Morning Telegraph*. The old lawman turned newspaperman made a show of covering his eyes.

"I'm blind! I'm blind!" he cried, then dropped his hands. "Damned if you ain't the prettiest man I ever did see, O'Farrell."

"Cut it, Bat," O'Farrell said. "You're not the only one who can get all duded up."

"'All duded up'?" Bat asked. "I don't think I've heard anyone say that since Wyatt Earp back in ninety-nine."

O'Farrell rushed on, afraid that his friend would start telling one of his stories which would end with him taking a replica of his old gun out of his desk drawer. O'Farrell usually enjoyed Bat's stories, but he had no time for them today.

"Bat," O'Farrell said, sitting down across from his friend, "what's the skinny on the beauty pageant out in Atlantic City?"

Bat sat back and smiled broadly. Approaching his late sixties both his waist and his face had filled out, but when he smiled like that it took years off him.

"I know I'm one of the judges," he said.

"How'd you get that job?"

"Hell, they just up and asked me," the old gunman said. "Who am I to say no to judging a bevy of beauties?"

"Who asked you?"

"Some fella from the—what's it called—Atlantic City something—"

"—Businessman's League?"

"That's it. Said they needed artists to judge and I qualified 'cause I'm a writer. You believe that? I never been called an artist before."

"Or a writer."

"You want me to shoot you?"

"Sorry."

"What's your interest?"

"I'll tell you," O'Farrell said, "but you've got to keep it under your hat for a while."

"That's a hard thing to ask a newspaperman to do, Val, but okay. For you I'll do it."

O'Farrell fed him the whole story, and Bat listened in complete silence.

"What do you want me to do?" Bat asked.

"I want to find out what you know about Balducci, and about the pageant."

"Like what?"

"Like are they on the up-and-up, both of them?"

"As far as I know the pageant is," Bat said.

"Does that mean that Balducci isn't?"

"There's been talk that Balducci is in bed with a certain criminal element."

"Like what?"

"Well, some of the crime reporters have been wondering if he's in with this new Mafia," Bat said. "They wonder if he's not involved with the giggle juice trade and other illegal activities."

"You sound like you're being real careful with your language. Why would a rich man like him want to run liquor with the mob?"

"Well," Bat said, "this new breed of—what do they call 'em— gangsters is a lot different from the bad guys of my day. You can't tell by white hats and black hats anymore, Val. And who knows why rich men do what rich men do?"

"Okay, so Balducci might be in bed with the Mafia," O'Farrell said, "but the pageant is on the level?"

"As far as I can tell," Bat said. "I wouldn't have agreed to be a judge if I thought different."

"How are you getting out there?"

"They're sending a car for me."

"What time?"

"Around five, I think. Do you want to ride with me?" Bat asked.

"Yes, I would," O'Farrell said. "I think if I walk in with you I'll be able to get around easier."

"Fine," Bat said, "meet me here around quarter to five and we'll go look at some girls. What will you be doing until then?"

O'Farrell stood up. "Trying to find my client before the police do."

7

O'Farrell knew more about the Mafia and Johnny Torrio—which were natural offshoots of Paul Kelly and his Five Points Gang—than he wanted to let on to Bat Masterson. Friend or no friend, it wasn't wise to let a newspaperman know all that you knew. However, he'd met Vincent Balducci and didn't see him as a gangster. It was more likely he had some connections—crooked and lucrative—to Tammany Hall.

O'Farrell was unable to locate Balducci that morning and into the afternoon. He wondered if the police were having the same problem. At least he knew that the man was supposed to be at the Yacht Club in Jersey that evening.

He decided to make one more stop before meeting Bat Masterson to go to New Jersey. There were still things he needed to know, and his buddy Sam McKeever would have the answers.

O'Farrell had decided not to change his clothes after leaving Bat Masterson, so when he returned to the offices of the *Morning Telegraph* he was still dressed for the Yacht Club party.

He met Bat in front of the building as a boxy, yellow Pierce Arrow Roadster pulled up. He and Bat got in and the driver pulled away and headed for New Jersey.

"Find your man?' Bat asked.

"No."

"Think he's in hidin'?"

"I doubt it," O'Farrell said. "Men with his money—and his

connections—rarely go into hiding, even if they are suspected of murder."

"And is he?"

"He's on the list," the detective said, "since he was paying the bills for the girl."

"And what's your interest in this, Val, other than him bein' your client?"

"I met the girl and liked her, Bat," O'Farrell said. "She shouldn't have died like that."

"Like what?" Bat asked.

"She was shot, once, in the temple."

"Any chance of suicide?"

"The word I got from the cops was that she was shot from close range, but there was no gun at the scene."

"Well, that rules out suicide—unless someone removed the gun."

"Too complicated," O'Farrell said. "I've found, in my experience, that the simplest answer is usually the right one. Once you start factoring in 'what ifs' you just muddy the waters."

"What about the gangster angle?"

"That muddies the waters," O'Farrell said, as if it was a perfect example of what he had been talking about. "I'm looking for a clean, simple solution."

"You're gonna solve this thing?"

"Bat," O'Farrell said, "I think I already have."

When they pulled up in front of the Yacht Club there were many other vehicles already there, Pierce Arrows, Rolls Royces, even some sporty Stutz Roadsters.

O'Farrell and Bat were dropped in front of the club. A tent had been erected to accommodate all the guests for the party. Festivities seemed to have already begun. A man dressed as King Neptune arrived at the docks on a barge surrounded by twenty women in costume and twenty black men dressed as Nubian slaves. A second barge brought the beauty contestants in. There were eleven of them, O'Farrell knew, because Georgie Taylor would have been the twelfth.

The contestants were allowed to wear their new risqué bathing suits on the barge, showing lots of skin, but were then whisked away to don something more appropriate for the party.

"Well," Bat said, when the girls were gone, "it won't be easy judging the most beautiful out of that lot, tomorrow night. I'd better find the officials and ask them what they want me to do."

"I'll see you inside the tent, then," Val O'Farrell said.

"Better stick with me, Val," Bat said, "at least until I get you introduced to someone in the know."

That was wise, O'Farrell knew. On his own he might end up being kicked out before he could find Vincent Balducci.

8

The pageant officials pinned a button on Bat's lapel that identified him as a judge and agreed to give O'Farrell a guest button. So armed, both O'Farrell and Bat joined the party in the tent.

There was a stage with a big band on it, playing their hearts out while a male and female singer alternated songs. Guests filled a dance floor or milled about holding champagne glasses or martinis or wine, all of which were being circulated by uniformed waiters. Money had been paid, whether it was for a license or just a bribe, and the giggle juice was flowing freely.

The men were wearing expensive suits and in some cases tuxedoes. The women flaunted jewelry—rings, bracelets, even tiaras—and the fashions of the day, some with six-inch hems flying higher while they danced the Charleston, the Shimmy, the Fox Trot, or the Black Bottom. It seemed as if many of the women who were young enough to care thought they had to do something to compete with the bathing beauties, some of whom were on the dance floor. He could imagine Georgie out there, and it made him angry—angrier than he'd been since he first discovered her body.

A male singer started to sing "My Time Is Your Time," and couples moved in to dance closer together.

"See him?" Bat asked.

"Who?"

"Your client?"

"Not yet."

"I see somebody you know," Bat said, pointing to Detective Sam McKeever of the New York Police Department, who was fast approaching with another man in a suit and some uniformed New Jersey police in tow. Right on time.

"Val," McKeever said, "this is Detective Willoughby, of the Atlantic City Police."

"What did you find out?" O'Farrell asked McKeever, after tossing Willoughby a nod.

"She was killed sometime Thursday night. Both doormen have alibis," McKeever said. "They were both seen on duty by other tenants."

"They could have slipped away long enough to kill her," Bat offered.

"You're muddying the waters again, Bat," O'Farrell said. "There are three logical suspects for this crime."

"And you've cleared the doormen?" Bat asked, looking at McKeever.

"Yeah," McKeever said, then, "Hey, you're Bat Masterson."

"At your service," Bat said.

One of the uniformed policemen said to the others, "That's Bat Masterson."

O'Farrell saw Bat's chest inflate until another officer said, "Who's he?" and a third said, "Newspaperman, I think.'

"Did you manage to keep this from Lieutenant Turico?" O'Farrell asked.

"Yeah, but he ain't gonna like it."

"I wanted you to get the collar," O'Farrell said.

"Wait a minute," Bat said. "You said there were three logical suspects."

"Well," McKeever said, "four, but I'm clearin' Val, here."

"Okay," Bat said, "so if you've cleared Val, and the two doormen, that leaves—"

"There he is," O'Farrell said cutting Bat off. He started to push through the crowd, causing several people to spill their drinks.

"Follow 'im," McKeever said to the other cops, and Bat followed them.

O'Farrell was faster than they were and was not being careful about who he bumped. As he got closer Vincent Balducci turned and saw him coming towards him. The millionaire was impeccably turned out in a black tuxedo and was holding a champagne glass. He was chatting with some people—one of whom was a matronly lady covered in jewels that did nothing to hide the fact that she was *not* one of the contestants. He frowned when he saw O'Farrell coming towards him, then saw something in the detective's face he didn't like. He turned and started pushing through the crowd. O'Farrell increased his speed, leaving McKeever and Bat and the other police to struggle through the crowd behind him.

The band started playing an up tempo number and people started doing the Charleston, again. Balducci was trying run now, and as he burst out onto the dance floor a heavyset woman trying to keep up with the music slammed into him with her hip and sent him flying across the floor. He bumped into a man whose arms and legs were flailing about in an obscene caricature of the dance and they both fell to the floor. The man shouted, but Balducci—in excellent physical condition—jumped up and began running again. He got a few steps when a slender but energetic girl in a flapper's dress banged into him with a sharp-boned hip and knocked him off balance. He managed to stay on his feet and finally made his way across the dance floor to the exit next to the bandstand.

O'Farrell, following in his wake, managed to avoid all the traffic Balducci had encountered and was right behind him.

It was dark out and Balducci headed for the marina. O'Farrell wasn't even sure why the man was running, but he took his forty-five from his shoulder holster just the same.

The millionaire ran to the end of a dock, then turned to face O'Farrell.

"You can't shoot me!" he cried out, waving his hands. "I'm not armed."

"Why would I want to shoot you, Vincent?" O'Farrell asked. He holstered his gun. "In fact, why are you running from me?"

Balducci was sweating so much that some of the dye from his hair was running down his forehead.

"Wh-why were you chasing me?"

"Was I?" O'Farrell asked.

"You came at me . . . the look on your face . . . I thought . . ."

The man was too fit to be winded from running. He was out of breath for another reason.

Suddenly, there was a small automatic in his hand. O'Farrell cursed himself for holstering his gun.

"I—I didn't mean to," Balducci said. "She told me about the sex . . . and I just went crazy . . . it wasn't my fault."

"Is that the gun?" Georgie had been shot at close range with a small-caliber gun. "Where'd you get it?"

"It was hers," he said. "I gave it to her for protection. I—I never thought she'd try to use it against me."

"You must have frightened her."

"She . . . she was mine! She wasn't supposed to be with anyone else."

O'Farrell felt badly about that. Maybe if he hadn't slept with Georgie she'd still be alive now. Or maybe it would have happened later, with someone else.

"Come on, Vincent," O'Farrell said. "If you shot her by accident, then you're not going to shoot me deliberately."

"You know," Balducci said, "you know . . . I knew it when I saw your face. I—I can't let you tell anyone."

O'Farrell wondered where the damned police were. And where was Bat Masterson? He was wondering how close he'd get to his gun if he tried to draw it now.

"Vincent—"

"I'm sorry," Balducci said, "I had no idea it would come to this when I hired you. I'm so sorry . . ."

Balducci tensed in anticipation of firing his gun, but before he could there was a shot from behind O'Farrell. A bullet struck Balducci in his right shoulder. He cried out and dropped his gun into the water, then fell to his knees and clutched his arm. O'Farrell turned to see Bat Masterson standing at the end of the dock with an old Colt forty-five in his hand. He turned to check that Balducci was neutralized, then walked over to Bat.

"Thanks, Bat."

"I still got it," Bat said.

"Where'd you get that?"

"Hey, all the guns in my desk aren't harmless replicas, you know."

Behind Bat, Sam McKeever came running up with the other policeman.

"Damned Charleston," he said. "How'd you get across that dance floor without slamming into somebody?"

"I'm graceful."

"Did he do it?"

"He did it," O'Farrell said. "He confessed. I'll testify, but I don't think I'll have to."

The other detective, Willoughby, waved at his men and said, "Go get him."

"You'll need divers," O'Farrell told both detectives. "The gun fell in the water when Bat shot him."

"The same gun?" McKeever asked, surprised.

"Yeah," O'Farrell said, "for some reason he was carrying it around. He said he gave it to her for protection."

The uniformed police helped Balducci to his feet and started walking him off the dock. When they reached O'Farrell and the two detectives they stopped.

"I'm sorry I slept with her, Balducci," O'Farrell said. "It just happened, but she shouldn't have died for it."

Balducci's mouth flopped open and he said, "*You* slept with her, too?"

As they marched him away McKeever said, "One of the doormen. Apparently he went up there when Balducci wasn't around."

"So he didn't know about me and her," O'Farrell said.

"He does now," McKeever said.

"And so do we," Bat said.

"You dog," McKeever said.

"I wonder if his money will be able to buy him out of this?" Bat asked.

"Don't matter to me," McKeever said. "My job's just to bring 'im in."

Bat and McKeever started after the other policemen. Let them rib him, O'Farrell thought, bringing up the rear. It wasn't his fault she was dead. That's what counted. Now he could be sad for her, and not feel any guilt.

The Final Nail

1

When Val O'Farrell entered Muldoon's he immediately spotted his friend Sam McKeever sitting at the bar. It was early, and the basement Bowery speakeasy was pretty empty. Even the regulars didn't start drinking in earnest until after noon. Of course, at one corner of the bar was Eddie Doherty, who started drinking the minute his eyes opened and didn't stop until they closed.

O'Farrell approached the bar and shook his head at Lars, the Swedish bartender, indicating that he did not want a drink. When Lars picked up the coffee pot and raised his eyebrows, O'Farrell nodded. A steaming mug was on the bar by the time he seated himself next to McKeever.

His friend was staring morosely into a shot glass of what O'Farrell had no doubt was Irish whiskey.

"Kind of early for that, don't you think, Mac?" O'Farrell asked. "Especially when you have to go in to work."

Without looking at the private detective, the cop said, "No, it ain't early, and no, I don't have to go to work."

O'Farrell picked up his mug of coffee and asked, "You takin' a day off?"

"A career off," McKeever said, raising his glass. "I've been suspended."

"A disciplinary thing?" O'Farrell asked. "They'll make you stew, and then reinstate you."

"I don't think so," McKeever said. "I'm finished."

"Why, Sam?"

"They say I've been taking pay-offs."

"It's nineteen twenty-four," O'Farrell said. "We're in the midst of Prohibition. Who isn't taking pay-offs?"

"Well," McKeever said, "I guess I'm getting' roasted for it. That's the difference."

"Let 'em go to hell, then, Sam," O'Farrell said. "Come in with me."

For the first time the cop looked at the shamus.

"Me? A private dick? Don't make me laugh. I'm a cop. My father was a cop. He'd turn over in his grave."

"Then don't just sit here and take it," O'Farrell said.

"What am I supposed to do?"

"Fight them."

McKeever laughed and turned his attention back to his whiskey. "With what?"

O'Farrell grinned and said, "Me."

O'Farrell got McKeever off the stool and told him to go home to his wife. He'd been up all night and hadn't seen her since the previous day, when he went to work.

"I can't go home, Val."

"Isn't she going to be worried when you don't show up?"

"She's used to me not coming home," McKeever said. "What she's not used to is me coming home without my gun and badge, suspended pending a murder investigation."

"Murder investigation?"

McKeever nodded. "Yeah, didn't I mention that? It's the icing on the cake."

O'Farrell dug into his pocket for his key. "Go to my place, get some sleep."

As he installed the police detective behind the wheel of a roadster, the cop asked, "How'd you know where to find me?"

"Lars called when you started drinking Irish whiskey at 6 a.m."

"Snitch."

"He's a good friend," O'Farrell corrected, "and an even better bartender."

Luckily, he'd gotten to McKeever before he could have a third drink, so he was okay to drive. With McKeever on his way, O'Farrell went to his own car, a yellow Pierce Arrow Roadster, and drove to Police Headquarters.

2

Headquarters had been located on Mulberry Street until 1909, when it moved to 240 Centre Street. O'Farrell had spent his last ten years on the job working out of that building, so he knew his way around. He also knew a lot of the men who still worked there, some by name, others on sight.

It was surprisingly easy for him to get in to see Captain Mike Turico, even though he'd sent his name ahead. Turico was not only McKeever's commanding officer but O'Farrell's old boss as well. They never got along when they were colleagues, and since O'Farrell left the department and made a name for himself as a private detective, their relationship had not gotten better.

"Whataya want, Val?" Captain Turico demanded as O'Farrell walked in. "I'm busy."

"Putting the final nail in Sam McKeever's coffin?" O'Farrell asked.

Turico looked up from his desk and locked eyes with O'Farrell. They were both middle-aged, had joined the police force at the same time. O'Farrell knew that Turico resented him, not so much for leaving the force as for becoming so successful as a private ticket.

"Your buddy McKeever supplied all the nails himself, O'Farrell."

"Is that a fact?" O'Farrell asked. "You mind if I take a look at the file, then?"

"Why? Is he askin' for your help? That figures."

"What figures?"

"That he'd go outside the force to get help—and from you."

"I guess if he thought he could get help from inside the force—like from his boss—he'd be here instead of me."

"So he did hire you?"

"Let's just say I'm here on my own," O'Farrell said, "to satisfy my curiosity."

"You wonderin' if your boy could be guilty?" Turico asked.

"I'm wondering why, if he got caught with his hand in the till, you're persecuting him for it. It's not like he'd be the only boy in blue on the take." O'Farrell gave Turico a long, knowing look. "I know a few pads with your name on them, Mike."

Turico's face clouded. He pointed his pen at O'Farrell, but the look on his face said he wished it was a gun.

"That's old news, O'Farrell," he said. "The days of you and me linin' our pockets is gone. I'm clean."

"If you're clean then you should be able to recognize it when you see it, Mike," O'Farrell said. "Sam McKeever's the straightest arrow we know. As for murder, you should know better."

"That's what I thought, too," Turico said. "Maybe that's why he's such a disappointment."

"What are you talking about?"

"Here." Turico opened his top drawer, pulled out a file and dropped it on his desk. "Take a look for yourself."

O'Farrell reached for the file, but Turico slapped a ham hand down on it.

"You look at it right here," he said. "It don't leave this office."

"Fine by me, Mike."

It didn't take long for O'Farrell to read through the file and take some notes. He closed it and tossed it back on the captain's desk. He hadn't bothered to hear McKeever's side of it because he knew the man was innocent. He wanted to see the evidence against him, and it didn't look so cut and dried.

"This is bullshit."

"Which part?"

"All of it," O'Farrell said. "The money, the girl—"

"The dead girl, you mean? Just because he's a cop don't mean he won't be charged with murder."

"You don't believe that."

"The hell I don't," Turico said. "I'm the one took his gun and badge from him."

O'Farrell rubbed his jaw, thought a moment, then got it. "You don't think he did it."

"What makes you say that?"

O'Farrell tapped the file with his forefinger. "There's no way you'd let me look at this file unless you wanted me to work on this. You hate my guts, and you'd eat nails before you help me normally."

"That's true enough."

"So why did you let me look at it?"

"You wanna help your buddy, O'Farrell?"

"You know I do."

"Then why are you lookin' a gift horse in the mouth?" Turico said. "Get out of here, Val."

O'Farrell stared at Turico, then decided there was nothing worth arguing about. Turico obviously thought McKeever was innocent but had to act on the evidence and suspend him. The captain didn't particularly like McKeever any more than he liked O'Farrell, but McKeever was the best detective he had. Every time McKeever closed a case it made Turico look good. With McKeever off the job or in jail, who was going to take his place?

"I'm going to clear Sam," O'Farrell said. "You can count on it."

"Sure," Turico said, "you clear your squeaky clean friend, Val, and I'll give him his badge back."

O'Farrell stood up, headed for the door and said, "You better polish it up, then."

3

O'Farrell left the headquarters building, walked two blocks to Crosby Street and entered the speakeasy he knew many off-duty cops frequented. He'd asked at Headquarters for McKeever's partner and had been told he was out.

He didn't know the new partner, Ed Melky, didn't know what he looked like. McKeever went through partners faster than some men went through women.

He went to the bar, got a coffee, and walked over to a trio of cops he recognized. They were drinking illegal hooch.

"Hello, boys."

They looked up at him, and while two of them looked away the third man said, "Hey, Val. How's it goin'?"

"Pretty good for me, Dooley," he said, "not so good for McKeever, I hear."

"Yeah," Kevin Dooley said, "yeah, I heard about that."

Dooley was a detective O'Farrell had worked with a few times while he was still on the job. He knew the other men on sight but not their names.

"What do you know about it, Kevin?" O'Farrell asked.

Dooley frowned, then stood up and said, "Over here, Val."

They walked away from the other men and sat at a small table. O'Farrell took of his fedora and set it on the table. The hat had cost more than the suit the police detective was wearing. He knew Dooley didn't hold his success against him, though, like a lot of cops did.

"Why you interested, Val?"

"I'm going to clear Sam," O'Farrell said.

"I don't know how you're gonna do that," Dooley said. "The evidence is pretty damning."

"You know McKeever," O'Farrell said. "You know he's married and loves his wife, so he wouldn't be messing with a two-bit whore, and you know he doesn't take money. Never has, never will."

"I do know that," Dooley said. "McKeever's always been clean, but you know as well as I do that it's the clean ones that fall hard."

"Not Sam."

"I don't know what to tell you, Val," Dooley said. "I don't know that much about it."

"Where's his partner?" O'Farrell said. "This fella Ed Melky. Do you know him?"

"I know Ed," Dooley said, nodding. "He's only been partnered with McKeever for about a month, since he transferred from Brooklyn. Might be why he's not catchin' any fallout from this. He and McKeever really don't know each other that well."

"I read the file, Kevin," O'Farrell said. "It didn't have the name of the detective assigned. Who's working the case?"

Dooley hesitated, then said, "Ed Melky."

"Sam's own partner is making the case against him? Why would he do that?"

"Maybe because he's also the main witness."

"The file said some Madam named Sadie fingered McKeever for killing one of her girls."

"Melky ain't about to appear in the file as a witness."

"You know anything about this place where the girl was killed?"

"It's over on Varick Street," Dooley said. "It's a speak downstairs, a whorehouse upstairs. Owned by a guy named Jay Watson."

"And Watson pays off?"

"Oh yeah."

"So why was McKeever supposed to be there collecting?" O'Farrell asked. "He's no bag man."

"Supposedly," Dooley said, "he was just making some extra dough."

"And then he goes upstairs with one of the whores and kills her? This stinks."

"Don't I know it."

"Do you know anything else, Kevin?"

"You saw the file, that means you know more than me," Dooley said. He looked over at his buddies, who were eying him. "I gotta get back."

"Is anybody on McKeever's side in this, Kevin?" O'Farrell asked.

"You are, Val," the other man said. "You are."

4

O'Farrell drove to the Varick Street building, knocked on the door of the speak downstairs. An eye slot opened and two beady eyes regarded him.

"Yeah?"

"I'm here to see Jay Watson."

"What's your business?"

"Police."

"You ain't no cop."

"I used to be, but I'm here on police business, anyway."

"You mean that cop what killed Lulu?"

"Yeah."

"What's you name."

"Val O'Farrell."

"I know you. Hold on." The slot closed, a bolt was thrown and the door was opened. A small man appeared, kicking aside a stool he'd used in order to look out the slot. "I hearda you."

'What did you hear?" O'Farrell asked.

"That yer all right. You was friends with Bat Masterson, right?"

"That's right." Masterson had died at his typewriter recently, in his office at the *Morning Telegraph*. "Is Watson in?"

"He is."

"What's your name?"

"Canto."

"Take me to him, Canto."

"Okay. Follow me."

O'Farrell followed Canto across the floor, half a dozen sets of eyes tracking him. When they reached a door Canto knocked.

"Come in," a voice called.

Canto opened the door, said, "Somebody to see you, Jay."

"Who—"

O'Farrell moved past Canto and into the room, then turned and told the little man, "Shut it."

Canto closed the door.

Jay Watson stood up from a rickety looking desk, alarm on his heavily lined face. It was hard to guess his age.

"Who are you?" he demanded. "Whataya want?"

"My name's O'Farrell. I'm here because you claim Sam McKeever took a payoff from you and killed one of your girls."

"You a cop?"

"Private," O'Farrell said, "but I'm working this."

"I don't hafta talk to you—"

"Yeah, you do, Jay," O'Farrell said. "And so does Sadie. Get her down here."

"Sadie? She's workin' upstairs—"

"Send Canto to get her. I want to talk to both of you at the same time."

"Why should I do that?"

O'Farrell opened his jacket to show the man the gun in his shoulder rig.

"Canto!" Watson yelled.

Sadie was a worn out, faded forty, thinner than she used to be. O'Farrell could tell because she no longer filled out her dress. When she entered the room she looked at Watson with frightened eyes—one of them still yellowish from a recent shiner.

"Now I'm going to tell the two of you something," O'Farrell said. "Sam McKeever never took a payoff in his life, and he wouldn't mess with any whores—especially not the diseased lot you likely have upstairs."

"My girls are clean—" Sadie started to object.

"Shut up, sister," O'Farrell said. "Who gave you that shiner? And don't tell me McKeever."

Her hand instinctively went to her eye.

"Um—" she said.

"I give it to her," Watson said. "Gotta keep her in line. Also, she let one of my girls get killed."

"You?" O'Farrell said. "I don't think you can hit that hard, Jay."

"I . . . I had somebody do it."

"Who? Canto? Or maybe Ed Melky did it for you."

At the mentioned of Melky's name both of them stiffened up. It was pretty clear to O'Farrell what had happened. It was Melky taking payoffs from Watson, and using the girls upstairs. It had to be, for the simple reason that Sam McKeever was clean—cleaner than any cop O'Farrell ever knew, including himself. That was why nobody was on his side. By not taking payoffs he made the others look bad. O'Farrell didn't know why McKeever wanted to keep his badge.

"Sit down, both of you," O'Farrell said. "We're going to go over this until I get the truth."

"But—" Watson said.

"Sit!"

5

O'Farrell decided not to search the city for Ed Melky. Instead, he went back to Headquarters, because sooner or later the man would have to show up there.

Melky didn't have an office, just a desk that sat opposite Sam McKeever's. That meant O'Farrell was going to be able to brace him in front of his colleagues. He was sitting in McKeever's chair when Melky finally appeared. In fact, he'd just hung up the phone that sat on McKeever's desk.

O'Farrell could see why Jay Watson and Sadie were afraid of the man. He was a bull, well over six feet with bulging biceps and broad shoulders, but a thick waist. Even seasoned detectives moved out of his way as he crossed the floor to his desk.

He stopped short when he saw O'Farrell. He had a jaw like granite, covered with stubble, and a fat cigar right in the middle of his face.

"I'm not a replacement, if that's what you're thinking," O'Farrell said.

"I know who you are, O'Farrell," Melky said. "What are ya doin' here? This place is for cops. You ain't a cop no more."

"I'm here on behalf of Sam McKeever."

"Jesus," Melky said, seating himself behind his desk. "He hired you to clear him? That's rich."

"Well," O'Farrell said, "he couldn't count on his partner, could he?"

"Hey, I ain't gotta back no murderer." Melky pointed at O'Farrell with the soggy end of the cigar. "He shoulda thought of that before he beat that girl to death."

"He didn't beat her to death, Melky," O'Farrell said. "You did. And he wasn't making Jay Watson pay extra money to stay open, you were.

And he wasn't beating up on Watson's girls regularly, you were. And it all started happening just about last month, when you got here."

"That what he told you?"

"I didn't bother hearing what McKeever had to say, Ed," O'Farrell said.

"That how you run an investigation?"

"It is when I know a man is innocent."

"Figures you'd try to clear your buddy by puttin' the blame on me. What about the witness?"

"The witness? Oh, you mean Sadie? You sure put a scare into her, blackening her eye right after you killed that girl, Lulu. I had a talk with Sadie, Ed. Jay Watson, too. They're changing their stories. Sadie says you like to pay rough with her girls and you finally killed one. I also spoke to a couple of other girls you brutalized. They couldn't work for a while after you finished with them. I sort of assured them you wouldn't be coming by anymore. And no more payoffs from Jay Watson. You're through."

The other detectives in the room had stopped what they were doing and were watching and listening. Mike Turico had come out of his office.

"You're a liar," Melky said. "You got nothin'."

"I just got off the telephone with your old boss in Brooklyn," O'Farrell said. "Great invention, the telephone. I was able to sit right here and listen to him complain about you. Seems you got in some trouble in Brooklyn, too, only they couldn't prove anything, so they shipped you here so you'd be somebody else's problem. And once you got here you couldn't wait to start up again, so you found the house on Varick Street and started working it."

"McKeever killed that girl," Melky said, with a sneer. "And he was takin' money."

"That's where you made your mistake, Ed," O'Farrell said. "I would have believed that of any other detective in this room." He looked around. "No offense, boys." Then back at Melky. "But not McKeever. See, you might as well have tried to frame a priest. Mike would cut his hands off before he'd take a payoff, and he'd cut off his dick before he'd stick it in a whore."

O'Farrell stood up, and Melky quickly got to his feet. He had a gun in a holster on his belt, but O'Farrell had removed his jacket and the cop could see the gun in the shoulder rig.

"Want to shoot it out here, Ed?" O'Farrell asked. "This isn't the Old West."

"You're lyin' about the washed out bitch," Melky said. "She's too scared—" He stopped short, but not short enough.

"Too scared to finger you?" O'Farrell asked. "Too scared to testify against you? Not anymore, Ed. I guaranteed her safety, personally. Jay's, too. You're through."

Melky went for his gun. O'Farrell didn't move, but suddenly the room was filled with the sound of hammers being cocked. More than half a dozen guns were trained on Ed Melky, including Mike Turico's.

"Take his gun, Owens," Turico said to one of the other detectives. "You're done, Melky. Going for your gun, you might as well have confessed."

"This is bullshit," Melky said as Detective Owens took his gun. "Them two would never testify against me! They're too scared!"

"You're right, Ed," O'Farrell said. "I lied."

He had, indeed. No matter how much he interrogated Jay Watson and Sadie they were just too afraid of Ed Melky to say a word. The only way they'd say anything was if Melky was behind bars.

"I made it all up, but now that you went ahead and fingered yourself, I think they'll come forward and testify. You can't hurt them anymore."

Turico approached Melky and said to Owens, "Take him downstairs and put him in a cell."

"I'll need help," Owens said.

"Take as many men as you need."

Four detectives ended up escorting Ed Melky down to the cell block. Turico holstered his gun and looked at O'Farrell.

"You're pretty slick, bracing him here in front of all of us."

"By all accounts," O'Farrell said, "he has a pretty bad temper. I figured he'd finger himself."

"So everything he said about McKeever was true of him?"

"Yes, everything."

"Your buddy owes you big for this."

"You just have that badge nice and shiny for when Detective Sam McKeever comes walking back through that door, Mike. And you can forget about that final nail."

Midnight Pass

1

The only thing that Truxton Lewis and his son-in-law ever agreed on was that he should go to Florida. . . .

As Tru Lewis unpacked his suitcase, his daughter's words echoed in his ears as she had spoken them in the living room of his house in Queens, New York, just days before.

"You're sixty-two years old, Dad!

"Sixty-one."

"Sixty-one, sixty-two, what's the difference?"

He'd smiled at his thirty-five-year-old daughter and said, "When you're sixty-one you'll know the difference, sweetie."

"My point is," Margaret Lewis Statman went on, gritting her teeth, "that you're too old to go traipsing off into unknown territory—"

"You make it sound like I'm going gold-panning in the Yukon," Tru had said, cutting her off. "I'm going house-sitting in Florida."

"You don't *know* anybody in Florida—"

"Sarasota, to be exact."

"My point is—"

"Or to be truly exact," he'd gone on, "Siesta Key."

At that she had turned to his son-in-law the Jewish dentist and asked, "Murray, help me out here."

To his everlasting credit, Murray Statman said, "I think it's a good idea, Maggie."

"What?"

"Since your mother died," Murray went on, `I've thought your father should get out of this house, and now—a year later—he is."

"Thank you, *boychik*," Tru Lewis—who was not Jewish—had said.

For the first time since they'd met, they agreed on something. . . .

Truxton Lewis, ten years removed from his job as a detective with the New York City Police Department, and a widower for just over a year, was unpacking his suitcase in a two-bedroom condo in Siesta Key, on Midnight Pass, the Key's main drag. He had put some ads in newspapers all over the country—well, papers from places he wanted to go—that said MATURE MALE IN SIXTIES AVAILABLE FOR HOUSE-SITTING. NONSMOKER, NO PETS, WIDOWER. Actually, he'd gone back and added the word "early" in front of the "sixties" part. He'd been delighted to get a call from a realtor in Florida about a condo in Sarasota—on Siesta Key—that needed looking after for a couple of months, and he'd jumped at it.

He stopped in the middle of unpacking and walked to the sliding doors of the balcony off the living room. He unlocked them, slid one door open, and stepped outside. While there was a parking lot just below him, Midnight Pass went right by the condo, and he could see the water beyond it. The Gulf, he thought, although he wasn't all that sure. The sand was white and there was a lot of beach, only dotted with people rather than packed the way the New York beaches were. It was January, just after New Year's—off-season down here. He thought he could see a couple of women in bathing suits, but for the most part the people seemed to be wearing long pants and windbreakers.

He decided to put off his unpacking and walk down to the beach.

Tru Lewis did not own a pair of Bermuda shorts, white shoes, or a white belt. He was determined not to dress like an old man or a tourist. Oh, he knew he was old—sixty-one was old in any society—but he didn't feel old, so he refused to dress like some out-to-pasture golf duffer. He put on a pair of lightweight khaki pants, a light blue T-shirt, and a light brown windbreaker. The only concession he made to the fact that he was in Florida was a pair of black sandals—but not the kind where he had to have something between his toes. He hated that. Because it was breezy out, he put a Yankee cap on his head to cover his full complement of white hair, left the condo, and headed for the beach. He made sure he had the key to the front door before he locked it behind him. That reminded him that he still had his Brooklyn house key around his neck. He used to lock himself out of the house all the time when Virginia was alive, but he'd had to learn not to do that over the past year, because she was no longer there to let him in.

He started down the hall toward the elevator when the door of another condo opened and a woman stepped out.

"Oh!" she said, putting her hand to her chest. "You startled me."

"I'm sorry, I didn't mean to. I'm Truxton Lewis, your neighbor."

"My neighbor?"

"Yes, I'm in . . . fourteen?"

She appeared puzzled for a moment, then brightened and said, "Oh, you're the housesitter?"

"That's right."

"I'm Evelyn Smith," she said, extending her hand. "Mr. . . . . Lewis, did you say?"

He shook her hand and said, "Yes, Truxton Lewis."

"'Truxton,'' she repeated. "That's an unusual name."

"Yes,'' he said. "It is. My friends call me Tru."

"Did you just arrive today . . . Tru?" she asked.

"Yes. I haven't even finished unpacking. I thought I'd go for a walk on the beach."

"Well," Evelyn said, "I was just going to run some errands, so I'll ride down in the elevator with you."

"I'm glad to have the company."

As they rode down, Tru was totally unaware that his attractive fiftyish neighbor was "checking him out." He'd have been pleased. though, to know that she was guessing his age at fifty-five or -six, a good half-dozen years younger than he actually was. Widowed for only a year after over forty years of marriage, he was still very much unaware that women of varying ages found him attractive.

As they left the building, Evelyn asked, "Will Mrs. Lewis be joining you down here?"

"No," he said, "I'm a widower."

Having gleaned the information she wanted on the first try, she said, "Well, enjoy your walk on the beach, Tru. I'll see you later."

"It was very nice meeting you."

He headed for the beach without a backward look, and Evelyn, noticing this, started to worry that she needed to get her hair done again.

He was surprised at how much space there was on the beach. He'd thought that an illusion from his fourth-floor balcony, but it was the same up close. It wasn't that there were no people around, it was just that there was so much sand.

Most of the people were scattered about, seated on lounges or folding chairs. Others—more intrepid, since it was January—were down by the, water. He was surprised and pleased to notice that there were not a large number of small children. He found that, at his age, he had little tolerance for small children--even his own grandchildren, if he was around them long enough. Oh, he loved his grandchildren, but in small doses.

He noticed there were quite a few men and women of his age on the beach. Most of them were couples, but he noticed one man who had made himself comfortable on a lounge chair, tugged his cap down over his eyes, and gone to sleep. He thought that when he found a chair available later in the week he might try that himself.

He checked out the snack bar, getting himself a Diet Coke—he thought he detected the hint of a New York accent in the speech patterns of the guy working there—and then the gift shop, picking up some postcards to send home to friends and family. After about an hour he left the beach and went back to the condo to finish unpacking.

2

Several hours later Truxton was unpacked and had made himself a cup of tea. He carried the cup around with him as he familiarized himself with the apartment. It was much too big for one person to live in, with a large kitchen and living room, a smaller dining room, and the two bedrooms. There was also a small room off the front door that could have been a family room or a small office. At the moment, there was a wicker chair and desk set in there.

He found the master bedroom and decided to do what snooping he could without opening any drawers or doors. He ended up simply studying some framed photographs on the dresser top. They were only shots of the same two people, a man and a woman, apparently middle-aged. There were pictures of each of them alone, and then some of them together. He decided that while they made a handsome couple, they each looked decidedly happier in the photos where they were pictured alone.

He finished the tea and carried the empty cup into the kitchen. He rinsed it out immediately rather than set it down in the sink. That done, he went back into the living room and looked out the window at the beach. The sun was going down and the beach was empty, except here and there where someone was walking. In the area where he had been that afternoon he noticed that someone was still in a lounge chair. He thought it might be the man he'd seen, with his cap pulled down over his eyes. Could he have remained asleep this long?

While familiarizing himself with the condo, he had seen a pair of binoculars. Where had they been? Oh, yes, on a shelf—there they were. Good ones, too. High-powered. He took them to the sliding doors with him, stepped out onto the balcony, and trained them on the beach. Sure enough, he recognized the cap and jacket the sleeping man had been wearing. It was windy now; and a flap of the man's jacket was blowing in the breeze. Wouldn't that be enough to wake him up?

Briefly, he considered calling nine-one-one, but what if he was wrong? He'd be taken for an old retired cop with an overactive imagination. Certainly a wrong impression to make on his first day.

He shook his head and went back inside. Better just to forget about it and not go looking for trouble where it didn't exist.

He tried to watch the TV, surfing the seventy or so cable channels that serviced the area, but half an hour later he was back at the balcony door, and the man was still on the lounge chair. Blowing air out of his mouth, he donned his jacket and left the condo to walk across to the beach and have a look himself.

When he reached the beach there was no one on it but the man on the lounge chair. No one within a hundred yards in either direction. The snack bar and gift shop were closed, and it was getting dark and cooler. If nothing else, maybe he'd just wake the man and keep him from getting cold and damp, maybe sick.

He approached the still figure and spoke.

"Hello?"

Nothing.

"Excuse me?"

No reply.

"Damn it," he said, aloud, "you better be a sound sleeper."

But he knew better, even as he approached. He'd seen enough dead bodies in his twenty-seven years with the department to have a sense about them. He stopped at the chair, reached out, and removed the cap from the man's head. His eyes were closed, but he still could have been asleep.

"Yeah, yeah," Tru Lewis said aloud. He reached out and pressed two fingers to the man's neck, but he could not locate a pulse. It was then that he saw the blood, inside the jacket, on the man's chest. Not only was he dead, but somehow, in the middle of a populated beach, he'd managed to get himself shot to death with no one the wiser.

3

Tru had to deal first with the sheriff's department before he could get to the city detectives. He told his story to a deputy, then to the sheriff, then to a sheriff's detective, then to the city cops, then finally to a couple of Sarasota detectives. He told them all the same thing. He was a retired New York City cop vacationing here, and he had stumbled upon a dead body on the beach.

It was pitch dark out, with very little light from a sliver of a moon. Most of the light came from the police cars that had trained their headlights on the body. They were still waiting for a coroner's wagon to come for the body, which remained on the lounger as if the man were simply asleep. Tru was sitting in the back of the Sarasota detectives' unmarked car. The back door opened and one of them got in with him, holding two containers of coffee.

"We sent somebody for these," he said to Tru. "One with milk, one without. I can take it either way, so you get your choice."

"Black," Tru said, and accepted the container. "Thank you."

"Sugar?"

"I don't use it."

"Yeah," the man said, "I shouldn't either," but he proceeded to put three packets into the cup before stirring it with a red plastic stirrer. This was Detective Bradley, middle-aged, with an open, pleasant face. His partner, about ten years younger, was Detective Simms, dark, glowering, not friendly looking at all. Who played good cop and who bad cop was never an issue, Tru'd bet.

"Mr. Lewis," Bradley said, "we appreciate you sticking this out with us."

"My fault we're all here," Tru said. "After all, I found him."

"Excuse me, but it's the killer's fault we're here," Bradley said, "not yours."

"Good way to look at it, Detective."

Bradley studied Tru for a few moments in the light from the dome lamp and then said, "You were a boss, weren't you?"

Tru hesitated, then said, "I retired a captain of detectives."

"I knew it," Bradley said. "The way you talk to us, and hold yourself—"

"I mean no offense, Detective—" Tru said hurriedly.

"No, no," Bradley said, "none taken. I'm just pleased with myself that I picked it up, is all."

"I see."

"Would you mind, Captain, telling me again how you figured out this man was dead?"

"I saw the blood—"

"I mean," Bradley said, cutting him off, "from your balcony."

Tru tried to be patient. After all, he'd been through this himself, asking the same questions over and over again during an investigation. However, he was finally getting to experience how it felt from the other end. He explained again about arriving that day, interrupting his unpacking to walk on the beach, when he first noticed the man. Then explained about going back to the condo and spotting the man again from his balcony. "It made me curious, is all," he said. "How somebody could just sit that way for so long."

"Did it occur to you he might just be asleep?'

"It did," he said. "His jacket was flapping in the wind, though. I thought that should have awakened him."

"And how did you notice that?"

"With binoculars."

"Oh, right. Go ahead, please."

"After I used the binoculars and determined it was the same man, I decided to walk down here and check it out."

"Why not just call nine-one-one?"

"That would have been embarrassing if I was wrong," Tru said. "I didn't want to be the old geezer who jumped to conclusions."

"Not so old," Bradley said. "When did you retire?"

"Ten years ago."

Bradley looked surprised.

"After how many years?"

"Twenty-seven."

"If you don't mind me asking," Bradley said, "how old are you? I mean, you don't look old enough to have been in that long, and retired that long."

"I'm sixty-one."

"God bless you," Bradley said, "I hope I look that good when I'm sixty-one."

Tru was aware he looked younger than he was, but allowed himself to enjoy the comment—heartfelt or not. He still didn't have a handle on Detective Bradley, so didn't know if the man was buttering him up or not.

"Again, if you don't mind me asking," Bradley said, "you retired pretty young . . ."

"Twenty-seven years seemed to be enough," he said, "and I wanted to spend some time with my wife, maybe travel a little."

"Did you travel?"

"As it happens, no," Tru said "My wife's health began to fail. She wasn't up to traveling."

"And is she with you?"

"She died a little over a year ago, after a long and debilitating illness."

"Oh, I'm sorry . . ."

"We never did get to travel," he repeated, "so I thought I'd do it myself."

"Which condos did you say you were in?"

"The place is called Key Waves."

"Expensive for a retired cop."

"I don't own it, Detective," Tru said, "I'm house-sitting."

"For free?"

"Actually," Tru said, "I'm paying something, but much less than it would normally rent out for."

"That's some deal," Bradley said. "How do you get a deal like that?"

"You advertise."

The front passenger door was opened abruptly and Bradley's partner stuck his head in. "Coroner's here."

"About time," Bradley said. He looked at Tru. "You might actually get to go home tonight, Captain."

"Captain?' Detective Simms repeated.

Bradley opened the door on his side. "I'll explain later," he said, getting out.

4

They finally let Tru Lewis go home, with the understanding that they would come to the condo the next day to take a statement from him. "I can come to your precinct—or whatever you call it down here—to do that," Tru had said.

"No, no," Bradley had said, "we'll come to you. Just call it professional courtesy."

"Well," Tru had said, "I appreciate that."

"Besides," Simms chimed in, "we want to get a look at this balcony of yours."

So much for professional courtesy. . . .

They arrived the next morning after breakfast. Tru had a fresh pot of coffee going and offered them both some. They accepted, and all three carried cups out onto the balcony.

"Where are those binoculars you told us about?" Bradley asked.

"I'll get them." Tru stepped back inside long enough to grab them, brought them out, and handed them to Bradley.

'Whoa!" he said, when he held them to his eyes. "Is this how they were set when you used them?"

"Yes."

Bradley handed them to his partner.

"You can see every grain of sand," he said.

Simms nodded and held them to his eyes.

"You could only have seen the man's back, though," he said.

"And the part of his jacket that was flapping in the wind."

Simms turned and looked at him. "And that was enough to tell you he was dead?"

"That was enough," Tru said, "to make me curious about why he was still out there."

"Let's go back inside," Bradley said.

They did, and Tru closed the door behind them.

"Don't do that," he said. He'd caught Simms starting to put his cup dawn on the expensive-looking coffee table in front of the sofa. "I don't live here, I'm just house-sitting."

"I'm finished with it," Simms said.

"Would you like some more?"

"No, thanks."

"Give it to me, I'll take it into the kitchen."

Simms handed Tru the cup.

"And you?"

"I don't drink mine as fast as my partner drinks his," Bradley said. "Thanks."

Tru took the empty cup and put it in the sink. He poured himself some more and went back to the living room. Bradley was sitting on the sofa. He noticed the detective was using a magazine as a coaster. Simms was sitting in one of the easy chairs. Tru sat in the other one. "Captain, I told my partner your background," Bradley said. "I'm afraid he's not impressed."

"I don't like ex-cops who go private," Simms said, frankly.

"Were you under the impression that I was a private eye or something?' Tru asked. "I'm here on vacation."

"And you found a body," Simms said.

"By accident."

"From up here."

"What are you implying, Detective Simms?" Tru asked. "That I arrived yesterday and decided to go down to the beach and kill a man?"

"Of course he's not implying that," Bradley said. "He's just being a jerk. Isn't that right, Hal?"

"Yeah," Simms said. "I'm bein' a jerk."

"Why don't you go down to the beach and talk to some people? The snack bar and gift shop should be open by now."

"I guess I'll do that," Simms said, and left without another word to Tru.

"He's like that," Bradley said when he'd gone.

Tru wasn't sure if they were trying to play good cop/bad cop with him or not. "Tell me what you want, Detective Bradley," he said, "without any games. Just come out and ask me."

"I just want to know that you're telling us all there is to tell, Captain," Bradley said. "That's all."

"Everything I've told you is the truth."

"But have you told me everything?"

"Yes."

"I wrote down most of what you told me last night," Bradley said. "Enough to have it typed up." He took the typed statement from his pocket and handed it to Tru. "If it looks okay to you, you can sign it. If not, let me know."

Tru scanned the document and found it accurate. "You either listen well or take good notes," he said, signing it and handing it back. "A little of both, I think."

He put the statement away and then sat looking at Tru. "Were you a good detective, Captain?"

Tru smiled. "I'll bet you checked already."

Bradley smiled sheepishly, caught.

"You're right. I called New York and spoke to your chief of detectives. He said he'd take you back on the job right now if you'd go."

"That's nice of him."

"Said you were the best detective he ever saw."

"That's generous of him."

"Let me ask you this, Captain," Bradley said. "How does someone walk up to a man sitting on a lounge chair on a crowdedbeach, shoot him, and then get away without anyone hearing or seeing anything?"

"He doesn't," Tru said. "Can't be done."

"What about a gun with a silencer?"

"He'd have to swim to shore from somewhere—a a boat. Maybe he'd have to wear a wetsuit to swim that far. He'd have to keep the gun dry. After all that, he'd have to be able to shoot the man with no one noticing. Same thing with somebody just walking along the beach. They'd still have to stop by him and shoot him. I don't think it can be done. It's off-season and the beach is not that crowded. But somebody would have to have seen something."

"Well," Bradley said, standing up, "that's what my partner and I are going to try and find out today. Thanks for your time, Captain."

Tru walked Bradley to the door.

"Did you identify the man?" he asked at the door.

"Yes," Bradley said. "His name's Philip Williams. He's retired, living in a condo across the bridge."

"What business was he in?"

"He was a stockbroker, from New York."

Maybe that explained why the two detectives seemed so suspicious of him. He and the dead man were from the same city.

"The name ring a bell?"

"No," Tru said, "never heard of him. Did he have a wife?"

"A wife. And a mistress," Bradley said. "We're looking at both of them. One or both may have a boyfriend."

"I wish you luck."

"We've got to find out who did it in order to find out how," Bradley said. "That's what's driving me nuts. How?"

Tru let the detective out, then retrieved the detective's cup from the living room and put it in the sink. Again, he freshened his own cup, then took it out to the balcony with the binoculars.

He watched the two detectives for a while as they questioned people on the beach. No doubt they'd find some folks who had been there the day before and who'd be there again tomorrow. Regulars who might have noticed something out of the ordinary.

He went back out onto the balcony several times over the next few hours. The detectives were gone when the sun started to set, and as the huge orange ball was slowly swallowed by the water he watched the snack-bar guy close up. Apparently, the gift shop had closed already. Except for the cars belonging to some couples who wanted to watch the sunset, the snack-bar guy's car was the last one in the lot. Slowly, the couples drifted away as the sun disappeared, and then finally the guy came out of the snack bar, locked it, and walked to his car. After that, the beach was empty. Anyone could have come and gone as he pleased. . . .

Anyone.

5

Under normal circumstances, Truxton Lewis was an early riser. On this morning, however, he was up before the sun, sitting on the balcony with a jacket on, and the binoculars in his hands. As it started to get light, a car pulled into the parking lot of the public beach where he'd found the body yesterday. He trained the binoculars on the car and watched as the man who worked in the snack bar—and who probably owned it—got out. First to arrive in the morning, last to leave at night. . . .

He went inside and made a phone call.

Later that day the doorbell rang. When he opened it, Detective Bradley was standing there.

"Where's your partner?"

"He didn't want to have to come here and tell you that you were right," Bradley said. "Can I come in?"

"Sure."

Tru closed the door and followed the detective into the living room.

"Maybe we should talk about this on the balcony," Bradley said. "Probably fitting."

They stepped out onto the balcony together. Tru didn't have the binoculars, but he could tell from where they were that the snack bar had closed, early. He only needed glasses for reading.

"You were right, Captain," Bradley said. "The owner of the snack bar is one Andrew Cranston. He's owned and operated it alone down here for about sixteen years. Everybody on that beach knows him as Andy."

Tru waited for the rest.

"Old Andy lived and worked in New York twenty years ago," Bradley went on. "You spotted what little was left of his New York accent. You've got a good ear."

"Thanks."

When we approached him," Bradley said, "he denied it, at first, but the more we pushed the weaker his denial became, until he finally spilled it."

"What's his story?"

"He and the dead man were partners on Wall Street years ago. They got into some trouble with the SEC—insider trading, I think. The dead man—Philip Williams—saved himself by rolling over on his partner. Cranston served two years in a country club, came out and spent two more years as an alcoholic. After he dried out, he came down here and he's been here ever since. The other day, who should walk up to his snack bar than his old partner? Retired and moved down here. Some coincidence, huh?"

"Lots of people retire and move down here," Tru said. "Lots of people come here from New York."

"Yeah, maybe," Bradley said, "but I still say it's a big coincidence."

"So how did he arrange to kill him?"

"Williams recognized him, greeted him like an old friend. And you know what? Cranston knew what he was going to do right away. He claims he had never had a thought of revenge in twenty years, but as soon as Philip Williams came up to his counter he knew he was going to kill him. He went along with the old-friend act, eventually lured him down here early one morning and did what you said."

"He shot him," Tru said, "dragged him out to a lounger before anyone came to the beach, and left him there, looking like he was asleep."

"Right. Nobody noticed him all day. You called it, Captain. How did you do that? From up here with binoculars?"

"I didn't call it," Tru said. "I just happened to notice that he was the first to arrive and the last to leave, and I caught a hint of a New York accent. Also, I remembered that while the victim had been shot in the chest, there was no hole in his jacket. That meant that someone had shot him while the jacket was open, and then zipped it to hide the wound from people on the beach. That was enough for me to call you and just suggest that you check his background."

"And we did," Bradley said. "But I don't know that we could have got Cranston if he didn't confess."

"Well, you said he had no thought of revenge for twenty years," Tru said. "Maybe it was more than he could take."

"You might think that, except for one thing," Bradley said.

"What's that?" Tru asked.

"He left him out in the open, right on the beach where he owned the snack bar. You'd think he would have dumped him someplace out of the way, given his connection with the dead man."

"I was wondering about that, myself," Tru said. "What possessed him to just lay him out there on the beach?"

"I asked him that," Bradley said. "You know what he said?"

"What?"

"He wanted to watch him out there all day, baking in the sun," the detective said. "He said he just wanted to enjoy it as long as he could, before we found him."

"And you did."

"No," Bradley said, "you did, Captain. Another day in the sun and the body would have started to smell and bloat. We'd have had a panic on the beach on our hands."

Bradley put out his hand and Tru shook it.

"You've been here two days." Bradley said, before he left. "Hate to see what's going to happen when you're here two weeks."

Black & White Memories

1

Guilt had long since bled the color from Truxton Lewis's memory of Elizabeth Bennett. Whenever the first strains of Dusty Springfield's "You Don't Have To Say You Love Me" started playing it all came back to him, but always in black and white. He wondered for years why that was. Then it came to him. It was the guilt.

Despite the guilty sinking feeling when he remembered the one time in his forty years of marriage he had been unfaithful, he would not have given up the memories for any reason—no matter what color they came in. The song was playing on the radio as Tru Lewis pulled up in front of the house owned by Jack Langston. Since retiring from the police department more than ten years ago—and since the death of his wife several years earlier—Tru had been house-sitting across the country in an attempt to relieve the boredom of being retired and a widower. One was bad enough, but both were too much to handle. The house was on Seven Mile Beach in Port May, New Jersey, a beautiful, Victorian town a county over from Atlantic City. It was October, which meant the tourist season was over. When Tru discovered that there was a house available in Port May he hurriedly made the call that got him the job of house-sitting the place for a month. He stopped the car in front of the house, one of the largest on the beach. Apparently, Jack Langston had made a ton of money dealing in commodities, and this was his family's summer home. Tru would "sit" in it for the month and then someone else would take over. A month was Tru's personal limit.

He retrieved his suitcase from the trunk and a bag of supplies from the back seat of his car, an '89 Ford Galaxy he'd borrowed from a friend, and let himself into the house with the key the real estate office had supplied him with. There were several keys, and he'd been well schooled in their use. He had not been in the house before, but had seen a diagram and knew where the guest room—his room—was. He'd learned early on in his house-sitting career that owners did not appreciate a stranger invading their master bedroom and usually insisted on an alternative.

He left the bag of supplies in the kitchen, then went directly to the guest room and dropped his suitcase on the bed, which was full-sized and comfortable looking.

Next he took a walk through the house, checking each of the rooms to make sure it was secure and had not been violated since the owner's departure. Finding everything in order he tried to decide whether to go back to the bedroom to unpack, or to the kitchen to put away the supplies. He opted for the kitchen.

His "supplies" consisted of six bottles of his favorite beer—Michael Shea's—and a box of one hundred Tetley tea bags. It took him a moment, but because the beer was warm he decided to put it in the refrigerator and make himself a cup of tea.

Armed with the steaming cup he went to the sliding doors at the back of the house, off the living room, and went out onto the full deck. There was a breeze coming off the water. He stood there and enjoyed it, sipping the tea, thinking about the last time he'd been in Port May.

2

Port May, New Jersey
September 1966

Tru Lewis was twenty-nine years old, had been a member of the New York City Police Force for seven years. From the beginning he seemed to be on the fast track to the top. He'd made detective after four and a half years, much of that spent working undercover. However, it was that time that was the cause of his recent problems. Suddenly, two and a half years after his last undercover assignment had ended, he was under investigation by the Internal Affairs Division, which suspected him of skimming part of three million dollars in drug money that had been confiscated by Tru and his partners. What made it worse was that his "partners" were apparently testifying against him.

"You have to get away, Tru," his wife told him. "I know that. I can understand that. But why can't we get away together?"

He couldn't tell her why. He couldn't bring himself to tell her he was sick to death of the smell of baby powder and puke. It seemed to him that babies smelled of either one or the other, and recently those smells had attached themselves to her, as well.

"I'm not good to be around, sweetie," he told her. "Let me do this. The verdict comes down Monday. I just want to spend the weekend alone. I'll be back Monday, I promise."

She'd held tight to the front of his shirt and asked, "You're not going to do anything foolish, are you?"

"Like swallow my gun? That's not my style, hon. I'll be back. I swear."

She'd kissed him fiercely and he'd left and driven to Port May, New Jersey, where his uncle—a retired cop—had a cottage he said he could use.

"Fuck 'em, kid," his uncle had told him. "Go to my cottage and don't think about it."

Not thinking about it was easier said than done, but going to the cottage did seem like a good idea. He could get away from the suspicious stares of his "friends and neighbors," as well as the constant crying and spitting up of his new daughter.

And his wife. Suddenly the love of his life had become someone he wanted to run away from. Her solicitous behavior around him, combined with the fact that their daughter had become an appendage on her hip, served only to irritate him.

His uncle's cottage was on Seven Mile Beach. He hadn't been there since he was a kid. When he pulled up in front it looked the same. He stood in front and studied the corner of the house where his uncle had once tried to smoke out some hornets from a nest but had only succeeded in setting the house on fire.

He used the key his uncle had given him to open the door. Even the inside looked the same. The furniture worn and musty, the walls cracked and peeling. He was carrying a small duffel bag with extra clothes in it and a paper bag with a six-pack of his favorite beer, Ballantine. He put the beer in the fridge, dumped his duffel in the smallest of the two bedrooms, and then went out back on the porch to look at the water. He left the front and back doors open to air the place out.

After twenty minutes he decided to close up the house again. He put on a windbreaker, because the salt air was cool in September, stuffed his hands into the pockets of his jeans, and started walking.

□   □   □

Being alone turned out to be a bad idea. All he could think about was what he would do if he was kicked off the force—or worse, kicked off and arrested. He replayed each scenario over and over again. Just when he started to think that swallowing his gun might not be such a bad idea he came to the end of the beach and saw the shack. Not actually a shack, but a small restaurant. It almost looked like what his old man used to call a roadhouse.

It was getting dark and the place was lit, though not brightly. He looked around and was struck at how black and white everything seemed. The sand was white, the sides of the building were white, the water was dark, there was not a hint of color anywhere. It was as if he had stepped through a portal into an alternate dimension where color had been drained from everything. He could smell fish frying, and hunger suddenly gnawed at his belly. He realized he hadn't eaten since that morning, when his wife had tried to force breakfast on him. He'd finally agreed to eat some toast before leaving, just to shut her up.

He walked towards the little café and as he got closer he could hear music coming from inside. It was Dusty Springfield singing "You Don't Have To Say You Love Me." As soon as he opened the screen door and stepped inside he saw her.

The interior of the place continued to foster the colorless illusion of the moment. The floor was laid with black and white tile, the walls, tables and countertops were also white. The leather of the booths and counter stools was black. A man behind the counter wore a long white apron over a white T-shirt and black pants. What hair he had left was black, a wispy fringe around his head and a thick mat on his forearms.

And in the midst of all this she stood, a shining oasis of color in a desert of black and white.

And the color was gold.

3

Her skin was pale, and her waitress uniform was a white apron, a white peasant blouse and a black skirt—but her hair was golden blonde, and it made her stand out, although she would have done so anyway. Her figure was Monroesque, with full, round breasts, the nipples of which were prominent, probably because the place was air-conditioned to the point of freezing.

A few of the booths were occupied and some of the tables. Since the tourist season was over Tru decided the people had to be locals.

"Sit anywhere," the man behind the counter said.

Tru only saw the one waitress, so it didn't matter where he sat, she'd be waiting on him. He chose a booth with no one seated directly in front or behind him.

When she came over he saw that she was older then he'd first thought, maybe late-twenties instead of early. She had blue eyes, which he hadn't been able to notice until now. The blue of her eyes and gold of her hair were the only hints of color in the place.

"Can I get you something?" she asked, and he realized this was the second time she'd spoken, He'd been staring and hadn't heard her the first time, but now he did and her voice had a smoky, throaty quality.

"Oh, uh, a burger," he stammered, feeling fourteen again, when being near any girl, let alone one as beautiful as this one, had made him stammer.

"How'd you like it?"

"Well done."

"Fries?"

"Sure."

"A shake?"

"Why not?"

She smiled and his stomach fluttered. That annoyed him. He wasn't fourteen anymore, and he was married, so why should he be reacting this way?

"I could just about sell you anything, couldn't I?" she asked, lowering her pad.

He nodded and said, "Just about."

"Well," she said, staring at him with a look of amusement, "why don't we just leave it at a burger, fries and shake for now?"

"Um . . ." he said, and she walked away, leaving in her wake a scent that tickled his nostrils and drove out all memory of baby smells.

She returned briefly with a glass of water and a smile and he breathed in her scent once again. He found himself waiting anxiously for his food, though his hunger had suddenly become a secondary concern. It was only because she would be bringing it.

While he waited he noticed three men come into the place and immediately seat themselves in a booth. They were all dressed similar to the way he was, jeans and windbreakers, but they all had Elvis hair and were eight or ten years younger than him. At that point the waitress started toward him with his plate of food in one hand. One of the new arrivals grabbed her free arm, halting her progress.

"Come on, Lizzie, we need some service, here."

She yanked her arm away and said, "Don't grab me like that again, Hal. I'll get to you when I finish with this guy. And don't call me Lizzie!"

"You love me," Hal called after her. "I know it."

She made a face that he couldn't see and walked to Tru's booth.

"Old boyfriend?" he asked, without stammering.

"He wishes," she said, setting his plate down. In doing so she bent over and brought her cleavage tantalizingly close to him. If her scent had teased him up to now it was suddenly heady, wafting up from between her breasts and making his head swim. "Can I get you anything else?"

"Uh, that shake."

"Oh yeah, right," she said, laughing, full, ripe lips parting to reveal perfect white teeth. "I'm sorry. What flavor?"

"Strawberry."

"Comin' up."

She had to walk past the booth with the three men and the one called Hal reached for her again. She avoided him, causing his friends to laugh at him. She went behind the counter, made Tru his shake, and started for his table again. As before Hal grabbed her free arm.

"Come on, Lizzie," he said, "don't be like that."

She tried to pull her arm away again, but he held fast this time.

"You're hurting me!" she snapped.

"Liz—"

Abruptly she overturned the shake glass and poured the contents onto his head. He shouted, released her arm and jumped up. His friends were now shedding tears, they were laughing so hard.

"Goddamn it, you bitch!" Hal swore.

Tru could see that Liz looked frightened so he got up and hurried over to the action. He got between her and Hal before the man could do anything.

Abruptly, his two friends stood up and got behind him. He started to reach for his badge before he remembered it wasn't there. They'd taken it from him pending the investigation—that and his gun. All he had left was the adrenaline rush he always got in situations like these.

"I think you boys better go and eat someplace else," Tru said.

"What's it to you?" Hal demanded.

"That was my milk shake," Tru said. "Because of you, I have to wait for another one."

The strawberry colored liquid was still dripping from Hal's chin and there was clumps of it in his hair and on his shoulders.

"That bitch had no call—"

"She asked you to stop grabbing her and you didn't listen. I think you got what you deserved, don't you?"

Hal stared at Tru, looking ridiculous and more pink than strawberry. Behind him his friends gave Tru the meanest looks they could muster, but he saw they weren't going to do anything without their leader's say so. He closed the distance between himself and Hal, invading the man's space, causing him to step back a pace before he could stop himself.

"Time to leave, Hal," Tru said, quietly.

Hal tried to match Tru's stare but in the end he couldn't, and looked away.

"Hal?" one of his friends asked.

"Let's go," Hal said. "Burgers in this place stink, anyway."

They backed away a few steps, then turned and shuffled out the door, Hal pushing them from behind.

He felt her hand on his shoulder and then he turned and faced her. She was taller than his wife, who had dark hair and dark skin and brown eyes. This girl was all pale and golden, and took his breath away.

"My hero," she said. "Thanks."

"No problem," he said. "I was kind of mad he got my shake."

"Go sit down and I'll bring you another one—on the house."

"Thanks."

He went back to his booth and started on his burger, not really tasting it. He was coming down from the rush of facing those three punks without a gun and badge, but was still high from the girl.

"Cop?"

He looked up at her standing there with another shake, smiling down at him.

"What?"

"I asked, are you a cop?" She put the shake down, this time without bending over.

"Why did you ask that?"

She shrugged. "Because you act like one."

"Well," he said, "it's a long story, but yes I am—I was . . ."

"Hey," she said, waving her hands in front of her, "none of my business. I'm sorry I asked. How's the burger?"

"It's fine."

"Look," she said, "I just want to warn you about those guys . . ."

"They didn't seem so tough."

"Well, you were facing them," she said. "Just be careful, okay? And really . . ." She put her hand on his shoulder and leaned over to kiss his cheek. She was so plush that for a moment he was blinded by the paleness of her skin. "Thank you," she said. "It's been a long time since anyone stood up for me." He couldn't understand that, at all.

4

After the last of the customers left she came over and sat opposite him in his booth.

"Close up for me, Liz?" the boss called out.

"Don't worry, Lenny," she said. "I'll lock everything."

The boss left and she leaned forward, a move which pressed her breasts against the table so that they swelled, threatening to spill out of her blouse. And there were those blue eyes, that full, soft mouth.

"Give me a quarter," she said.

"A quarter?"

"For a song."

He reached into his pocket and handed her one. She went to the jukebox and punched in the number she wanted. Then turned and walked slowly toward him while the song started. Once again he heard Dusty Springfield's "You Don't Have To Say You Love Me."

"Dance with me?" she asked, ample hips already swaying.

He pushed away his partially eaten burger and got up. She came into his arms and pressed against him. He forgot about everything—his wife, the baby, Internal Affairs, his badge . . . everything. Nothing else existed except her in his arms. He knew he should be feeling guilty. After all, his wife was at home taking care of their new daughter, his career was on the line, and here he was dancing with a woman he'd only just met, but wished he could stay with forever.

"You're married, aren't you?" she asked. Her head was on his shoulder, her mouth near his ear.

"Yes."

"The good ones always are."

They danced until the song ended and then he didn't want to let her go. They stepped away and looked into each other's eyes.

"I know this is crazy," she said, "but would you like to come home with me tonight?'

"More than anything else in the world."

"No strings," she said. "Just tonight."

"No strings."

"I don't want to break up a marriage," she said, "but I feel like if I don't take this chance I'll always wonder . . . you know?"

He nodded. "I know."

"I'll lock up," she said, and began to scurry about, turning off burners, and lights, and locking doors, until finally they were going out the front door together.

They were on him like a pack of wild dogs.

Her arm was linked with his so that when they pulled him from the steps she went sprawling into the sand as well, away from the action. They rained down punches and kicks on him. He tried to give back as good as he got, but it was three against one and they had caught him unprepared. He had no doubt that it was the three punks from earlier in the evening. In fact, one of them still swelled sweetly of the shake Elizabeth had poured over his head.

She finally got back to her feet and decided to join the fray rather than call fruitlessly for help. She jumped on the back of one of the men and began to pummel him.

"Get her off me!" he shouted.

"Stop it!" she cried. "You're killing him!"

The other two stopped kicking Tru long enough to pry Elizabeth off the third man's back, sending her into the sand again.

"We're not gonna kill him, Lizzie" Hal said. "We're just teachin' him a lesson."

"Yeah," one of the others said, "No big city asshole better come here and mess with our women."

"What the hell are you talking about?" she demanded. "You losers don't have any women."

The three men exchanged glances, wondering how to respond to that.

"Besides," she said, before they could make up their minds, "you're really in trouble now."

"And why's that?" Hal asked.

"Because he's a cop," she said. "You three dimwits just assaulted a cop."

"A cop?" Hal said.

"Jesus," one of the others said. "We didn't know."

"A cop, Hal," the third one said. "We gotta get outta here."

"Lizzie—" Hal started.

"Just get out of here," she said, cutting him off, "and don't call me that."

"He started it," Hal said. "He stuck his nose—"

"I can keep him from reporting this if you'll just get out of here!" she said, urgently.

"Come on, Hal," one of the others said, grabbing his arm. "Let's go."

Hal gave one last look at Tru, lying in the sand, bloody and battered, and then allowed his friends to pull him away.

"Jesus," Elizabeth said, and dropped to her knees next to him. "Are you all right?"

"I—I think so," he said, spitting blood from a split lip.

"You're not dead, or anything?"

He laughed, then hissed because that split his lip even more.

"No," he said, "I'm not dead."

"Do you have a place around here?"

"Just up the beach."

"Well," she said, "I guess we better go there so I can look after you. Can you get up?"

"Yeah," he said, his head clearing somewhat. "Where did they go?"

"They ran off when I told them you were a cop." She helped him to his feet. "You don't want to go after them or anything, do you?"

"No," he said, "I just want to forget the whole thing."

"Well then, lean on me," she said. "This isn't exactly what I had in mind, but I guess I'll have to play Florence Nightingale."

"Not what I had in mind, either."

She tended to his wounds, which were more annoying than serious, and then helped him into bed. She'd kissed his forehead then his mouth and said, "You're not in shape for much more than this," which he later thought had probably been for the best.

She'd walked to the door then, turned and said to him, "I'm not leaving my number."

He nodded. "I understand."

"Too bad," she'd said, "Mr. Cop."

She left, the taste of her on his lips, and he'd never even told her his name.

The Present

He took the tea cup back into the house and put it in the sink. Then locked all the doors, going out the back and walking down the deck steps to the sand. He started down the beach, then turned and frowned at the house. He hadn't noticed it before, but it was apparently on the same lot his uncle's house had been on. He'd thought it a coincidence that a house on Seven Mile Beach had become available for sitting, but not this much of a coincidence. He continued down the beach as dusk came and seemed to bleach the color out of everything, The sand was white, the water was getting dark. He wondered if the small café would still be there, and if it was she couldn't possibly still be working there as a waitress, could she?

When he finally came to the end of the beach he saw it. Only one wall still stood, but it was the one with the front door in it. He walked to the steps that the three men had pulled him down. He'd gone home the next day, hugged his wife and baby, told her that he'd come home early because he'd gotten mugged—and because he missed them. That Monday he found out that IAD had cleared him and his career would continue.

He'd thought about Elizabeth over the years once in a while, especially when he heard that Dusty Springfield song. He'd recall how they talked, how their eyes met, how they'd danced in the café and what they had almost done—and would have done—if the three punks hadn't jumped him outside. He'd felt guilt all these years because of how good he'd felt just dancing with her. How bad would he have felt if he'd spent that night with her?

He'd never cheated on his wife in all the years they'd been together and had always considered this café the place where he'd come the closest. As a younger man he'd felt that even the dance had been a betrayal, but now, thinking back, he knew it hadn't been. It had simply been a cleansing time for him, a few moments respite from a life that had suddenly become filled with turmoil.

There was no harm in that.

The Guilt Edge

1

It always amazed Truxton Lewis how many people were willing to leave a key under a mat, a rock, or in the mailbox.

This time the owners of the house in Montville, Connecticut had used a flower pot by the front door. He dug into the dirt and came up with the mud-covered key. He opened the door and stepped inside with his suitcase in hand. After his first three house-sitting jobs he'd gotten his packing down to one suitcase. It was even easier when house-sitting for someone who had a washer/dryer.

The house was spread out over one floor—four bedrooms, twelve rooms in all. It was one of the larger house-sitting jobs he'd taken on, but when he'd seen the job come up on the Web he'd put his name and credentials in right away. It gave him an opportunity to return to the East Coast. Since moving from New York to Bourbon, Missouri, he didn't have that chance very often. His qualifications made him desirable as a live-in caretaker—no kids, no pets, and no smoking.

He'd found his instructions on the dining room table. The family had even gone so far as to make a map of the house. He guessed they were afraid he'd get lost looking for the bedroom they'd put aside for him.

He walked past three bedrooms where all the furniture was covered by sheets and found the fourth room laid out for him. He put his suitcase on the bed, left the unpacking for later. Retracing his steps to the kitchen, he checked the refrigerator. They had left bottled water, Diet Coke—which he had asked for—and iced tea. No beer. He'd have to pick his own up later, as soon as he found a grocery store. He pulled out a bottle of Diet Coke, opened it and took a couple of good swallows, then carried it with him while touring the rest of the house and the grounds. By the end of the day he had the place scoped out. By the end of the second day he had his routine down pat—which included keeping the plants watered. By day three he found the Mohegan Sun Casino, a few miles away.

2

It was an Indian reservation casino that was actually split into three sections—Casino of the Wind, Casino of the Sky, and Casino of the Earth. These casinos had popped up all over the country since Congress passed the Indian Gaming Regulatory Act in 1988. The Act recognized the right of Indian tribes in the United States to establish gaming facilities on their reservations as long as the states in which they were located had some form of legalized gambling.

Tru had been to several of these casinos since he started house-sitting but never one of this magnitude. It was almost as large as the other casino in Connecticut, Foxwoods; too big for his taste, but he went anyway. His game was blackjack, and since it was just a way to pass the time, he was happy to see the casino had five-dollar tables. On his first few visits, he had run into several different dealers but decided he liked a girl named Tina the best. She was young, obviously Native American, with a strong profile and beautiful, sleek black hair. He even found himself flirting with her, which surprised him. She was in her twenties and he was over sixty, yet they seemed to fall into an easy rapport.

After the first week he sought Tina out when he visited the casino, then followed her from table to table when the dealers had to switch. The casino did not allow a dealer to remain at one table for more than half an hour. That way they couldn't form a working relationship with a player to cheat the casino.

"If you keep following me," she told him one day, "I'm going to think you're sweet on me."

"What if I was?" he asked. "Would you be embarrassed to have an old man sweet on you?"

She laughed. "You're not so old."

"You're a very nice girl, Tina," he said.

One day, after he'd been coming to the casino for almost three weeks, he ran into somebody he knew.

"Captain Lewis?" the man said from behind him.

Tru turned. The voice wasn't that familiar, but he immediately placed the face.

"Jimmy Diver?"

"That's right," said Diver, who had been a New York City police detective during Tru's watch. "Hey-hey, I heard you retired years ago!"

The two men shook hands. Diver, who was a few years younger, had gone totally gray since their last meeting. His handshake was as powerful as ever, but he was carrying around a bit of a belly.

"You tryin' to get rich at the tables?"

"No," Tru said, "just passing time, flirting with the pretty dealer."

"Hey-hey," Diver said, smiling at Tina, who grinned back. It was early, with Tru the only player at the table. Tina just waited—and listened.

"When did you put in your papers?" Tru asked.

"Coupla months ago," Diver said. "Got divorced, too, so I thought I'd try makin' some money at blackjack. I got a system."

"Don't we all."

"You livin' around here?"

"No, I'm just a tourist."

"Well, it was good to see you, Cap," Diver said. "I gotta go hit my twenty-five dollar table."

"Good to see you, Jimmy," Tru said. They shook hands again, and Diver moved on.

After a few hands, Tina said, "He called you Captain. Are you in the Army?"

"No, no. I used to be a New York City cop. Captain of detectives. I retired years ago."

She nodded, got quiet while she dealt. Her silence lasted about ten minutes.

"Do you think you could help me?" she asked.

"Help you?"

"I—I have a problem, and I need some help," she said.

"The kind of help a policeman could offer?"

"Yes."

"Well, I'm not a policeman anymore, Tina. Maybe you should go to your local police. Or—don't you have tribal police?"

"Yes," she said, "I could do that. But—I couldn't hire you?"

Tru liked the young dealer, but he didn't really relish the thought of getting involved in her private life.

"I'm not a private detective, Tina," he said. "Maybe you should check the yellow pages for a real one? Or, like I said, go to the cops?"

"Oh, sure," she said, "sure, I should do that. I'm sorry. Forget I asked."

At that moment her relief came along. She clapped her hands, showed her palms to the eye in the sky, and moved on to another table.

Tru didn't follow her.

In fact, he didn't return to the casino after that day. He didn't want to run into Jimmy Diver again, and he thought it would be awkward to sit at Tina's table.

Rather than find another dealer, or table, he decided to find another way to pass the time.

3

He was on the back veranda spraying the plants after dinner when the doorbell rang. It had been three days since he'd left the house. He had the refrigerator well-stocked and had brought plenty of paperbacks. Staying away from the casino was saving him money, and embarrassment.

He walked through the house, still holding the spray bottle, and opened the door. A state trooper stood in the doorway, complete with hat and Sam Brown belt.

"Mr. Lewis?"

"That's right."

"Sir, I'm Sergeant Ben Holmsby. I'm the resident state trooper to the Montville Police Department."

"Okay."

"Can I come in?"

"Sure." Tru backed away to let the young man enter. As he did the trooper removed his hat.

"What's this about?" Tru asked.

"Do you know a woman named Tina Jordan?"

"Jordan?" Tru repeated.

"She was a blackjack dealer at the casino."

"I know a Tina," Tru said. "I don't know her last name. She works at the Mohegan Sun."

"This her?" The trooper held out a casino photo ID.

"That's her."

"Can you come with me, sir?"

"Where?"

"To Headquarters."

"Not till you tell me what's going on."

"This woman—Tina Jordan—she was killed today."

The Montville Police Department was on Fort Shantok Road in Uncasville. On the way Holmsby explained that it was a twenty-one-man police department with the Mayor serving as Chief of Police.

"We have a lieutenant who acts as administrative head," the trooper said, "and I handle operational aspects of the department."

"Do you have detectives?"

"Not at the present time," Holmsby said.

The trooper did not ask any questions of Truxton Lewis until they arrived at the Montville Police Department and joined the Mayor/Chief of Police in his office.

"Why isn't this man handcuffed?" the man demanded, without waiting for an introduction.

"He hasn't done anything, sir," the trooper said. "He's here voluntarily."

"Are you the Mayor?" Tru asked.

"That's right."

"And the Chief of Police?"

"Yes."

"Excuse me, sir, but do you have any law enforcement experience?"

Instead of answering, the Mayor/Chief looked at the trooper. "Why is he the one asking questions?"

"I think we need to be introduced," Tru said to the trooper, who looked amused.

"Sure," Holmsby said. "This is Mayor Harold Schiff. Mr. Mayor, this is Truxton Lewis."

Tru took out his voided NYPD ID, showed it to both men. "Retired Captain of Detectives Truxton Lewis."

Now the trooper really looked amused, as the Mayor appeared flustered.

"Sir," the trooper asked, "would you mind telling me what your last assignment was in your department."

"I don't mind at all," Tru said. "I was in command of a homicide unit."

4

They left Truxton in the Mayor's office. The trooper came back without the Mayor, handed Tru a cup of coffee, then seated himself behind the desk. "He's a politician. Doesn't know a thing about police work."

"Then why is he also chief?"

"To tell you the truth? I don't know. Maybe they're saving money that way."

"And how did you end up here?"

"I came in under the Resident State Trooper Program," he said.

"And you get the murder investigations?"

"Actually," Holmsby said, "this is the first."

"Well, I suppose I could help you."

"That's a possibility," Holmsby said, "but first two things have to happen."

"What are they?"

"I'll need to check you out, and I'll need you to tell me how you knew Tina Jordan."

"We can take care of both of those."

Holmsby made a call to the New York City Police Department's main number, asked to be put through to the Brooklyn South Homicide Squad, which Truxton Lewis had commanded for five years prior to his retirement. The trooper talked for five minutes to the squad's present commander, Captain Ed Samuelson, who confirmed everything Tru had said. Samuelson had been Tru's lieutenant and had been given command of the squad at his recommendation.

Trooper Holmsby hung up. "He said to tell you he still hasn't entirely cleaned up the mess you left behind."

"He's a good man."

"Okay, now tell me about you and Tina Jordan?"

It took all of two minutes.

"That was it?"

"That's it. She was a blackjack dealer, and I played at her table for a while."

"And she asked you for help?"

"Yes."

"Because she knew you were a retired detective."

"That's right."

"How did she know that?"

"I ran into another retired cop while I was sitting at her table. It wasn't hard for her to figure that out from our conversation."

"I don't get it," the trooper said. "Why would she ask you for help but not come to the police?"

"I don't know. I recommended she do just that, or hire a PI, and she said she might. I didn't see her anymore after that."

"Why not?"

"To tell you the truth, I didn't feel comfortable there anymore. So she never came in?"

"I'll have to check with Lieutenant Brennan," Holmsby said. "He takes care of all administrative matters."

"Aren't there tribal police? Maybe she went to them."

"I'll check that, too. What about family? Brothers? A father who could've helped her?"

"I never asked," Tru said, feeling bad for having to admit that. "During the times we talked she said she had no family. Just her daughters. Where are they?"

"Social Services has them. So you've had no contact with Tina since she asked you for help?"

"No. How was she killed?"

"She was shot."

"Do you have any leads?"

"No, we don't."

Now Tru felt horrible. The girl had asked for help, he'd shrugged her off with lame advice, and she was dead. He felt not only shame, but guilt.

"Are you satisfied with my answers?" Tru asked.

"Yes, I am."

"So I'm not a suspect?"

"Should you be?"

"No, I shouldn't," Tru said. "And if I'm not, I'd like to offer you my help." It was the least he could do for her, he thought. Or, maybe, for himself.

"Why would you want to do that?"

"By your own admission this is your first murder. I've investigated many. Also, I . . . sluffed her off. Maybe if I'd helped her she'd be alive."

Holmsby sat back in his boss's chair and rubbed his jaw. "I like the idea, but I'll have to clear it with the Chief." He got up and stopped at the door. "He's probably gonna want to talk to you. I think he'll ask some pretty dumb questions."

"I'd expect nothing less from a politician," Tru said.

"He's a small town politician, which is probably worse than anything you dealt with in New York."

"I'll keep that in mind."

5

As Trooper Holmsby and his Chief reentered the room Tru could see the Mayor was not happy. The scowl on his face gave him extra wrinkles.

"Mr. Lewis," the politician said, "the trooper tells me you've volunteered your services to this investigation."

"That's right," Tru said.

"If we agree to accept your help, is it understood that the investigation will be run by this office?"

"By you?"

"No, of course not. By Sergeant Holmsby, but under the auspices of this office."

"I understand that."

"As far as credit for solving it—"

"The captain isn't interested in credit, sir," Holmsby said, cutting his boss off, "he just wants to help."

"How altruistic."

Tru decided the Mayor had some issues that had nothing to do with Tina Jordan.

He turned to Holmsby. "I think we should go to the house."

"Good idea," the trooper said. "Let you have a look at the scene."

"Yes." Tru looked at the Mayor. "Anything else?"

"No," Mayor Schiff said. "Sergeant Holmsby will see that you have whatever you need."

Tru stood up. "Thank you."

He turned and followed Holmsby. Outside the office, after he closed the door behind them, he stopped.

"We can go and talk to the lieutenant, see if Tina Jordan ever did come in—" Holmsby started, but Tru stopped him.

"Let's go to the house first," he said. "I want to have a look for myself."

He followed the trooper through the building and out to the parking lot.

"Do you want me to give you a car to use?" Holmsby asked.

"No," Tru said, "the people I'm house-sitting for left one for me, but I only know my way from the house to the casino and back. If we're going to work together I'd rather we stay together—if you don't mind driving. It'll save me the time it'd take to learn the way."

"It's fine with me."

They stopped at a four-door Toyota that looked a few years old. Trooper Holmsby unlocked the doors and they got in.

As the trooper started the engine Tru asked, "By the way. How did you know where to find me?"

Holmsby reached into his pocket and came out with a piece of paper. "Found this on her refrigerator."

It had "Truxton Lewis" on it, and "the Lawford house."

"And you knew where the Lawford house was?"

"I looked it up."

6

When they got to a small wood frame house a few miles from the police station, Holmsby told Tru that they were still in Uncasville.

"And we're right on the edge of the reservation," he added.

"Really?" Tru looked around, saw similar houses on the block.

"Yes. What did you expect, teepees?"

"Well . . ."

As they pulled in front of Tina Jordan's house, there was an old Chrysler in the driveway.

"Hers?" Tru asked.

"No," Holmsby said. "Looks like the tribal police are here."

They got out of Holmsby's car, walked over to the other car. As they reached it the driver's side opened and a man in uniform got out.

"Trooper," he said.

"Officer Standing Hawk."

The tribal policeman looked to be about thirty, tall, broad-shouldered with hair as black as—well, as black as Tina Jordan's had been.

"This is my colleague," Trooper Holmsby said, "Captain Lewis."

"Captain?" the officer asked.

"Retired Homicide captain," Tru said, "NYPD."

"You sent for help," Standing Hawk said to Holmsby. "That's good."

"Not exactly. Seems the captain met Tina Jordan at the casino. When he heard she'd been killed he offered his services, since we're not exactly experienced at conducting homicide investigations."

"What about you, Officer?" Tru asked. "Investigated any homicides?"

"Not lately."

"Then how'd you get assigned to this case?"

"I'm not assigned," he admitted. "In fact, my boss said we got to leave this to the regular police."

"Then what's your interest?"

"Simple," Standing Hawk said. "Tina Jordan was my sister."

Tru's guilt suddenly multiplied tenfold as he looked into the man's sad eyes.

"Why don't we go inside and talk," he said. "Since you're her brother do you have a key?"

"No key," Standing Hawk said, "but I'm sure the trooper can oblige."

Holmsby fished a key out of his pocket and approached the house. Standing Hawk and Tru followed.

"Where was she found?" Tru asked.

"Living room. This way."

They followed him into the living room, where Tru immediately spotted the blood-soaked patch of rug.

"Who found her?"

"A girlfriend of hers," Holmsby said. "Works with her at the casino."

"Where were the kids?"

"Sitting next to her," Holmsby said. "They had her blood on them."

"How old are they?"

"Two and four."

"Not much good as witnesses, then. Forced entry?"

"Not that we could see."

Standing Hawk walked over to the sliding glass door, checked the lock. "No scratches here or on the front," he said.

"Very good," Tru said. "What else?"

"If there's no forced entry," the Mohegan said, "she must have known her killer and let them in."

"Could be," Tru said.

"What other explanation could there be?" Standing Hawk asked.

"I've got a question for you, before I answer any more."

"What's that?"

"Why did Tina tell me she had no family?"

"I'm kind of curious about that one myself," Trooper Holmsby said.

Standing Hawk stared at the two of them for a few moments, then asked Tru, "Did she also tell you she had no father?"

"That's what she said."

"Well," Standing Hawk said, "my sister chose to get married against my father's will. When she did, my father disowned her."

"Does that mean you disowned her, too?"

The man had the good grace to look uncomfortable.

"It happened at a time when I . . . I didn't have any choice but to go along with my father."

"But that time passed, didn't it?"

"It did," he said, "but by the time I developed a mind of my own she wouldn't have anything to do with me."

"What about her daughters?"

"What about them?"

"Well," he said, "why should they be with Social Services when they have family?"

"I didn't know about you, or your father," the trooper said. "I had no choice."

"Well, I—I guess I'll look into it."

"Are you married?" Tru asked.

"No."

"Any women in your family?"

"No," Standing Hawk said. "My mother died years ago, and I have—had no other sisters."

"Well, maybe—"

"Look," the tribal cop said, "I came here to find out what happened to my sister."

"How did you hear about it?" Tru asked.

"We keep in touch with the Montville Police."

Tru suddenly decided that he'd rather work with the tribal policeman than with the state trooper. Maybe it was because the policeman was Tina's brother, or maybe because he didn't have a politician to answer to.

"Hey Trooper, could you do me a favor?"

"What's that, Mr. Lewis?"

"My name is Truxton," Tru said, "or you can call me Tru. Would you go back to your station and talk to your lieutenant?"

"But . . . how will you get back?"

"I'm sure the officer, here, wouldn't mind dropping me."

"Not at all," Standing Hawk said, tucking some chewing tobacco into his cheek.

"Well, okay," the trooper said. "I'll see you back at the station."

"Okay."

Holmsby looked at the tribal cop.

"You really her brother?" he asked.

"Yes," Standing Hawk said, "I really am."

Holmsby nodded and left.

"So," Standing Hawk asked, "what was that about?"

"I have the feeling you and I should work together on this, Officer."

"Why's that?"

"Because I think we're responding to the same impetus."

"And just what would that be?" Standing Hawk asked.

Tru hesitated for only a moment, then said, "Guilt."

7

"What do you have to feel guilty about?" Standing Hawk asked.

Tru noticed that the man did not try to deny his own feelings.

"She asked me for help," Tru said.

"I envy you, then," Standing Hawk said. "She would never ask me for help."

"Well, if she'd asked you instead of me—"

"Captain Lewis," the other man said, cutting him off. "Why don't we stop measuring guilt and blame and see what we can do about finding out who killed her?"

"Okay," Tru said.

"And just how do we do that?" Standing Hawk asked.

"How long have you been a cop?"

"A rez cop for about five years," Standing Hawk said. "I did two years before that in the Military Police."

"Here or abroad?"

"Germany, but I've never been a detective, so I'm just going to have to follow your lead."

"Okay," Tru said. "As I understand it, this house is not on the reservation."

"That's true," Standing Hawk said. "This entire block is off the rez. It's probably why she chose to live here."

"But the casino is on the reservation, right?"

"Right."

"So you have jurisdiction there?"

"Yes."

"That means you can get us their surveillance tapes, right?"

"Probably. I've never had to do it before," Standing Hawk said. "I guess I can. I'll check with my boss."

"Can you do that by phone?"

Standing Hawk took out a cell phone.

"I want those tapes today," Tru said.

"Tapes of what?"

"Tina's blackjack table," Tru said, "and the employee parking lot."

"Okay, Captain."

"Listen, you can start calling me Tru, and I need something else to call you besides officer, or Standing Hawk."

"Steve," Standing Hawk said.

Truxton Lewis walked through the house, looked in every room, including the one the little girls shared. In Tina's bedroom he found a box that had held a gun. He searched for a receipt that would tell him where she bought it, but there was none. He kept the box open and held it by the inside lining so he wouldn't leave prints, then carried it back to the living room as Standing Hawk finished his call.

"What've you got?" the Tribal cop asked.

"Empty box," Tru said. "Looks like she bought a gun."

"Any receipt?"

"No." Tru put the box down on an end table. "You know anybody in the area who's selling guns?"

"Yeah, but Tina wouldn't go on the rez. She hasn't been there in five years, since she got married—except to work at the casino."

"Where's her husband?"

"He took off after the second girl was born. Hasn't been back."

"Okay," Tru said, "maybe somebody bought the gun for her. We'll have to check with the seller."

Standing Hawk walked over and picked up the box. "Guy I'm

talking about sells out of his trunk," he said. "He wouldn't have something in a box like this."

"We don't have a choice, if he's the only seller you know of. We'll have to ask him. But first the tapes."

"My boss says we'll need a warrant," Standing Hawk sad. "He's making a call to see—wait." His cell rang. He answered, listened, then said, "Thanks," and broke the connection.

"We don't need a warrant if we look at the tapes on the premises. The head of security will show them to us."

"Okay," Tru said, "then let's go."

"Okay."

"Wait," Tru said, at the last minute. "Let me take a look out back."

They slid the glass door open and stepped out. There was no patio, just grass. Tru walked around the yard while Standing Hawk waited. There were some brown patches in the grass. Against the back wall, on the ground, he bent over and picked up a cigarette butt.

"Did Tina smoke?" he asked.

"No, she hated it."

"Couldn't she have started? I mean, you haven't seen her in a while."

"I kept tabs on her."

"How?"

"The same girl who found her used to let me know how she was."

"The girl who works at the casino?"

"That's right."

"I'll need to talk to her, too." He held the butt up and squinted at it. "Can't see a brand. There's no filter."

"That's because it was hand rolled."

Tru looked again and saw that the Tribal cop had it right.

"Lots of men on the rez roll their own."

Tru put the butt in his pocket.

"Let's go to the casino."

8

In the car , Tru used Standing Hawk's cell to call Holmsby. The trooper had found out that Tina Jordan had tried to swear out a complaint against a stalker about a week before she'd asked Tru for help.

"And what did they tell her?"

"She was told that the man hadn't broken the law, so we couldn't do anything. They never even took his name."

"She was told wrong, Holmsby," Tru said. "There are stalking laws, you know."

"I understand that. I'm going to address that with the men for the future."

Tru told Holmsby where he'd be, then hung up thinking that the future wouldn't help Tina Jordan much.

A good indication of the sheer size of the Mohegan Sun Casino was the fact there were twenty restaurants on the grounds.

They sat in the security office with the head of security—a Native American Standing Hawk knew from the reservation—viewing surveillance tapes for several hours.

Standing Hawk called him Danny, but waitresses and other employees called him Mr. Leaphorn.

Leaphorn had a waitress bring them coffee. Watching the tapes of Tina's table didn't yield anything. It showed Tru as a regular for a number of days, but not much else. They studied the tapes of her table going back at least two weeks before she'd asked Tru for help. When they found nothing, they switched to the parking lot cameras.

After two hours of that, Tru's mouth was sour with coffee when he spotted something.

"Wait," he said, "who's that?"

Standing Hawk and Leaphorn both leaned forward to have a look. Tru froze the picture.

"That's Eddie Tall Bear," Leaphorn said.

"Who is he?"

"He works at the casino," the security man said.

"Did he know Tina?"

Standing Hawk said, "Since they were kids."

Tru turned in his chair to look at Standing Hawk. "Boyfriend and girlfriend?"

"In their teens."

Now he looked at Danny Leaphorn. "She ever talk to you about him? Complain?"

"She never complained to me about anybody," the security man said.

"Wouldn't it have been your job to help if someone was bothering her?"

"On casino grounds, yes," Leaphorn said. "I wasn't responsible for her once she went home."

"Nobody's accusing you, Mr. Leaphorn," Tru said.

"She could have asked me, though," the man said. "I would have done something."

"I want to talk to the girl who found her," Tru said to Standing Hawk, then pointed at the frozen image on the screen and said, "and I want to talk to him."

"Why him?" Leaphorn asked. "All he's doing is standing there rolling a cigarette."

"Exactly," Tru said.

Tina's girlfriend's name was Jesse Campbell. Danny Leaphorn went and got her, then left her alone with the two men. She knew Standing Hawk.

"Jesse, you found Tina," Tru said.

"That's right." She appeared nervous. She was wearing her casino dealer's uniform.

"What were you doing there that day?"

"We were going to go shopping."

"Had she ever told you she was being stalked?"

"No."

"Not a word?" he asked. "You didn't know a man was bothering her?"

"No."

Tru looked at Standing Hawk, who was staring at the girl.

"Jesse—" the tribal cop started.

"I don't know anything, Steve!" she said. "Honest!"

"Why are you so nervous?" Tru asked.

She bit her lip. "I don't know *you*."

She risked a glance at Standing Hawk, then looked away. Tru realized he wasn't the one making her nervous, at all.

"You can't talk in front of him?" he asked.

"N-no."

"What the hell—" Standing Hawk started, but Tru cut him off.

"Why don't you just step outside for a minute, Steve?" he suggested.

"Yeah, sure," Standing Hawk said, reluctantly, "okay."

Tru and Jesse waited until the door closed behind the tribal cop.

"Okay, Jesse," Tru said, "spill the beans."

9

"The only man Tina told me had been stalking her was . . . her brother."

"Her brother?" Tru asked. "How many brothers does she have?"

Jesse pointed to the door and said, "Just one."

"Okay, wait, explain this to me."

"Since her father and brother disowned her she's wanted nothing to do with them," Jesse said. "Lately, her brother's been trying to talk to her, but she's been putting him off."

"Talk about what?"

Jesse shrugged. "She didn't want to know."

"So you want me to believe her brother killed her because she wouldn't talk to him?" Tru asked. "Her brother the cop?"

"I didn't say that," she said. "You asked me if she told me about anybody stalking her. Steve's the only one she mentioned."

"What about this guy, Eddie . . ."

"Her old boyfriend? What about him?"

"Does he bother her?"

"No," she said. "He works here, they see each other, but he don't bother her."

Tru frowned. Was Tina Jordan trying to use him to help get rid of her own brother? Even if he had been stalking her, it didn't necessarily follow that he killed her. Maybe it was a stranger, a burglar, who broke in—no, no forced entry. And why would Tina let a burglar in?

"Okay," Tru said. "You can go."

"Really?"

"Yeah."

She stood up, headed for the door, then stopped. "Are you gonna find out who killed her?"

"Yes," he said, "yes I am."

She nodded shortly and left.

Moments later the door open and Danny Leaphorn came in.

"Standing Hawk out there?" Tru asked.

"Said he'd wait for you in the parking lot. I guess he figures you're done."

Tru looked at the monitors. They switched feeds every ten seconds or so. He watched and saw Standing Hawk out in one of the parking lots, waiting. As Tru watched, the man patted his pocket, then took the makings out and began to roll a cigarette.

The feed switched.

"Hey," Leaphorn asked, "didn't you want to talk to Eddie?"

"Does he smoke?" Tru asked.

"Huh? Yeah, he does."

"You know his brand?"

"Camels," the man said. "Won't smoke filters, and too damn lazy to roll his own. You wanna talk to him?

"No," Tru said, "I think I've seen enough. Can I make a call?"

Out in the parking lot the tribal cop flicked his cigarette away when he spotted Tru. He took a round tin of tobacco from his back pocket and put a hunk in his mouth, started to chew.

"Where to?"

"Time to go back to the station," Tru said. "You can drop me."

"You sure?"

"Yeah," Tru said. As he followed Standing Hawk to his car Tru very quickly bent and picked up the cigarette butt. "I've seen enough," he said, again.

10

Tru could tell by the scenery that Standing Hawk was not driving them to the police station but to his sister's house. When they got there the tribal cop pulled into the driveway and turned off the engine.

"We've got to talk," he said and got out.

Tru sat where he was, looked around the inside of the car. Unlike most police cars he'd been in, there were no weapons available. He got out.

Standing Hawk was pacing in front of the house. Tru could see the outline of the tobacco can etched into the right rear picket of his jeans. The man was probably a long time smoker and chewer, and couldn't control either habit while standing outside his sister's back door. Standing Hawk's gun was still in his holster.

"What happened, Standing Hawk?" Tru asked.

"My father died," Standing Hawk said. "My family was falling apart. I had to bring Tina back, with her children, and then it would've been all right."

"But she said no."

"She wanted nothing to do with me," he said.

"So you kept at her, harassing her, until that night, when you came here and waited outside the back door, smoking and chewing."

"She finally let me in," he said. "It got out of hand. We argued, I don't even know how, but the gun was in her hand. She told me to get out or she'd shoot me. Me! Her own brother! With my father gone I'm the head of my family. And she was threatening to shoot me."

"So you grabbed for the gun, there was a struggle? What?"

"No struggle," he said. "I-I did grab the gun from her, but then . . . I shot her."

"Just like that?"

"No!" Standing Hawk stopped pacing, faced Tru. "Not just like that. For a moment I thought someone else had shot her, but . . . but it was me. How . . .how could I shoot my own sister?"

"Why don't we go and talk to Trooper Holmsby, Standing—"

"No." The tribal policeman drew his gun, finally. "You figured it out. I knew you did. When you picked up that cigarette in the parking lot?"

"Well, you did leave one behind the house, along with a couple of patches of tobacco juice."

"Damn it!"

"What are you going to do now, Standing Hawk? Kill me? Kill a cop? Well, a retired cop."

Standing Hawk flexed his hand on his Ruger.

"I don't know," he said. "Let me think."

"No time to think, Standing Hawk," Tru said. "The time to think was when you were pointing a gun at your sister, not me. Now you just have to lower it, or Trooper Holmsby will have to shoot you."

"W-what?"

Tru inclined his head to his right. Standing Hawk looked, saw the trooper in a shooter's stance, aiming his service weapon at him.

"Sorry, Standing Hawk," the trooper said, "but you're under arrest."

It took only a moment, but Standing Hawk lowered his gun.

Three days later Trooper Holmsby and Truxton Lewis were sitting on the patio of the Lawford house, beers in hand.

"You took a big chance calling me from the casino," Holmsby said. "What if he hadn't taken you to the house?"

"But he did," Tru said. "You got him."

"Yeah, but only because he broke down and confessed while I was listening."

"You had the DNA on the cigarette and tobacco juice."

"He could've just said he left it there when he went to see his sister. And he could have just admitted to buying her the gun. That would have explained the prints. We'd have nothing."

"And if he'd just stayed away and not tried to play the grieving brother he might have gotten away with it, too. Or maybe the guilt would have eaten him up and eventually he would have confessed. What does it matter? You've got him."

Holmsby pointed with the beer bottle. "You bucked the house edge and got lucky."

"Why *did* he get her the gun, though?"

"He did it a long time ago," Holmsby said. "For her protection. Ironic, huh?"

Tru took a long drink from the bottle of beer.

Bucked the guilt edge, and got lucky.

The Listening Room

1

The best way for Truxton Lewis to warm up on a frigid January night in St. Louis was to experience some hot jazz at a new club called The Listening Room. Located on Del Mar, in the heart of University City, the club had been operating for only a month and was owned by an old friend of his from his police department days.

The invitation had been extended to Tru Lewis from opening night on, but this was his first actual visit to the club. He was there because it was cold outside and hot inside, but also because the owner, Billy Danvers, had called him and asked him to come.

Tru had gotten the call that morning on his cell phone, while he was having breakfast in his new house in Bourbon, Missouri. . . .

"Hey, Tru?"

He recognized Billy's voice immediately, because it had a distinctive timber to it. Billy Danvers always had a great speaking voice. Rich in timber, some women even called it beautiful. Because of that Billy had always wanted to be a singer—specifically, a jazz singer—but the problem was that when he opened his mouth to sing nothing beautiful ever came out.

"Billy?"

"Yep," Danvers said, "it's me."

"I've been meaning to come to your club, but—"

"That's why I'm callin', Tru," Billy said, cutting him off. "I know I invited you to come to the club and listen, but now I need you to come so I can talk to you. I'm havin' some problems, man."

"What kind of problems, Billy?"

"The kind you can help me with," Danvers said. "You were always the best cop I ever knew, Tru."

"So this is serious."

"Very serious. Can you come to the club tonight?"

"I'll be there, Billy. What time?"

"Come for the nine p.m. set and we'll talk after. I'm leavin' your name at the door and everything's comped."

"That's not necessary, Billy," Tru said, "but I'll be there."

"Thanks, Tru. It means a lot to me."

"I'll see you tonight," Truxton said.

For Truxton Lewis the best thing about Bourbon, Missouri was that it had only about 1,380 people, give or take ten. For a man who liked his privacy, this was a good size for a town to be. He'd house-sat a four-bedroom, two-and-a-half bath with a finished basement and two-car garage for about two weeks a few months back, and had fallen in love with the town. The people who had built this house had also liked Bourbon for its size. However, the home they had constructed seemed grossly out of place in a small city where the mean value of a home was fifty thousand dollars. This house had to have cost a bundle to build, and when they decided to sell it they'd no doubt be asking close to one-fifty.

But for Tru Lewis, Bourbon was a haven, a place to hang his hat when he wasn't traveling around the country. House-sitting was a profession—no, more of a pastime—Truxton Lewis had taken on after the death of his wife of thirty years and his retirement from the New York City Police Department after twenty-seven. His daughter didn't like the new venture her father had taken up, and she'd liked it even less when he announced he was moving to Missouri.

The bad thing about Bourbon was that it was seventy-five miles from St. Louis. That didn't sound like a lot, but while Truxton Lewis enjoyed travel he detested driving. His preferred mode of transportation was walking and, being from New York, he'd always made the best use of public transportation. He used to enjoy flying but that had ceased to be fun even before the 9/11 debacle in New York. Too many families with kids, or hockey teams or glee clubs or the idiots who went on spring break. Also bad meals—or meals of peanuts and pretzels—served by a surly "flight attendant." He longed for the days of real meals served by pretty and attentive "stewardesses."

But those days were gone, and if he was going to go into St. Louis to The Listening Room, he was going to have to drive. Upon his arrival in Missouri two months ago he'd purchased a used Toyota just to use locally. Any extensive traveling he would do would still be done by train or—when the need arose—by plane. Even more locally, in Bourbon, he'd walk.

He drove into St. Louis, taking I-44, and found his way to University City. He still didn't know St. Louis that well, and in fact had only been to the city a few times since moving to Bourbon. The small-town life had been what he'd been looking for when he left New York. The big city held too many memories of his wife, and at sixty-three he was looking to start over again.

He had a computer in his small one-bedroom house which he'd gotten for a song—the house, not the computer—and had used MapQuest to get directions to the club. The Listening Room had a small parking lot and he claimed one of the remaining spots available and went inside.

The ambience was dark and warm as he stepped inside and gave his name to the man who was covering the door, clad in a tuxedo.

"Yes, sir, Mr. Lewis," he said, "we have your name right here. Will you be dining tonight?"

"No," Tru said, "I'm just here for the music." He'd had a fast-food dinner along the highway. Junk food was something else his daughter didn't approve of. Tru had eaten a lot of it as a street cop but had gotten away from it as a detective. Now, later in life, he was starting to eat it again and was finding it much better than the first time around, cholesterol be damned.

The man turned and lifted his hand and a twentyish waitress appeared, very pretty in a crisp white shirt and black skirt.

"Amy will show you to your table," the man said. "Enjoy the show."

"Thank you."

He followed the waitress's saucy butt to his table, feeling his age as he did around girls her age.

"Would you like a drink?" she asked.

"Yes," he said, "beer. Whatever you have on tap that's local."

"That would be Schlafley's."

"Fine. What time does the show start?"

"Nine on the dot."

"And how long does it run?"

"Usually sixty to seventy minutes, depending the performer."

"Okay, thank you."

"Mr. Danvers says you're comped, so if you want anything else just let me know."

"I will, Amy. Thanks."

She smiled and flounced away while Tru watched, feeling like a dirty old man.

2

Truxton took a moment to look the club over. It was a good-sized room with space between the tables. He knew some places would have pushed the tables closer together and sacrificed privacy for volume. He was glad his friend had chosen to go this way. The walls were dark wood, the tables were solid, with white cloths on them. When Amy came back with his beer it was in a traditional tapered glass, the way Tru liked it. So far he didn't see Billy Danvers skimping anywhere. Next time, he vowed, he'd sample the food. Tonight he was wondering what kind of problems Billy was having, and that would have interfered with his enjoyment of food.

As for the entertainment, he had never before heard of the woman who was singing, but she was good. He'd find out from Danvers if she was well known. As far as jazz was concerned, he knew the historical names Boots and Bird and Chet Baker. Of the new artists, he only knew Harry Connick Jr. and Diana Krall. As for instrumentalists, his knowledge was limited to Kenny G and Candy Dulfer.

He was on his second drink by the time the lights went down and the woman came on stage. The stage was close, the room intimate. She had a piano player, a base player and a drummer. At one point she even replaced the piano player for a couple of songs. She was good, entertaining, not spectacular.

As she started a new song, someone touched his shoulder from behind. He turned and looked into the face of his waitress.

"Mr. Danvers said I should send you back when she started her last song."

"Oh, okay."

"Follow me."

He tried not to watch her tush while he followed her but then thought, "What the hell, I'm not dead."

"It's the door at the end of the hall."

He walked to the end of the hall, past several other doors, and knocked on the office door. When there was no answer he turned to look behind him, but Amy had moved on already. He knocked again, and when there was no answer tried the doorknob. It turned, so he opened the door and walked in.

"Billy—" he said, but that was far as he got because the man seated at the desk in the leather chair had a silver letter opener sticking out of his chest. There was very little blood, but that didn't matter.

He was dead.

Truxton turned and hurried back down the hall. There was a good chance the murderer was still in the building and he knew that after the singer finished her last song people would start to leave.

He went to the front to the man who had let him in and grabbed his arm.

"Wha—"

"Your boss is dead," Tru said. "Somebody killed him. You can't let anybody leave, and you have to call nine-one-one."

"What the hell—who are you?"

Tru did something he didn't like to do. He took out his badge, which had the abbreviation "Ret." on it, but lots of people wouldn't notice that, and the doorman was one of them.

"Call nine-one-one, tell them a man's been murdered and give them the address."

"Jesus," the man said, "Mr. Danvers—"

"Yes," Tru said, "Billy Danvers, your boss, is dead. Now make the call—and remember, nobody leaves!"

"But how do I keep them all here?"

"You have bouncers, don't you?"

"Well . . . yeah, but—"

"Place them at the door," Tru said. "I don't care what it takes. Nobody leaves."

3

Tru went back to the office to wait and that's where he was when the cops arrived. First he had to deal with the uniforms. He showed them his badge and they agreed to let him remain at the door of the room while one of them waited inside with the body and the other waited outside for the detectives.

"You might want to call for some backup. You'll need help keeping the crowd inside."

"Yes, sir," one of them said, "we intend to do that."

The detectives were next, a mismatched pair of men named Helmuth and Cloutier.

Helmuth, the younger, had an attitude. Cloutier, in his fifties, with a head of steel-gray hair, looked at Truxton's badge closely.

"Retired?" he asked.

"Captain of Detective," Tru said.

Cloutier nodded and handed the badge back.

"Fill me in on the victim."

The body would not be moved until the M.E. arrived, so there was time.

"Billy Danvers. I knew him in New York. We were both cops together, came out of the academy together. He retired before I did, even though he's younger. He's always loved jazz and decided to become involved in that world. I don't know all that he's done in the past ten years, but it brought him here, to St. Louis, and to this club."

"And to this," Cloutier said, looking at the body behind the desk.

"That's a fairly heavy-duty letter opener," Tru said; "it must have taken a lot of strength to plunge it into his chest."

"You're thinking a man?"

"Or a hefty woman."

"Did you see any hefty women in the club tonight?" Cloutier asked.

"I'm afraid I was either looking at the woman on stage, or my waitress's butt."

"Can't blame you there," Helmuth said, with a smirk. "Probably all an old coot like you can do now is look, huh?"

Tru ignored the man, but the remark seemed to anger his partner.

"Go out front and wait for the M.E., Phil."

"Why do I have to—"

"Just go!"

Helmuth made an annoyed noise and left the office.

"I'm sorry," Cloutier said, "he's young."

"I took that into account when he made the remark."

"You're more understanding than I am."

"I'm older."

"Not by much."

Cloutier turned back to the body. He and Tru were alone in the office. He started studying the photos on the walls.

"That's Bill Withers," he said, pointing, "and that's Lou Rawls. And Diana Krall! Are these photos genuine?"

They were framed and hanging on the wall, photos of Danvers with famous jazz artists. Cloutier examined the rest of the photos while Truxton looked around the room. He noticed the room smelled of something—freshener, or disinfectant. On the floor were two cigarettes, smoked halfway down and squashed flat.

"I can't say for sure," Tru said, "but knowing Billy I'd bet they were. It was his dream to meet those people, so I guess he did."

"Wouldn't mind meeting them myself," Cloutier said.

He turned around suddenly and looked at Tru.

"I'm sorry," he said. "You've lost a friend and I'm talking about jazz."

"I hadn't seen him in five or six years, I think," Tru said. "I'm kind of . . . numb about the whole thing. We were friends in that we worked together for a while, but we certainly weren't close."

"You said he called and said he had a problem you could help him with?"

"That's right."

"He didn't say what it was?"

"Only that I could help because I was an ex-cop."

"He was an ex-cop," Cloutier said. "I wonder why he couldn't help himself?"

"I never got the chance to ask," Tru said. "I wish I'd insisted on seeing him as soon as I arrived. Maybe he'd still be alive."

"Can't berate yourself, Captain," Cloutier said. "How were you to know?"

"Not Captain," Truxton said. "You can call me Tru."

"Unusual name, Truxton."

"My parents were unusual people."

Helmuth stuck his head in the door and said with attitude, "M.E.'s here. Should I let him in?"

"We're waiting for him, aren't we, Phil?"

Helmuth withdrew without reply. Moments later an older man— older than Truxton—entered and raised bushy eyebrows at the body.

"Oh my," the M.E. said.

"Doctor Doyle, this is Captain Lewis, retired from the New York

City Police Department. He's a friend of the deceased, found the body."

"Bad business," the doctor said. "I'm sorry for you."

"Thanks."

The doctor went to the desk and performed a brief examination of the body.

"Looks like the letter opened went right through the heart. He died instantly, not much blood." He turned and looked at Cloutier. "Can I have him?"

"If you're done with him here, so am I," Cloutier said.

"I'll have my boys come in and bag him."

"Let's get out of the way," Cloutier said to Truxton. "I've got to start questioning people. You want to sit in?"

"Why not?"

They started down the hall together. Tru noticed that two of the doors he'd passed earlier went to rest rooms—men's and women's. Another door was unmarked.

"You mind if I open this?" he asked Cloutier.

"No, go ahead."

Tru opened the door and both men looked inside. It was a closet, with a broom, mop, bucket and room for a person or two.

"Think somebody waited in here for a chance at him?" Cloutier asked.

"No," Tru said, closing the door.

"Why not?"

"Because somebody waiting to kill him would have brought their own weapon," Tru said. "A letter opened, that's a weapon of opportunity."

"So you think this was unplanned?"

"Yes, I do," Tru said. "This looks like a spur-of-the-moment killing. Maybe there was an argument, maybe the person felt threatened, grabbed the letter opener . . ." Tru shrugged.

"Is there a back door, I wonder?"

"I don't know."

They continued back into the club, where people were sitting, and milling about, waiting impatiently to be allowed to go home. The singer and her group were seated on the stage, and she was smoking impatiently.

"We'll have to split them up, Phil," Cloutier said. "You question the staff, I'll start on the patrons. You can help me with them when you're done."

"What about the musicians?" Truxton asked.

"We'll treat them as staff, I guess."

"Why don't I pitch in and help?" Tru asked. "I'll question them."

"You don't have any authority here—" Helmuth started to say, but Cloutier cut him off.

"No, that's okay," he said. "We can use the help."

"You're in charge," Helmuth said.

"I'll take the heat, Phil," Cloutier said. "Why don't you get started."

"Fine," Helmuth said, and walked away.

"He might be right," Tru said. "Maybe I should just take a seat—"

"No, it's my call," Cloutier said, "and we're shorthanded. Go ahead, do it."

"Okay, thanks."

Cloutier went off to start questioning patrons. Tru knew the detective would question them, then take their names and addresses and send them home. Once everybody was gone, Billy Danvers's murder was going to be harder to solve.

He walked up to the stage where the singer was squashing a cigarette out in an ashtray. On the floor were two half-smoked cigarettes, squashed flat. Tru looked up at the four people on the stage—the singer, the pianist, the bass layer, and the drummer. Sometimes, he thought, it's a matter of where you look. Cloutier had been looking at the pictures on the wall, not at the floor. Not at the scene.

"My name is Truxton Lewis," he said to the quartet. "I'm . . . working with the police."

The singer looked at him. Up close he could see how heavy her makeup was. She also looked more fifty than forty this close up.

"You were in the audience," she said.

"Yes," he said. "I heard most of your set." For a moment he felt that he still couldn't recall her name.

"Carla Jenkins," she said, smiling. "You were trying to remember my name."

"I'm sorry."

"Don't be." She turned and pointed to the musicians. "Hal Joseph, Dave Malden, and the bass player is Vic Cantone."

Truxton nodded to all three men. Hal, the drummer, was grayhaired, fiftyish, wearing a T-shirt and jeans. Vic was a young man, early thirties, wearing a suit and tie. Dave Malden looked forty, might have been fifty, was delicately built, probably didn't weigh one-fifty.

He had a sports jacket over a shirt buttoned to the neck. The other two men were over six feet.

"I heard the owner was murdered. Are we suspects?" Carla Jenkins asked.

"At this point everyone is suspect."

"With him dead we may not get paid for this gig," she pointed out.

"That might not matter to the killer."

She laughed and said, "Matters to me."

"Who does the negotiating?" Tru asked.

"I do," Carla said. "I'm the headliner. The guys back me up."

"So you were in the office at some point?"

"Of course," she said. "That's where one does the negotiating."

"And none of you fellas have been in the office?"

"Nope."

"Never."

"Not me."

Truxton bent over and picked up the cigarettes from the floor of the small stage.

"Whose are these?" he asked.

"Not mine," Jenkins said, indicating the one she had just lit. "Mine are in the ash tray."

"They're mine," Hal, the drummer, said. "What about it? It's not a non-smoking building, is it?"

"They're only smoked halfway down."

"I'm tryin' to quit."

"He smokes 'em exactly halfway," the woman said. "Doesn't want to miss a drag."

"Sit tight," Truxton said to them. "You might be able to go home soon."

"What about getting paid?" Carla Jenkins asked.

"I can't help you with that."

He didn't bother pointing out that only three of them might be going home.

4

There were four flattened cigarettes sitting on top of Billy Danvers's desk. "These two," Truxton said to Detective Cloutier, "I took from the floor of the stage. These two, I took off of this floor."

"You brought us in here to show us cigarettes?" Helmuth asked.

"Very special cigarettes," Truxton said. He directed his comment to Cloutier, who was more receptive. "Two things you've got to know about Billy Danvers. He was a clean freak. Can you smell it in here?"

Cloutier sniffed the air. "Cleaning solution of some kind."

"Right. I found two of these cigarettes right here on the floor in front of his desk. No way he'd leave those here."

"If he saw them," Cloutier said.

"Right."

"So chances are he was dead when whoever stomped out these cigarettes left the room."

"Chances are."

"But it's not certain," Helmuth said.

"Not at all," Truxton said, "but like I said, I found these other two cigarettes on the stage."

"Who smoked 'em?" Cloutier asked.

"The drummer."

"Don't mean he killed anybody," Helmuth said. "Just means he was in here."

"You're right," Tru said, "but all three of those men told me they weren't in here."

"So he lied," Cloutier said.

"He lied." Tru also told the detectives what he knew about the drummer—Hal Joseph—trying to quit smoking.

"So me smokes 'em all down to exactly the same place," Cloutier said.

"That's right."

The older detective turned to Helmuth.

"Bring the drummer in here," he said. "Let's see what he has to say for himself."

Helmuth, looking unhappy about it, said, "Yeah, okay."

After he left, Cloutier passed a hand over his face and said, "I gotta retire. I missed those cigarettes."

"Could have happened to anyone."

"You got any idea why I agreed to let you help here?" the man asked.

"Crossed my mind."

"It's 'cause I'm losin' it, and I know it," Cloutier said. "Oh, I'm not sayin' I'm a bad detective. I've had my day, but I just don't have a taste for it anymore."

Truxton didn't know what to say, and he was saved from saying something trite when Helmuth walked in with Hal Joseph.

"Have a seat, Mr. Joseph. My name is Detective Cloutier, this is my partner Detective Helmuth. I believe you've already met Mr. Lewis."

"What's this all about?"

Cloutier hesitated, then said, "I'll let Mr. Lewis answer that, since he's the one who spoke to you earlier."

"Is he a cop?" Joseph asked.

"He used to be."

"Then I don't have to talk to him, do I?" the drummer asked.

"Uh, yes, you do," Cloutier said. "Sit down. Phil, close that door."

Helmuth closed it and put his back to it.

"Truxton?" Cloutier said.

Tru, unprepared for Cloutier to hand the play over to him, stepped forward.

"Mr. Joseph, you told me you'd never been in this office."

"Did I say that?"

"Yes, you did," Tru said, "and yet I found these cigarettes on the floor tonight—smoked halfway down, and crushed under foot."

"Lots of people crush cigarettes out under their feet," Joseph said. "Doesn't mean a thing."

"Are you still maintaining that you've never been in this office?"

The drummer hesitated, coughed into his hand, then said, "Okay, well, so maybe I've been in here before."

"Maybe you were in here tonight," Truxton said.

"Maybe," Cloutier said, stepping forward, "you stabbed Billy Danvers with this letter opener and killed him."

The detective held the letter opened in his hand, in a plastic bag. It was the first time Truxton had seen it out of Billy's chest. It had a heavy blade and a leather handle. A fancy instrument with which to open letters—and sturdy enough to kill.

Joseph stared at the letter opener in Cloutier's hand and said, "No."

"Then why don't you tell us what you were doing in here earlier tonight, Mr. Joseph," Truxton said.

"Look," Joseph said, "look . . . I didn't kill him. Okay, we had a little, uh, argument."

"About what?"

"Money."

"He owe you," Truxton asked, "or did you owe him?"

The man squirmed uncomfortably.

"Look," he said, "this goes back a ways. Billy used to be involved with a record label that I recorded on."

"How far back are we going?" Tru asked.

"Ten years, maybe more," Joseph said. "He . . . lost the job because he got caught with his hand in the cookie jar."

"And some of the cookies were yours?" Cloutier asked.

"Huh? Oh, yeah, right. I was playing with a trio at the time and we felt he stole some money that belonged to us."

"So you thought you'd get it back from him tonight?" Truxton asked. "Is that why you took this job?"

"Yeah," he said. "When Carla called me and told me about this, she told me who the owner was. I figured I could get some of the money back from him. I—I'm not doin' as well as I once was."

"And how did you figure you'd get the money back?" Tru asked. "Just by asking nicely?"

"Well . . . he owns his own club. I figured he had to have some money somewhere."

"So you asked him for it?"

"Sonofabitch said he didn't remember me," Joseph said. "But he did. He bitched about me smoking in his office, so I lit up two cigarettes just to piss him off."

"Not exactly the right way to go when you're asking for money, was it?" Cloutier asked.

"He'd already said no," Joseph said. "He told me he wasn't about to pay a debt he didn't remember."

"And then what?" Tru asked.

"And then I . . . left his office."

"And he was alive?" Cloutier asked.

"Sittin' right there," Joseph said, indicating the chair the dead man had been in.

"Mr. Joseph," Truxton said, "I think there's something you're not telling us."

"Huh? Like what?"

"Where do you live?"

"Baltimore."

"You want us to believe you came all the way here from Baltimore to ask Billy Danvers for the money he stole from you, and when he refused to give it to you, you just walked out of his office?"

"That's what happened," Joseph said, "but I also came here for the gig. Carla calls me to play drums for her most of the time."

Cloutier looked at Truxton, obviously wondering what he had in mind. Helmuth, still leaning against the door with his arms folded, rolled his eyes.

"I think," Truxton said, "that since you feel certain Billy was skimming money from the record label you were signed with, that when he refused to give you any money you threatened him."

"Wha—no."

"I think you threatened to ruin his reputation here in St. Louis, which he couldn't afford since this club has only been open a month."

"Blackmail?" Cloutier said. Tru looked at him and nodded. "That makes sense," the detective said. He looked at Hal Joseph. "What about it? You want to cop to some attempted blackmail now so we don't find out about it later, when it'll really look like a motive?"

"Motive?" Joseph asked. "If I was tryin' to blackmail him, wouldn't that give him the motive to try and kill me?"

"And did he?" Truxton asked. "Did he grab the letter opener and try to use it on you, so you had to defend yourself. Are you claiming self defense, Mr. Joseph?"

"N-no, I'm not," the drummer said. "Wait—"

"Wait for what, Mr. Joseph?" Cloutier asked. "Do you want a lawyer before you confess?"

"Confess? Wha—I'm not confessing."

"To what, Mr. Joseph?" Truxton asked. "Are you not confessing to murder, or to blackmail?"

"No, no, wait," the musician said, "you're confusing me. I am not confessing to murder."

"And what about blackmail?"

"Okay, okay," Joseph said, "I may have told him I was gonna spread it around town that he was a thief."

"If what?"

"If he didn't pay me."

"How much?"

"Ten thousand."

"Is that what you think he owed you?" Truxton asked.

"I—no, I figured . . . you know . . . with interest . . ."

"If it's ten grand with interest, then it couldn't have really been much ten years ago, could it?" Truxton asked.

"It was the principal," Joseph said. "He shouldn't have stole anything!"

"So you made him pay the hard way, right?" Helmuth asked,

springing away from the door. He grabbed the baggie containing the murder weapon from his partner's hand and waved it under Hal Joseph's nose. "You made him pay with his life!"

"No!"

"Come on, Joseph," Cloutier said. "Your cigarettes are on the floor, and I'll bet your fingerprints will be on the letter opener."

Suddenly, the man looked stricken. "Wait," he said, "wait . . . when I first came in and sat he . . . he asked me to hand him the letter opener."

"So you're saying your prints are on it," Truxton said.

"Well . . . yeah, I guess . . . b-but I never took it back from him. He held it the whole time."

"Did he ever threaten you with it?" Truxton asked.

"N-no—"

"Not even after you tried to blackmail him?"

"N-no, he never threatened me."

"You're full of shit, Joseph!" Helmuth said. He threw the plastic encased letter opener onto the desk. "You're saying he never threatened you because that way you had no reason to defend yourself."

"Back off, Phil," Cloutier said.

"This asshole's lying'," Helmuth said. "He did it."

"Maybe," Cloutier said, "but if the three of us keep yellin' at him he's not gonna be able to get a word in edgewise. Back off."

Reluctantly, Helmuth backed away.

"Why don't we three step outside and give the man time to think," Truxton suggested.

"Good idea," Cloutier said. "There's no other way out of here, anyway. Take five, Mr. Joseph. We'll be right back."

"Can I smoke?" the man asked.

"I think you've done enough damage to your credibility with your smoking, Mr. Joseph," Truxton said. "Try to hold off."

The three detectives left the room together after Truxton started to make a move for the desk but was waved off by Cloutier shaking his head.

Out in the hall Truxton said, "What did we get from the staff?"

"Not much," Cloutier said. "No one saw anybody go back to the office during the show."

"Billy must have been dead before the set started," Truxton said.

"The M.E.'s guess at time of death would support that."

"Hey," Helmuth said, "ain't we givin' him a chance to tamper with evidence, leavin' him in there alone?"

"What evidence, Phil?" Cloutier asked.

"There was the body, which is gone, and the letter opener, which is—hey, where is it?"

"Don't worry, Phil," Cloutier said, "I've got—"

"Don't worry, hell!" Helmuth said. "He could be—" He cut himself off and charged into the room. Cloutier looked at Truxton, shrugged and they went in after him.

"He wiped it clean!" Helmuth said, looking down at the letter opened in the bag. "See? It ain't sealed."

"Prove it!" Hal Joseph said. "I didn't touch it."

"Mr. Joseph," Cloutier said, "this is the letter opener you handed to Billy Danvers?"

"Yeah? So?"

"Well, if your prints are not on it now," Truxton said, "that would mean that you wiped it clean while we were in the hall. Why would you do that if you're not guilty?"

Hal Joseph looked trapped.

"I—I—oh, all right!" he said, finally. "I did it to protect Carla."

"Carla Jenkins?" Tru asked. "The singer?"

"That's right."

"You're sayin' the singer killed him with the letter opener?" Cloutier asked.

"That's what she told me," Joseph said. "She said they argued—Billy tried to put the moves on her, or something, I don't know—but they argued and she stabbed him."

"And he fell into the chair," Cloutier said.

"That's what she said," Joseph said. "I'm tellin' you. When you guys went outside I wiped off the letter opener to protect her."

"That's real noble of you Hal," Cloutier said, "except for one thing."

"What's that?"

Cloutier picked up the baggie with the letter opener and let the weapon drop out onto the desk.

"What're ya doin'—" Helmuth started.

"This isn't the murder weapon," Cloutier said. He took a baggie from his pocket with a silver letter opener in it—the one Truxton had seen sticking out of Billy Danvers's chest—and said, "This is."

"Wha—" Helmuth said.

"W-what? What?" Joseph stammered.

"I found that one in the desk drawer, and stuck it in a baggie," Cloutier said. "I wanted to see if you'd take the first opportunity to clean it off. See, now that you've told us that Carla Jenkins killed him, and all you did was touch the letter opener once to hand it to Billy Danvers, there should be three sets of prints on the murder weapon— the dead man's, yours and hers." Cloutier leaned over so his face was inches from Hal Joseph's. "If there's only two sets of prints—yours and his, and not hers—what do you think that means?"

"I—I-maybe she cleaned it."

"You're the killer, Hal," Truxton said, "and you didn't have time to clean the murder weapon. Or maybe you couldn't bring yourself to do it while it was sticking out of Billy's chest. Either way, the fingerprints will tell the story—and so will Carla."

"She'll lie! She'll say she didn't do it."

"You're the one who's lying, Hal," Cloutier said. He looked at Helmuth. "Cuff him and take him out."

Helmuth did as he was told, pouting the whole time that he hadn't been let in on the letter opener switch.

"I thought you said you lost your taste for this," Truxton said. "That was a nice trick, switching the letter openers."

"You noticed right away, didn't you?"

"I knew the one sticking out of his chest had a silver handle. What if Joseph had remembered that, too?"

"I think we'll find out that the murder wasn't premeditated, and was probably a result of him trying to blackmail Danvers. They probably fought—whatever. I banked on him being flustered and not remembering the letter opener."

"Well, it was a good trick."

"You placed him in the room with those cigarettes," Cloutier said. "All I did was give him a chance to hang himself."

"When did you make a switch?"

"Right after the M.E. left and gave me the weapon. When I saw the second one I thought it might come in handy."

The left the room and walked down the hall together. Hal Joseph was already outside in a police car. Truxton looked at the stage and saw that Carla Jenkins was still smoking, and the other two men were staring off at the front of the club. They had to have seen Joseph being led out in cuffs.

"Should we tell them they'll need a new drummer?" Cloutier asked.

"I think they know."

"Do you think Danvers called you about the blackmail?"

"Couldn't have," Truxton said. "The call came this morning, before Joseph tried it."

"What then?"

Truxton looked around The Listening Room, wondering what would happen to the place now. "I guess we'll never know."

The Hook

1

Denver, 1899
George's Weekly

> *Normally, this is a sports column, but something has happened in this city and no one seems to be doing anything. Three women have been killed on the streets of Denver and the police department seems to be unable—or unwilling—to do anything about it. All citizens of Denver—decent and otherwise-have a right to be able to walk the streets in peace and safety. The Old West—they keep telling me—is gone. The Twentieth Century is upon us, and yet these young women are dead and the killer is still at large. Shame on you, Chief Flaherty, and shame on the Mayor. . . .*

The banging on the door woke Bat, who reached out for Emma only to find her gone. This was not unusual. She often rose before he did, as she often retired before him. If she was up, she would answer the door, and would not allow anyone to disturb him unless it was . . .

"Bat?" she said, softly. "It's the police."

When Bat entered Chief Flaherty's office there was only one other man there, seated in front of the Chief's desk. Flaherty's normally florid face was redder than ever as he told the police officer who had delivered Bat, "You can go."

"What's this all about, Chief?" Bat asked. "I don't usually get up this early in the—"

"Masterson," Flaherty said, cutting him off, "this is Inspector House. Inspector, Bat Masterson."

House stood up and turned to face Bat. He had a genial grin as he extended his hand and said, "Quite a column in today's paper."

"Oh," Bat said, accepting the younger man's extended hand, "so that's what this is about."

"That's right, Masterson," Flaherty said. "Since you think the Denver police are so inept, I'm gonna accept your offer of help in this case."

"I didn't offer—"

"Or I'm gonna toss your ass in jail for obstructing the investigation."

"I didn't obstruct—"

"One or the other," Flaherty said. "The choice is yours."

Bat could see that the Police Chief was deadly serious. It had been a few years since he'd seen the inside of a cell, and his recent spate of soft living had not left him in shape to handle the food.

George's Weekly was owned and edited by Herbert George, who was so thrilled to have the likes of Bat writing for his paper that he allowed the western legend to cover any subject he wanted. Ostensibly a sports columnist, on this morning Bat was berating the Denver police for their inability to track down and capture the man who had, in recent months, killed three women on the streets of Denver. Two were what polite society called "decent" women, and the third was what that same group referred to as "fallen." To Bat Masterson, whether the women were somebody's wife or a street whore didn't matter.

Actually, it did matter to Bat. The person it didn't matter to was his wife, Emma. She was the one who was particularly upset about the murders, since she and her friends no longer felt safe on the streets.

"It's the job of the police to catch this maniac, isn't it?" she'd asked him yesterday morning while he dressed.

"Yes, dear."

"And they're not doing their job, are they?"

"No, dear."

"Well then, somebody should light a fire under their asses, shouldn't they?" she demanded.

"Yes, dear." Bat wasn't surprised at his wife's language. When they'd met she had been performing on stage at the Palace Theater, which at the time he'd owned (and had since sold). Stage people, he'd found, often "salted" their language.

"Somebody with the public's ear," she finished, and stared at him.

It suddenly became clear that she was talking about him, so he fixed his tie, turned to her, kissed her cheek and said, "Yes, dear."

He'd written the column, half expecting that Herbert George would not run it.

But he did. . . .

Bat sighed. "I guess you got yourself a volunteer, Chief."

"Excellent," Flaherty said. "House has been working on the case, so he will catch you up on what's been going on. I think you two should work well together."

"Shall we go?" House asked, standing up.

Bat stood and said, "Lead the way."

"Oh, and one more thing," Flaherty said before they reached the door. "When this thing blows up it ain't gonna be blowin' up in my face. It's gonna be your faces. You two got that?"

"Got it," Bat sad.

"Yessir," House said.

The two men left the office.

2

"I don't get it," House said, out in the hall.

"What is there to get?"

"You're Bat Masterson," House said. "Why would you agree to this just because of some threats from our blowhard police chief?"

"Are you married, son?"

"No sir."

"Then you wouldn't understand."

Inspector House led Bat to an office and closed the door behind them.

"Have a seat."

The detective walked around and sat behind his desk. On it were three folders. He put his hand on them.

"Want to read them, or do you want me to tell you what we have?" he asked.

Bat sat across from the man. "Just tell me."

"How much do you know?"

"Only what I read in the newspapers."

House sat back in his chair. "Well, forget everything you read," he said. "It's all false."

"Why?"

"We've kept the truth to ourselves."

"And has that helped?"

"No."

"All right," Bat said, settling back in his chair, "tell me what you've got."

"We reported that the three women were robbed and murdered," House said. "We deliberately left out the method that was used to kill them. Because of that, all these 'Jack the Ripper' rumors have started."

Bat had the good grace to experience some chagrin. He had, after all, mentioned Jack the Ripper to Herbert George only yesterday.

"And were they killed the same way Jack the Ripper's victims were?" he asked.

"Not at all," House said.

"So how were they killed?"

"We don't know," House said.

"What does that mean?"

"It means there was no sign of violence on them," House said. "They were just . . . dead."

"Natural causes?" Bat asked. "All three?"

"No," House said. "They had to have been killed. They were dumped where they were found. Somebody killed them, we just don't know how."

"It's impossible to kill somebody and not leave a mark on them," Bat said. "Where were they found?"

"Different parts of the city," House said, "but the odd thing is . . . the family of the third woman."

"What about them?"

"Well . . . she was found down by the docks," the Inspector said. "They claim she never would have gone down there."

"Why not?"

"She wouldn't have reason to," House explained, "and she was afraid."

"So maybe a man took her there?"

"They say no," the Inspector said. "She was married. Her husband can't explain what she was doing down there."

"How old was she?"

"Twenty-eight."

"Happily married?"

"By all accounts."

"Where were the other women found, exactly?"

"One was found in a Market Street alley, another at the train station."

"The train station? Where?"

"Behind one of the buildings."

"It sounds like all these girls were . . . discarded."

"Yes."

Bat sat and thought a moment. It was actually a smart move for Flaherty to bring in someone with a fresh perspective. He was just sorry it had been him.

House went on to explain how he had conducted his investigation, and how he had come up with nothing concrete to point to the killer.

"The women were all in their twenties," he said, "but that's the only similarity. The first was a whore, the second an old maid and the third happily married."

"Old maid? How old?"

"Twenty-nine. Not attractive. No prospects."

"What about the other two and where they were found?" Bat asked.

"Not unusual," House said. "The whore was the one found behind the train station. She could have been doing some business there."

"And the second woman? Was she known to frequent the area where she was found?"

"Not frequent, but friends didn't find anything unusual about it."

"Where did she work?"

"The other end of town," House said, "near where she lived."

"So she was found a long way from either."

"Yes."

"I'm not a detective, but it still sounds like they were dumped, like human refuse. Were they killed where they were found?"

"Hard to tell."

Bat rubbed his face. He hadn't even had a cup of coffee yet.

"What else did the bodies tell you?"

"The bodies?"

"They were examined, weren't they?"

"Well, yes, but . . . I told you, they weren't attacked."

"Was anything done to them after they were dead?"

"What do you mean? Do you mean . . ." House looked horrified.

"People have done things to bodies after they're dead, Inspector. I'm sure you know that."

"Yes, well . . ."

"How about autopsies?" Bat asked. "Were the bodies autopsied?"

"Autopsied?"

"You do know what an autopsy is, don't you?"

"Well, yeah, I guess . . ."

Bat knew that Doctor George E. Goodfellow had conducted autopsies during the time he spent as coroner in Tombstone, Arizona. He also knew until the 1860s autopsies were pretty much confined to execution victims. But this was 1899, the dawn of a new century. Autopsies were being used to find cures for disease, why not use them to find out other things?

"Maybe an autopsy would tell us something we don't know," Bat said. "Where are the bodies?"

"Well . . . the third is at the morgue. She was only killed a few days ago. The others are . . . I assume they've been buried."

"We might have to dig them up."

"What? Oh, no, the families . . . the Chief wouldn't like—"

"The Chief volunteered me for this and I've come up with an idea nobody else had. He'll go along with it."

"But—"

Bat stood up. "Let's go ask him."

3

Chief Flaherty went along with it, but only to a point. He agreed that the third girl should be autopsied but held off any decision about the others until after that.

Now they needed to find a doctor who would do it. At that time Denver had no coroner and would not have until 1902.

"Get a doctor the same way you got me," Bat told Flaherty. "Volunteer one."

"I got a better idea," Flaherty said, and that's how it became Bat's job to come up with a doctor. But it was actually Emma Masterson who had a suggestion.

After Bat returned home and told Emma what had happened she said, "I have just the woman for you."

"Woman?" Bat asked. "A female doctor?"

She folded her arms across her bosom. "And what's wrong with a female doctor?"

"Emma, we're going to be asking her to cut open these women."

"Justina is a doctor, Bat," she said. "Cutting into a body is not going to frighten her."

"All right, all right," he said. "How do you know her?"

"I came across her delivering babies in my volunteer work," she said.

"Delivering babies? This is a long way from delivering babies."

"I told you, she's a doctor." Emma actually stamped her foot in frustration.

"All right," he said, again. "Since it's your fault I'm involved, I'm going to go with your suggestion. Where does this Doctor . . . whatsername live?"

"Doctor Justina Ford," Emma said. "She moved here only a few months ago to practice. She graduated from medical school earlier this year—don't you dare interrupt me again, Bat Masterson!"

The buggy pulled up in front of 1880 Gaylord Street and Bat and Inspector House stepped out.

"A lady doctor," House said to him, as they approached the door.

"Yes."

"Women are supposed to be nurses," the Inspector said, "not doctors."

"House, I've already gone through this with my wife," Bat said, the exasperation clear in his voice. "We need a doctor, right?"

"Right."

When a black woman answered the door Bat said, "We're here to see Doctor Ford. Would you tell her that we're here, please?"

"I am Doctor Ford," the woman said. "You must be Bat. Emma said you would be coming by to see me. Please, come in."

She turned and went inside, leaving them to follow her or not. Bat and House exchanged a glance. Both men were obviously taken aback by the fact that she was black.

They followed her inside, Bat first.

They found her in a modestly furnished living room. She was in her late twenties, her hair pulled back tightly, her skin very dark and smooth.

"My surgery is through there," she said, inclining her head toward a door, "but we can talk in here. Would either of you like refreshments?"

"No, ma'am," Bat said. "We might as well just get to it, Did Emma tell you what we wanted?"

"No. She just told me that you needed a doctor and she recommended me. What is it you need done, gentlemen?"

"An autopsy," Bat said.

"Just one?"

"At first," he said. "Maybe two more, but those victims are already buried."

She looked at House.

"You're a policeman?"

"Yes, ma'am," he said. "Inspector House."

"Then this is about the three women who have been killed?"

"Yes, ma'am."

"And autopsies have not yet been done?"

"No, ma'am," House said. "We, uh, didn't even think of it until Bat mentioned it."

"You would be paid by the city," Bat said.

"I'm not worried about that," she said. "If I can help catch this maniac I'm happy to do it. May I perform the autopsy at the St. Joseph's Hospital, on Franklin Street?"

"You can have it done anywhere you want, Doctor," Bat said. "We'll have the body brought there . . . when?"

"As soon as possible," she said. "Immediately, in fact. I'll go there now."

"We'll have the body brought right over," Bat said, "and thank you, Doctor."

"Thank you for asking me, Mr. Masterson," she said. "I'm happy to help."

Bat and House left. The buggy they'd ridden there was waiting for them outside.

"We'll leave this one here to take her to the hospital. We can find a cab around the corner," Bat said.

"You really think she can do this, Bat?" House asked.

"She's a doctor, House," Bat said. "Let's just go and arrange for the body to be brought to her."

Bat headed for the corner and the Inspector followed him, still dubious.

Bat Masterson and Inspector House were waiting outside the operating room while Doctor Ford performed the autopsy on the dead woman, Jessica Williams. House kept nervously looking through the window of the closed door.

"Relax," Bat said. "She knows how to cut into a body."

"I hope so."

Bat hoped so, too. He wondered why Emma had not told him that Doctor Ford was black. He was careful not to mention it to Chief Flaherty. It was well known that the Chief hated black people.

House backed away from the door quickly and seconds later Doctor Ford came through, wearing a white surgical gown stained with blood.

"What did you find, Doctor?" Bat asked.

"It was a very good idea to have an autopsy performed, Mr. Masterson," she told him. "It's not what I found that's interesting—astounding, actually—but what I didn't find."

"And what's that?"

"There are no internal organs," she said.

"What?" House asked.

"This woman's internal organs have been removed."

"But . . . she wasn't cut open," Bat said, "the way the Jack the Ripper victims were."

"Exactly."

"And yet they're . . . missing?" House asked.

"Yes."

"But . . . that's impossible," House said.

"Yes," Doctor Ford said, "it is."

4

Flaherty was irate.

"You allowed a black woman to cut open a white girl?" he demanded.

"We allowed a doctor to cut open a dead girl, yes," Bat said. "If we hadn't, we wouldn't know about the missing organs."

"Does she know what she's doing?" the Chief demanded.

"Yes, Chief, she does," Bat said.

Flaherty rubbed his face with both hands. "The Mayor's gonna be livid."

"Come on, Chief," Bat said. "We need to dig up the other two girls so Doctor Ford can examine them as well, see if the same thing is true."

"The families . . ." Flaherty said. "The Mayor . . . the newspapers."

"I work for a newspaper, Chief, remember?" Bat asked. "I can slant this in a way that will make you look very good."

That seemed to appeal to the Chief.

"All right, Masterson. I'll get an order from a judge to exhume both bodies so this doctor can examine them. But I'm warning you. . . ." The man pointed a finger. "This better result in us catching this maniac." He looked directly at Inspector House. "Understand?"

It took two days but eventually Bat and House were standing outside the operating room at St. Joseph's Hospital again, waiting.

"If she finds the same thing," House said, "what are we gonna do? We'll have three impossible murders. Yet, how can it be impossible if it's been done?"

"That's a very good question," Bat said. "I guess we'll have to wait for the doctor to answer that one. I'll tell you one thing, I can't wait for this to be over so I can go back to being a sportsman and nothing else."

"I've heard people refer to you that way," House said. "As a sportsman? Is that how you prefer to be known these days?"

"It's as good a way as any," Bat said.

At that moment the door opened and Dr. Ford came out. "It's the same," she said.

"Damn it," House said. "This is too strange."

"Doctor," Bat said, "did you find anything at all that might explain what's going on?"

"I have found something," she said. "It's on all three women, but I don't know that I can explain it."

"Anything would help," Inspector House said.

"There is an incision, a very small incision, on their left side."

"All three?" Bat asked.

"Yes."

"And that's all?"

"Yes."

"Could the organs have been removed through that?" Bat asked.

"It doesn't seem possible, but . . ."

"But what, Doctor?" Bat asked. "If you've got an idea, don't hold back."

"That's all it is," she said, "an idea. Just something I remember from medical school. If I could have some time—"

"Give us an idea of what you're talking about," Bat suggested, "and then take the time you need."

"Well, I'm thinking about . . . mummification."

"Mummi—what's that?" House asked.

"Mummies?" Bat asked. "You mean like in ancient Egypt?"

"Yes."

"Egypt?" House asked, still looking confused.

"When they mummified their dead," Dr. Ford explained, "part of the ritual was to remove all the internal organs."

"But . . . through a small incision like the one you described?"

"I seem to remember . . . something about a small incision, but I don't recall how it was done. I can do some research at the museum, talk to the Egyptian expert there."

"Can that be done today?" Bat asked.

"I don't see why not."

"Then I'll take you there, Doctor."

"I don't need to be taken, Mr. Masterson—"

"Sorry, ma'am," Bat responded, "what I meant was, I'll go with you, if you'll allow me to."

"Well . . . why not?"

"Just let me walk the Inspector out and I'll have a cab waiting when you're ready."

"Very well."

Outside the hospital Bat said to House, "You go and tell Flaherty what I'm doing. After the doctor and I go to the museum I'll come and find you."

"What the hell, Bat," House said. "I can't go back to the Chief with this."

"This could be the only explanation we have for what seems to be impossible," Bat said.

"Ancient Egypt? Mummies? Do you believe all that?"

"Don't you ever do any reading, son," Bat said. "We're talking about history."

"Still," House said, as they headed down the hall, "it's hard to believe."

"Yes, it is."

5

"Who do we ask for?" Bat asked, as they entered the Denver Museum of History, located on Broadway.

"The Egyptology expert," Dr. Ford said.

"I'll let you start the talking."

"Shouldn't Inspector House be with us?" she asked. "After all, he's the policeman."

"Inspector House had something else to do. Don't worry, we have official standing."

They walked down a long hall until they encountered a man standing at a desk.

"Can I help you?"

"My name is Doctor Ford," she said, "and this is Bat Masterson, the columnist. We are hoping to speak to whoever is your expert on Egyptology?"

"Bat Masterson?" the man asked. He was a small man roughly Bat's age, but he stared at the frontier legend with a little boy's enthusiasm. "Really?"

"Yes," Bat said, "I'm afraid so. Do you have an expert in Egyptology?"

"Ooh, yes, we do," the man said. "You want Mr. Vartan. I'll get him for you."

"Thank you," Ford said.

"Doctor, how many of these experts could there be in Denver?" Bat asked while they waited.

"I would think only one."

"And would he know how to do this, how to . . . what? Mummify?"

"I know what you mean, and I don't know," she said. "I suppose we'll have to ask him."

They waited in silence, and after a few minutes the doctor looked at Bat curiously. "Did you mean that you . . . suspect this man, even though you haven't met him yet?"

"No, of course not. I just thought if he's the only expert that maybe the killer had come to see him, just like we have."

"Oh, I see."

But now that she mentioned it, why couldn't the one man in Denver who had the knowhow be a suspect in the crime? Bat decided he would give this jasper a real close going over.

They heard footsteps coming toward them and saw the small man returning with a very tall, dark-skinned man wearing a suit and tie.

"This is Mr. Vartan," the small man said.

"I am Michael Vartan. I understand you were looking for me?" Vartan asked. "Sam said one of you is a doctor?"

"I am Dr. Ford," Justina Ford said.

Vartan looked at her in complete surprise.

"I did not know we had any black doctors in Denver let alone a woman. How fascinating."

"Mr. Vartan?" Bat said. "My name is Bat Masterson. We would like to ask you some questions about—"

"The famous killer?" Vartan asked.

Bat closed his mouth and glared at the man.

"I am a columnist for the newspaper *George's Weekly*."

"Ah, but surely you are the famous Bat Masterson," Vartan said. "There could not be two men with such a name."

"I am perhaps famous," Bat said, "but not as a killer."

"I am so sorry," Vartan said. "I have offended you."

"Mr. Masterson has been many things, Mr. Vartan," Dr. Ford said, "among them a lawman."

"And now a writer," Vartan said. "How commendable. I apologize again. You have some questions concerning what?"

"The process of mummification," Dr. Ford said.

Vartan stared at them, then said, "I have an office. Would you follow me, please?"

He led them through hallways of the museum, allowing them only glimpses of displays through doorways as they passed. Eventually they came to a room with a desk and a few chairs. He invited them in to sit, and closed the door before circling his desk and seating himself.

"Please, tell me your problem."

Dr. Ford described the murders and her autopsy findings. "What we need to know is, could the organs have been removed through this small incision?"

"Interesting," Vartan said. He paused to consider and while he did he picked up an instrument from the desk. It was a bronze tool with a small hook on the end. "Do you see this? It was used by the Egyptians to remove the brain through the nasal passage."

"Could it be used for the organs, too?" Bat asked.

Vartan didn't reply to Bat's direct question, but went on, warming to his gruesome subject. "No one knows how the brain was removed, but it must have been in pieces. It could not have been removed this way as a whole."

"The organs couldn't have been removed as a whole either," Dr. Ford said. "At least, not through that incision."

"In ancient Egypt, the incision you refer to was indeed used to remove the organs," Vartan said, "and then they were put into a jar and buried along with the body."

Bat didn't like the way Vartan's eyes shined.

"But no one knows for sure how it was done," Vartan continued, "just as we don't quite know how the brain was removed." He set the tool down. "But we know that they were."

"So no one," Bat said, "not even you, who is an expert, would be able to do such a thing now?"

"I?" Vartan asked, looking shocked. "I would never—no, no, too bloody. I would be too . . . squeamish, I think."

Bat doubted that Vartan was squeamish about much of anything. The man seemed to be enjoying the spotlight. To Bat's trained eye, honed by years of gambling and sizing up men who might or might not try to kill him, Vartan also seemed amused.

"Mr. Vartan," Dr. Ford said, "has anyone else come to see you about these things in, say the past six months or so?"

"Unfortunately, no," Vartan said, making a steeple of his hands and fingers and regarding them above it. "I rarely get to speak of these things in this way."

Another thing Bat noticed about Vartan was that the man's gaze never wavered from his own. Even when he speaking to the doctor, he was looking at Bat. Many men had looked at Bat that way over the years, as if they had or were getting his measure. They had all been disappointed.

Oddly, the room seemed bare. There were no Egyptian objects of any kind on the walls, and the only one on his desk was that bronze tool sitting on the edge of his desk.

"I am so sorry these women were killed. How was it done?"

"That's still something of a mystery," Dr. Ford said, "but their organs were removed after death."

"Shocking . . . in this day and age, I mean."

"Yes," Dr. Ford said, "quite."

"They were peaceful in death, Mr. Vartan," Bat said. "What would make them die so peacefully?"

"Well, certain poisons would have that effect," Vartan said. "There are poisons which cause horrible, painful deaths, but there are several which could cause a person to simply . . . fall asleep . . . forever. Some of these were used in ancient Egypt."

Poison was not a common form of killing in the West—at least, not in what people were now calling the "Old" West.

"And you would know what kind of poisons those were, wouldn't you?" Bat asked.

Vartan looked embarrassed and said, "Well, I am an expert on things Egyptian."

"Yes, you are," Bat said.

"That's fascinating," Dr. Ford said.

"Well," Bat said, "I think we're done here, Doctor. Obviously, Mr. Vartan won't help us with anything more."

Bat got to his feet, stumbled and almost fell, righting himself by catching the edge of Vartan's desk. He knew the man must have been thinking, "What an old fool."

"Can't," Vartan said.

"Excuse me?" Bat asked, back on solid footing.

"You said I won't help you with anything more," Vartan said. "You meant 'can't.'"

Bat looked the man in the eyes and said, "Did I?"

Outside the museum Dr. Ford said, "What a rude man. He never looked at me the entire time."

"That's because he was lookin' at me," Bat said. "He's the one."

"I beg your pardon?"

"He did it. He killed those women and removed their organs."

"How can you—"

"He looked me in the eyes the whole time, challenging me. Believe me, Doctor, I know what that look means. He did it."

"Is that what you will tell the Chief? Would they arrest him on your word?"

"No," Bat said, "they wouldn't, but I don't think they'll have to."

"Why not?"

Bat put his hand in his pocket and came out with the bronze hook from Vartan's desk. Carefully, he wrapped it in a handkerchief and handed it to the doctor.

"How did you—you took that when you stumbled."

"Yes. Check it and you might find some flecks of blood on it. He's so arrogant that he still keeps it on his desk."

"You think he used this?"

"Even if he didn't, he knows I know," Bat said. "He knows if he stays in Denver, I'll have him."

"But . . . if he leaves, and goes somewhere else . . . is that good enough?"

"It'll have to be, Doctor," Bat said. "It'll have to be."

□ □ □

But it wasn't, not for Bat Masterson.

That evening, as Vartan came out of his apartment carrying a suitcase Bat was waiting, leaning against the building. He hadn't been wearing a gun that afternoon in the museum, but he was wearing it now. He'd chosen one with a pearl handle that gleamed in the moonlight.

Vartan saw him and stopped. There was no slump to the man's shoulder, no diminishment of his arrogance.

"You stumbled on purpose," he said. "I realized it afterward."

"I was going to let you go," Bat said, "let you run, but I decided I had to know why. Why would you do that to those poor women?"

"I am afraid my explanation will not give you much satisfaction."

"Try me."

The man shrugged. "To see if I could. I have studied the Egyptians for so long. I believe they were a master race. I wanted to see if I could do what they did. And after I did it once, I knew that if I kept trying, I would succeed."

"Did you do more than those three?"

"No, just those—so far."

"Just those, period, Mr. Vartan."

"Now that you know the why, perhaps you would . . .?"

"Put the suitcase down, Mr. Vartan," Bat said, pushing away from the wall so Vartan could see the pearl handle, "you won't need it where you're going."

The Knights of Liberty

Baltimore, Maryland
October 1861

"**D**amn you, Timothy Webster, you're a goddamned spy!" the man
shouted. His name was Mike Zigler, and while he was known to
some of the men in the saloon, he was not as well liked as good ol' Tim
Webster.

"What are you babbling about, Zigler?" one of the others asked.

"This man's a damned Yankee spy!" Zigler shouted. "I saw him in
Washington yesterday."

Webster rushed to his own defense with the truth.

"He's right," he said calmly. "I was in Washington yesterday. Many
of you know that already."

"Yeah," Zigler said, "but do they know that you were in the
company of the chief of the Yankee detectives?"

Now Webster had no choice but to call the man a liar by being one
himself. "You are a liar!" he cried, with as much indignation as he
could muster.

"Damn you!" the man shouted, and sprang at him. . . .

When Timothy Webster was summoned by Major E. J. Allen he knew
he would once again be placed in danger while performing a service
for his country. He had no problem with that. It was the way he
preferred to live his life, risking it from time to time. From the time he
first went to work as a detective for the major's agency his life had
become worth living. Prior to that he'd just been marking time. He'd
come to America from England with his parents when he was twelve.
They'd lived in Princeton, New Jersey, where he had worked as a

mechanic. Eventually, he went to work for the New York City Police Department. It was the kind of work he wanted, but still not enough. So when he met the major and was offered a job to work for him, he jumped at the chance.

Now, five years later, he was working for the major in a different capacity. This time he was a spy for the newly formed secret service, serving President Lincoln and the Union cause. However, it was not so much patriotism that brought him to this work—even though he had adopted the United States as his country—as it was loyalty to the man for whom he'd worked for five years.

When President Lincoln decided there was a need for a "secret" service he went to the one man he thought could head up such an operation. That man was now known as Major E. J. Allen—but, in reality, his name was Allan Pinkerton.

Webster had been a Pinkerton detective for five years, and only recently had he been pressed into service as a secret-service man. Pinkerton had closed his offices and, in accordance with President Lincoln's specifications, had formed his secret service—and many of the men he pressed into service were his own operatives. Of them all, Timothy Webster was the best. This was not vanity on Webster's part, but Pinkerton's own opinion. That was why he summoned Webster for the dangerous job of becoming the country's very first double spy.

"Come in, Tim," Pinkerton said, using a firm handshake to draw the man into his office. As usual Pinkerton was looking prosperous in a tweed three-piece suit, a gold watch fob hanging from a vest pocket. He accepted President Lincoln's appointment on the condition that he would not have to wear a uniform. He preferred to worry about blue and gray only when talking with his tailor. He proffered a well-fed appearance which he attempted to temper with sideburns and a heavy mustache.

"How are you, my boy?"

"Fine, sir."

"Sufficiently recovered from your last assignment to take another, do you think?"

"I'm ready when you are, sir."

"Good man!" Pinkerton went around behind his desk and indicated the chair located directly in front of it. "Have a seat and let me explain it to you. This one might be extremely dangerous."

Webster was a tall, impressive man, sometimes referred to as "Big" Tim Webster, but it was not his size, nor his courage, which made him an effective double spy. Rather it was his ability to ingratiate himself to anyone, to make friends at a moment's notice. In addition, there was his incredible good luck. It was the sort of luck that Pinkerton, his fellow operatives, and his friends thought could only be brought by a Guardian Angel. Some thought Webster depended too heavily on this luck, took it for granted, and would someday pay the price. Perhaps he would, but that did not stop him from putting it to the test.

This time, explained Pinkerton, it would be put to the test in Baltimore in pursuit of a group of hostile Southern sympathizers known as the Knights of Liberty.

"You would be alone among the enemy, using your uncommon charm to ingratiate yourself to the extent that you will be invited to join this brotherhood of Rebels. Do you think you can do this?"

Webster smiled and said, "It's a challenge I gratefully accept, sir."

"As I knew you would, my boy," Pinkerton said, proudly, "as I knew you would. . . ."

2

Baltimore, Maryland, was under a state of martial law when Webster arrived. Southern sympathizers were at work everywhere. Lincoln's administration had arrested people in authority, city officials, newspaper editors, and the like, but some of the Baltimoreans who were also Southerners had formed organizations whose purpose it was to undermine the government at every turn. One such organization was the Knights of Liberty, and it was Webster's assignment to insinuate himself into their service for the purposes of disbanding them and having the members arrested.

Webster had done his double-spy work in the South before, and had also been to Baltimore in the past. For those reasons, when he arrived this time he was recognized by some and greeted as a friend of Dixie. He arrived in grand style, too, as Pinkerton had supplied for him a generous expense account. He took up residence in the Miller Hotel, one of the finer establishments in Baltimore. Not as alone as he might have thought, he made contact with another agent of the North named John Scully, whose assignment it was to assist Webster in any way possible.

"In what way will you establish yourself?" Scully asked during their first meeting. They were sitting in the bar of the Miller Hotel, preferring to be seen in public rather than skulking about in private someplace. This way their meeting seemed very innocent, and no one else could hear what they were saying. They sat with a glass of sherry each, and sipped slowly. It would not do for a double spy to become drunk and loose-lipped.

"I have already taken steps to do so," Webster said. "I have railed openly against Union outrages and predicted victory for the Confederacy. Also, I have offered to transport papers, maps, and anything of that sort into Washington for any Southerners who have messages they need delivered."

"And will you deliver them?"

"Oh, yes," Webster said, "but only after we have opened them, copied them and sent them on to Mr. Pinkerton."

Only Lincoln, some of his staff, and the operatives who worked for him knew that "Major E. J. Allen" was actually Allan Pinkerton.

"That is devious," Scully said. "I don't understand how you do it, Tim. Everyone seems to trust you."

"It is a gift," Webster said, "and one I have always used to my best advantage."

"That is why I am glad we are colleagues," Scully said, "and not friends." Webster understood exactly what his "colleague" meant. You cannot betray a man with whom you are not friends.

"I propose a toast," he said, raising his glass, "to our business relationship."

And so, for the next two weeks Webster worked flawlessly at establishing his identity. He did make trips into Washington, lest anyone check his story closely, and he was able to send Pinkerton copies of many messages sent into the capital city by Southerners — some harmless, some not so. By the end of those weeks no one in Baltimore doubted his veracity, all thought him a fine fellow working for the cause of the South.

But perhaps not all. . . .

Webster had just returned from Washington, a trip which had not yielded very much in the way of information, but still he was in good spirits. Many of the Southerners he had ingratiated himself with were actually fairly good fellows whose company he enjoyed. That would not, however, keep him from doing his job and having them arrested if the need arose. Whenever an arrest took place as a direct result of his actions, he was the one who protested the loudest about the indignity and unfairness of it. This only endeared him that much more to his Southern friends.

On this particular night he was in one of Baltimore's popular saloons with a dozen or more of his "friends" around him. Nowhere in sight was John Scully; it was just Webster and a roomful of Southerners. Suddenly a man appeared, sullen and scowling, and pushed his way through the crowd so he could face Webster nose-to-nose.

This, then, was Mike Zigler, who was presently springing at Webster with very bad intentions. . . .

Before anyone could move, Tim Webster's fist caught the man in the face and sent him to the floor. He sprang up angrily, a knife in his hand. At this point Webster produced his pistol and pointed it at the man, unwaveringly.

"Get out of here before I kill you."

Zigler glared at Webster, then looked around him and shared the glare with the others.

"You'll get what you deserve if you befriend this man."

"Ah, you're crazy!" someone shouted from the back. "I'd just as soon believe that Jeff Davis hisself was a spy, as ol' Tim here."

Others piped in with their agreement and Zigler had no choice but to skulk from the saloon and melt into the darkness.

Webster holstered his gun and called out, "Drinks for everyone!" which was met with a chorus of cheers. The incident served to bolster Webster's position as a fellow Southerner, but he still had not achieved his ultimate goal—to be invited to join the Knights of Liberty.

He assumed that invitation would require a very special act.

3

After the incident in the saloon Webster decided he needed to do something drastic to further cement his position as a true Southerner. He decided that a few secret trips into lower Maryland and Virginia while carrying secret messages would do the trick. He decided to take Scully with him. His admiring Southern friends warned him to be on constant lookout for Union soldiers, because "those Yankees are capable of anything."

Webster and Scully were actually able to move very easily in and out of the areas because they carried secret Union passes. Meanwhile, the messages they were given to carry enabled the Union to connect to the South persons never even previously suspected. These forays into "Union territory" enabled Webster to facilitate the arrest of many Southern sympathizers while also serving to endear him further to his fellow Baltimoreans.

When he returned, he found himself hailed as a Southern hero, and waiting for him was the very invitation he had been waiting for.

He was several days returned from Virginia when a man came up beside him in a saloon and offered to buy him a drink.

"I have one, sir," Webster said, "but I'll gladly take you up on the offer when I've finished."

"No," the man said, "not here."

"Where, then?"

"Are you aware of the Knights of Liberty?"

Webster took a good look at the man now. Slightly built, thinning gray hair, probably in his mid-forties, with just the hint of a Southern accent. "I certainly am," Webster said.

"They have been watching you," the man said, "and have decided it is time to invite you to be one of us."

Webster looked around and then lowered his voice. "You are a member of the Knights of Liberty?"

"I am," the man said proudly, "and it is my duty to make you one. What say you?"

"What else could I say," Webster asked, "but 'Lead on.'"

"Not now," the man said, lowering his voice even more and glancing about. "We meet at midnight. Meet me here at quarter-to and I will take you there."

"I cannot wait, sir," Webster said. "This is indeed an honor."

"For us as well, Mr. Webster," the man said. "Your exploits are well known to us. No one has risked their life more for the South without actually donning a uniform. Quarter till midnight, sir."

"I'll be here."

The smaller man nodded, and then faded away into the crowded saloon.

□ □ □

Still later, seated at a table together, he made his arrangements with Scully. "You're going in alone?" the other agent asked.

"I must," Webster said, "tonight and other nights, as well. I must discover all I can before we take steps to disband them. We must know who all their members are, and who their contacts are, as well."

"But I could follow you, see where you go, and then bring troops to take them—"

"Not tonight, Scully," Webster said. "We must wait until the time is right."

"If you have another incident like that night in the saloon with that fellow Zigler—"

"I'll have to take my chances, John," Webster said. "I implore you, do nothing tonight but wait for me to contact you."

Scully worried his bottom lip but finally agreed.

Webster met with the slight man in the saloon as arranged. He was then taken to a deserted street corner where they stopped.

"What's wrong?" he asked.

"You must be blindfolded from here."

"But if I am to be a member, why can I not see where we are going?" Webster asked, contriving to sound confused.

"First you must be accepted as a member," the man said. "That is what tonight is for. Once you have been accepted you may come and go to meetings freely."

Webster wondered if this was a trap. Had they found out who he really was, perhaps from that man Zigler, or someone like him? Was he being blindfolded and led to his death?

He decided he must take the chance. He was so close to his ultimate goal, the disbanding of the Knights of Liberty, that he had to accept the risk. "Very well," he said. "Blindfold me."

4

Once the blindfold was in place he was led down the street, the slight man—whose name he still did not know—holding him by the arm. They stopped at a gate, where the man gave a proper password, and then they went down a concrete stairway and along an alleyway until they reached a door which was opened only after a second password was uttered. Webster fervently hoped, as he was led down another stairway, this one inside, that when the blindfold was removed he would not be facing cocked pistols and rifles.

Finally they reached a room and stopped. He could sense the others around him, knew he must be in a crowded room full of Southern supporters who, if they knew who he really was, would tear him apart.

"Timothy Webster?" a strange voice said.

"Yes."

"If you are to be a member of the Knights of Liberty," the voice said, "you must take an oath to support the South and to thwart, hate, and violate the Northern abolitionists until you draw your last breath, or until we have won this accursed war. Do you so swear?"

"I swear," Webster said. "With all my heart."

"Remove the blindfold."

Someone did so and Webster had to wait for his eyes to adjust before he could look into the faces of the men who surrounded him. Suddenly they surged forward, closing on him, and after a moment of panic he saw they were smiling. Then they were shaking his hand and patting his back heartily, and just like that he was a Knight of Liberty.

That night he was called on to make a speech and he did so with verve and vigor, denouncing the Yankees and all they stood for. In the end the place exploded with applause and he was truly accepted as a brother.

That night, and for many nights after, Webster attended the meetings and memorized names, and faces, and facts. He learned that they did, indeed, work in direct contact with the Southern army, and that they had branches outside of Baltimore. He stored enough information in his mind to cripple their organization, and yet he still would not allow Scully to close in and round them up.

Then one day Scully said, "I think you should contact Mr. Pinkerton, Tim. Let him decide what to do."

"And if I don't," Webster asked, "you will?"

"The longer you are inside, the more danger you are in. It is my duty to look after you," Scully said, "and that is what I intend to do."

"Very well," Webster said. "I will consult with Mr. Pinkerton."

Scully nodded his thanks and breathed a sigh of relief that the matter had been taken from his hands.

Webster got in touch with Pinkerton who, while he realized that

Webster could learn more and more, decided not to take any chances. He told Webster to close the group out at the next meeting.

"Put an end to it, Tim," he said, "and let's be on to something else."

"Is that official, sir?"

"It is."

At the next meeting Webster entered the room and looked around at the other men in attendance. It was actually a good night to close them out, as this was as large a gathering as he had been at since joining. While he recognized many of the faces, there were many more still which he did not. Then he saw a man approaching him with such purpose in his stride that he sought out the man's face, which was familiar to him, but not immediately—and then he knew!

Mike Zigler, the man who had attempted to denounce him in a saloon earlier in the month.

"You!" Zigler shouted, drawing the attention of the others. "You are here, you traitor?"

Webster wondered if he should draw his pistol and shoot the man dead before he could say anything more, but how would he explain it?

"This man is a Yankee spy!" Zigler shouted, frothing at the mouth, such was his anger. He glared at Webster and said, "You are among my people now, Webster, not yours. There's no help for you here."

"What are you saying, Mike?" It was the slight man who had invited Webster to join. Webster had discovered that his name was Rufus Blight. "What do you mean?"

"I mean he is sent among us to spy," Zigler shouted.

"Can you prove this?" another man called out.

"Mike's word is good enough for me," someone else called.

"Me, too."

Zigler's eyes shone as shouts of support continued to pour forth. He looked at Webster and a triumphant glint appeared in his eye, for this night he would have his revenge for the previous humiliation.

Zigler produced his knife, and as Webster went for his pistol his aims were seized and pinioned behind him.

Webster had no time to shout the words which were to have been a signal for Scully and a troop of Union soldiers to break in. He'd finally gotten himself in too deep, as friends and colleagues had said he someday would.

Unless he could talk his way out.

"Listen to me!" he shouted. "Zigler is lying. I am not—"

"None of your silver-tongued oratory will save you now," Zigler said, drowning him out. "Tonight I'll carve me up a spy."

Zigler came forward, his blade held low, and as Webster felt the tip of the blade prick him there was a crashing sound and suddenly men were shouting and pushing. His arms were released, but someone pushed him and he gasped as Zigler's blade went into his side.

A squad of Union infantry swept into the room and began herding the frightened, surprised Knights of Liberty against the wall.

Webster brought his hand down and clamped it around Mike Zigler's wrist. The knife had gone in barely an inch, but Zigler was trying to push it farther. They were jostled and the knife sliced sideways, opening a gash in Webster's side that bled freely. However, it also brought the knife free of his flesh and now he twisted and, with his great strength, snapped Zigler's wrist so that the man cried out in agony and released the knife.

Someone grabbed Zigler and pulled him away, pushed him against the wall with the others. Webster, his knees weak from relief and shock, felt his legs go out from under him, felt hands catch him and lower him easily to the floor.

"John?" he said, looking up at Scully.

Scully pressed his hands to Webster's wound and shouted to a Union soldier, "I need a medic, fast!"

"Yes, sir."

"John," Webster said.

"I'm here, Tim," Scully said. "You'll be fine. It's a tear, lots of blood, but you'll be fine."

"No signal . . . " Webster said.

"It took too long," Scully said. "When there was no signal I just had the soldiers break down the door."

"Looking after me?" Webster said, with a weak smile.

Scully nodded to his colleague and said, "Which is just what I am supposed to do."

In the days that followed the word got out that the Knights of Liberty had been captured, with only a few exceptions. Among those who had escaped was Timothy Webster. No one was surprised, for wasn't Webster a true and amazing son of the South, and wasn't he always able to escape the clutches of those damned Yankees?

About the Author

Robert J. Randisi, founder of the Private Eye Writers of America, is a publishing phenomenon. With more than five hundred novels under his belt, he shows no sign of slowing down. His latest work includes the "Rat Pack" series of Hollywood mysteries for St. Martin's Press and a new novel for Perfect Crime Books, *The Bottom of Every Bottle*.

Described by *Booklist* as "the last of the pulp writers," Randisi has published in the western, mystery, horror, science fiction and men's adventure genres. The current count: more than five hundred forty books, fifty-plus short stories, and editorial responsibility for thirty anthologies. He has also edited a Writer's Digest book, *Writing the Private Eye Novel*, and for seven years was the mystery reviewer for the *Orlando Sentinel*. In 1982 he founded the Private Eye Writers of America and created the Shamus Award. In 1985 he co-founded *Mystery Scene Magazine* and the short-lived American Mystery Award; a couple of years later he was co-founder of the American Crime Writer's League. In 1993 he was awarded a Life Achievement Award at the Southwest Mystery Convention. His latest recognition, in 2009, was the Lifetime Achievement Award from the PWA.

In the Western genre, as "J. R. Roberts" he is the creator and author of The Gunsmith series, which has been appearing monthly since January 1982.

Randisi was born and raised in Brooklyn, N.Y., and from 1973 through 1981 he was a civilian employee of the New York City Police Department, working out of the Sixty-Seventh Precinct in Brooklyn. After forty-one years in New York, he now resides in Clarksville, Missouri, an artisan community of five hundred people. He lives and works with writer Marthayn Pelegrimas in a small house on three acres, with a deck that overlooks the Mississippi.

5871111R0

Made in the USA
Charleston, SC
14 August 2010